Broken Promises

Book Two of the Barrington Family Series

Chris Taylor

LCT Productions Pty Limited

LCT Productions Pty Limited

18364 Kamilaroi Highway, Narrabri NSW 2390

ISBN: 9781925441017 (eBook)

ISBN: 9781925441024 (Print)

Broken Promises is a work of fiction. Names, places, characters, brands, media and incidents are either the product of the author's imagination or are used fictitiously. Any resemblance to persons living or dead, events or locales is entirely coincidental.

Other books by Chris Taylor

The Munro Family Series
(in order)

The Profiler

The Investigator

The Predator

The Betrayal

The Deception

The Negotiator

The Christmas Vigil (A novella)

The Ransom

The Defendant

The Shooting

The Maker

The Sydney Harbour Hospital Series (in order)

The Perfect Husband

The Body Thief

The Baby Snatchers

The Final Bullet

The Debt Collector

The Lab Test

The Stolen Identity

The Cliff-top Killer

The Likeable Fraudster

The Sydney Legal Series
(in order)

An Accidental Murderer

At the Hand of her Father

A Woman Scorned

Lies and Deception

Ordinary Evil

The Ties that Bind

The Perfect Crime

A Toxic Inheritance

Malicious Love

The Craigdon Family Series

(in order)

Callum

Joel

Isabella

Nicholas

Sophia

Flynn

Noah

Logan

Elizabeth

The Barrington Family Series

(in order)

Broken Lives

Broken Promises

Broken Bonds

Broken Spirits

Broken Minds

Broken Vows

Broken Hearts

Broken Dreams

Broken Homes

The Fairfax Family Series (in order)

A Cattleman in Disguise

A Cattleman's Quest

A Cattleman's Daughter

A Cattleman's Secret Baby

To Catch a Cattleman

The Doctor and the Cattleman

To Rescue a Cattleman

A Cattleman's Heart

For the Love of a Cattleman

Bachelors and Brides Series (in order)

Matilda

Austin

Farrah

Benjamin

Verity

Denver

Ebony

Tyrone

Willow

Books by Chris Taylor

Writing as

Bella
Christian

This Is Where It Ends Series
(in order)

Jessie's Story

Ryan's Story

Holly's Story

Sarah's Story

Veronica's Story

Love audiobooks? Check out Chris Taylor Books on audio

iTunes   Amazon Audible

Join Chris Taylor's Facebook reader group/fan page and be
among the first to receive news of book releases, read and
review books prior to release and other amazing offers.

Join Now!

VIII

This book is dedicated to my beautiful aunt, Vas Roberts. For her smiles, her good cheer, her love, laughter and her fighting spirit... Right until the very end... You are an inspiration.
And as always to my husband, Linden. My love, my life.

Chapter One

It was as if the heavens had opened up and decided to drop a year's worth of rain in one afternoon. The deluge battered Charlotte Barrington's BMW convertible as she strained to see through the torrent of water that bounced off her windscreen. Her wipers were going at top speed but they might as well have been motionless for all the effect they had.

Though the sky had been dull and gray and filled with heavy clouds before she left home an hour earlier, there had been no hint of the tsunami waiting right around the corner. Now she was stuck in the middle of it, fighting to get home.

She'd gone out for cat food. The thought of her chocolate point Siamese baby going hungry had forced her out to the shops when she would much rather have spent the afternoon binge-watching the current TV serial she was hooked on. There was something addictive about all those sexy doctors facing life-and-death situations on a daily basis—sometimes several times a day. Of course, it was only TV. Real life wasn't quite as dramatic, thank goodness. She ought to know.

As a detective with the New South Wales Police Force, she'd faced her fair share of drama and dangerous situations. Thankfully not so dangerous that she'd ever actually feared for her life. Her first post as a probationary constable had been to a rural town so far from Sydney it should have been described as the outback. The biggest excitement in Watervale had been a purse-snatching a couple of months into her twelve-month stint. Poor old Rosie Bennett—eighty-five if she were a day—had been sent flying when fourteen-year-old Jaxon Pitt had stolen her handbag. It was lucky the great-grandmother hadn't broken a hip when she'd landed hard on the concrete footpath outside the local supermarket.

Despite no shortage of eyewitnesses, Charlotte had still conducted a thorough investigation and Jaxon had been arrested and charged within the hour. That was one thing about small towns: Everyone knew everyone. Rosie had taught Jaxon's mother in high school. Everyone said he was the spitting image of his mother. And they'd been right.

Still, Charlotte had learned a lot from her fellow officers in Watervale. Detective Chase Barrington was her cousin and he'd taken it upon himself to show the probationary constable the ropes and a few tricks of the trade. Her brother Wade was also a resident of Watervale. As the local park ranger, he'd been only too willing to take her hiking on some of the trails. They'd even camped out in the bush once or twice, toasting marshmallows before a campfire and recalling adventures from their childhood. She'd enjoyed her time in the country, but it was the city where she had yearned to be.

Nothing beat the glitz and glamor, the noise, the excitement, the sheer vibrancy of the city. Directly after the end of her probationary year in Watervale, she'd been lucky enough to be posted to the affluent beachside suburb of Cronulla. It was sixteen miles south of the city of Sydney, but it was still a decent enough place to live. The combination of relaxed beachside living and the cosmopolitan vibe of trendy cafés, theaters and restaurants made the place popular with locals and tourists alike. Better still, it was only a ninety-minute drive to her parents' house outside Broken, in the southern highlands. She spent a lot more of her days' off at the house she'd grown up in, now that she was single again.

But not today. Today had been all about sleeping late, eating junk food and watching TV on her way-too-comfy couch. What better way to spend her last day off before tackling the challenges of her new job? The ink had barely dried on her promotion to the homicide department of the Sutherland Shire Police Area Command and she felt the need to impress.

Charlotte was most definitely the new kid on the block. So new she was yet to be part of a homicide investigation. She was itching to get started. Not only was she more than ready to cut her teeth on her first homicide investigation, she was also more than ready to have a decent distraction from her ex-boyfriend.

It had been three months since Keith had broken things off. Her self-esteem was still smarting. Her sisters accused her of hiding out in her unit every night, moping about the future she'd thought was hers for the taking, a future vision that had been blown to smithereens. And they were right. She hadn't been out since Keith had leveled the death blow to their relationship.

It's over... We both want different things... I don't love you... You're more devoted to your job than you are to us...

The accusations had come thick and fast. He'd even insulted her prowess in the bedroom. That had been unnecessarily hurtful and even though her rational, logical self had wanted to dismiss his cruel words, a part of her had wondered if there was some truth to them...

At least her career was on track. After five years of policing, she'd finally made detective. The only blight on the landscape was her work partner. Tony Sabattini was a veteran cop who should have retired a long time ago. Though his decades of homicide experience would benefit a rookie like her, his rude and taciturn attitude toward almost everyone and everything was proving difficult to take. Still, even that couldn't put a damper on the fact she'd finally made it. She was officially on the homicide team.

That thought triggered a slow smile of satisfaction.

Just then a jagged shard of lightning cracked against the sky. Charlotte yelped in alarm and jumped. Her thoughts went immediately to Raoul who was terrified of thunder and lightning. She hoped he was okay. She wasn't sure what caused the sheer terror he displayed at the slightest hint of thunder, but there was no denying he hated storms.

Her four-legged feline companion, Raoul, was currently the most important male in her life. She'd rescued him from an animal shelter when he was a few months old. She didn't know anything about his early days. No doubt there was some past trauma that made him the way he was. At least she had his favorite food in the back of the car. That would help him get through the rest of the day.

With a sigh of relief, she arrived at her complex and activated the remote to her garage. She'd never been more pleased to have undercover parking. The price tag on her unit had been worth every cent. It was a ground-floor unit in a three-story walk-up. Although the building was circa 1970s and had yet to be gentrified, the fact that it was two-bedroom, two-bath and within walking distance of the beach more than made up for the dated exterior.

She could never have afforded such a place on her cop's salary, but a year earlier she'd been given a generous sum of money from her parents as a twenty-fifth birthday gift, along with the BMW. She'd used the money as a deposit on the unit. Of course, the responsibility of the ongoing mortgage payments fell to her.

Though Frank and Evelyn Barrington were more than prepared to help out their nine children financially, they also expected each one to take responsibility for their lives and make something of themselves. There was no pressure for any of them to enter into the family mining business, but they'd all grown up knowing there was most definitely an expectation that they'd work hard and succeed in their chosen fields. For Charlotte, that was the police force. Two of her brothers, Trace and Zac, were also cops.

The extra pay from her recent promotion would certainly help with the mortgage. Even with the hefty deposit, the monthly payments were steep. After her weekly expenses, there was never a whole lot left over. She'd learned the hard way about the importance of sticking to a budget.

Dropping her grocery bag on the kitchen counter, she pushed her long wet hair back off her forehead. The sprint from the supermarket to her car had proven disastrous. The heavy rain had soaked her through. Kicking off her shoes, she padded barefoot down the hallway.

"Raoul? Puss, puss? Where are you, baby? Has the storm upset you?"

She passed the bathroom and stripped off her wet clothes. Grabbing a towel, she dried off and then wrapped the towel around her and continued her search.

"Raoul?"

She found him hiding under her bed, curled up in a ball and shivering with fear.

"Oh, my poor baby!" She drew him close and pressed a kiss against his soft fur. He burrowed in against the towel. She sat on the bed and petted him until he stopped trembling, reassuring him all the time that the storm was almost over and he was fine.

Satisfied at last that he was over the worst of it, she set him down on the carpet and headed back to the kitchen. Diving into the grocery bag, she found a tin of cat food and pulled open the lid. She spooned the contents into his dish then tapped the edge of the bowl.

"Raoul? Baby? Dinner's ready."

"Meow."

He rubbed himself against her bare legs and then began to eat. Leaving him to it, she padded back to the bathroom and dropped the towel on the floor. She opened the door of the shower and started the water. The hot spray felt good on her shoulders. After shampooing, shaving and moisturizing, she pulled on her old bathrobe and went back out to the kitchen. Raoul had finished his dinner and sat cleaning himself by the sliding door that led out to the covered patio.

"How was that, my gorgeous boy?" she crooned. "Are you feeling better?"

Pouring herself a glass of wine, Charlotte took it out onto the patio. The storm had passed as quickly as it had started and now the air smelled fresh and clean. She filled her lungs. Just then, the sun burst out from behind a cloud and the sky was filled with a brilliant rainbow.

Charlotte's spirits lifted. She might have been down in the dumps since Keith's abrupt departure, but life was looking up. The rainbow was a sign; she was sure of it.

The swish of passing cars outside reminded her there were people with places to go, things to do, dreams to fulfill. She was overcome with a sudden wave of discontentment. She was twenty-six. In the prime of her life. She ought to be out dancing, drinking, having fun with friends. Flirting.

Wow, I can't remember the last time I did that...

She and Keith had been together for three years. They'd met by chance at the train station and had bonded over books. She'd been reading an autobiography of a famous Australian cricketer. Keith had once played cricket for his state. He'd been cute in a slightly feminine way, with longish brown hair and glasses that kept sliding off his nose. He'd been sweet and funny and attentive. Their relationship had been more of a slow burn than an instantaneous combustion, but it had been nice. Comfortable.

Though they'd dated for three years, they'd never moved in together. They'd spent time at each other's places, including sleepovers, but Keith was an accountant and liked to think things over long and hard before he made a decision about anything—including whether they should share an address. Looking back, she just wished he'd called it quits before he'd broken her heart.

No, that wasn't right. She wouldn't lie to herself. He hadn't broken her heart. In fact, though she liked him a great deal and enjoyed his company, she was pretty sure she'd never been in love with him. Not the kind of heart-stopping, butterflies-in-stomach, sweaty hands kind of love she read about in romance novels. Then again, those romances were fiction. Make believe.

Does that kind of love really exist?

She didn't know and she sure as hell wasn't going to find out by hiding out every night in her home.

She took a sip from her glass and sighed. Another long, empty night stretched out before her. Raoul found the courage to venture out onto the wet tiles and wrapped himself around her legs. Setting her glass aside, she bent and picked him up, pressing her face against his soft fur.

"You're the only man I need in my life," she murmured.

A sudden image of her as a crazy old cat woman filled her mind. Living alone in her unit, surrounded by cats. The neighbors' children whispering about her as she walked by...

Charlotte cursed. Was that to be her lot? She set Raoul down on the tiles. A surge of determination went through her. She'd be damned if she'd spend another night moping about and bemoaning the sad and sorry state of her love life. It was time she went out and did something about it. Starting now, under a clearing sky.

Returning to the kitchen, she finished her wine and left the empty glass on the counter. She glanced at the clock above the fridge. Half past four. Though it was a little early to be hitting the bars, she was determined to get out and socialize. After all, it was five o'clock somewhere. She strode down the hallway to her bedroom. Dropping the bathrobe to the carpet, she flung open the doors to her wardrobe. She moved clothes aside, searching for the perfect something. At last she settled on a skintight, black leather dress.

She pulled it off the hanger and slipped it over her head. The sleeveless bodice cupped and lifted her generous breasts, leaving a fair amount of cleavage on display. The hem kissed the top of her thighs. A zipper ran up the middle from top to bottom, the zipper tab lying innocently near the cleft of her breasts. It was a dress she'd only worn once. Keith had taken one look at her in it and had nearly had a fit. He'd been overwhelmed and embarrassed by its blatant sexuality and had asked her to wear something else.

She remembered the night as if it had happened yesterday. They'd been going out on a date to celebrate their third anniversary. She'd bought the dress with that in mind, hoping it might re-ignite the spark. She should have known then that something was up.

She looked in the mirror at her reflection and ran her palms down the curves of her body. Though she was a diminutive five-foot-three, she was naturally slender and worked hard to stay fit, with regular visits to the gym.

What hot-blooded male wouldn't want a piece of this?

Determined to find out, she went into the adjoining bathroom and quickly and efficiently applied her makeup. Dark eye shadow, mascara, bright red lipstick. She set about blow-drying her hair and then brushed it into loose, shiny waves. What she lacked in height, she made up for by being perfectly proportioned and she knew just how to gain a few extra inches.

She padded back into her bedroom and pulled out a pair of four-inch stilettos. She slipped them on and then stood back to survey the results.

The woman who stared back at her was sophisticated, sexy and with enough mystery in her gaze to create interest. For a moment, she was paralyzed with indecision.

I'm not the kind of woman to indulge in a one night stand... Is that what I'm contemplating? Taking a stranger home for the night?

Charlotte would never have described herself as spontaneous. Her siblings often teased her about the length of time it took her to make a decision, especially about something important. That was something she and Keith had had in common. Like him, she preferred to examine an issue from all angles, make lists of the pros and cons and yet here she was, contemplating something that could have significant repercussions and she'd barely thought it through.

She stared at her reflection in the mirror. She looked good. She felt good. It was time to reclaim her life. Time to remember she was an attractive, single, twenty-something woman with her whole life ahead of her. With that thought in mind, she tidied her bedroom, picked up an evening bag and after tossing in her house keys, lip gloss and a credit card, snapped the clasp shut and slid the strap over her shoulder. Bidding Raoul a good evening, she left her unit.

Grayson Thorpe tilted the glass toward his lips and gulped the yeasty cold beer. Despite his best efforts, the numbness he sought continued to elude him. The Brass Monkey was a popular bar in Cronulla and it just happened to be his favorite hangout. Fortunately, it wasn't far from where he lived—although probably not for much longer. But that was a battle to come.

He'd been keeping the barstool warm, chasing morose thoughts since he'd left work more than two hours earlier. He'd probably already had more than his fair share of drinks, but he couldn't bring himself to go home. Earlier that day, he'd discovered his wife was cheating on him. He didn't know for how long, but he suspected it had been going on for several months.

It was at least that long since she had any interest in their relationship, including having sex. He'd tried to be understanding, but when she'd continued to reject his advances, he'd finally suggested they see a marriage counselor.

Lydia had merely smirked. "A marriage counselor? Really Grayson? How quaint. Have you forgotten I'm a psychologist? I counsel people for a living. You think I can't work through my own shit?"

He'd winced, upset by her callous response. He'd tried to explain he hadn't meant it like that, but she'd refused to listen. He'd ended up spending yet another night alone in the spare room.

A few days ago, he'd taken off his wedding ring. It was a big step and had filled him with desperate sadness, but he'd gotten to the point that he refused to wear it until he felt like Lydia's husband again. As far as he knew, she hadn't even noticed. Now he knew why.

Sadness at the demise of his marriage and a lingering anger toward the woman he'd committed himself to for life, overwhelmed him. With a weary sigh, he picked up his glass and drained his beer. The bartender moved closer.

"Can I get you another?"

Grayson looked down at the empty glass. "I probably shouldn't. I need to get home."

A knowing look passed over the bartender's face. "You got someone waiting for you?"

Grayson grimaced and was filled with another surge of pain. "Nope."

The truth was, Lydia was likely still at work. And after that, she took a Pilates class. At least, that's what she'd always told him. Now he couldn't help but wonder if she'd been meeting her lover instead. Whatever kept her occupied, she wouldn't think anything of the fact he wasn't home. On a normal day, he'd still be at the office. On a normal day, he wouldn't be home for hours.

And boy, had his wife taken advantage of that routine...

Lydia knew how much he wanted to make junior partner. It was one of the things they fought about. The fact he worked too hard, spent too many hours at the office. He'd tried to explain that it was important to work hard if he wanted to get promoted, but Lydia didn't seem inclined to accept that, or to understand. In the end, he'd stopped offering explanations and she'd stopped asking where he'd been.

The sound of raucous laughter behind him caught his attention. He swiveled on the barstool and surveyed the crowd. The place had filled up since he'd arrived. The clock over the bar showed it was now a little past five. The bar was buzzing with animated young professionals: men and women in their power suits, tasteful ties, shiny shoes. Everyone seemed in high spirits, laughing and joking and sharing conversation. He'd never felt so alone.

His gaze slid further along the bar and snagged on a woman. She sat alone at the bar and sipped from a glass of red wine. Her bare legs were crossed, drawing his attention to their shapeliness. His gaze moved higher. She was a little overdressed for so early in the evening, but what the hell. Maybe her day had been as shitty as his.

His gaze skimmed over her tight black leather dress and then paused on her breasts. They swelled generously above the zipper that divided the bodice, almost spilling over.

Maybe she's looking for someone to make a shitty day better...?

Reflexively, his cock hardened. Though he'd never been unfaithful to his wife, discovering her infidelity had left him feeling angry and impotent. He'd loved her with everything that he had and yet, it hadn't been enough. She'd thrown his love and devotion back in his face, as if it were of no value. It would serve her right for him to get even with her, even if she never caught wind of it. It might be just the thing to find a willing woman to help validate his masculinity, help him feel worthy of a woman's attentions.

As if sensing his scrutiny, the woman turned and saw him. She gazed at him for a moment, a slight smile on her ruby-red lips. Then she returned her attention to her wine. His heart kicked against his chest. Another rush of blood filled his cock. It strained against his boxers. It had been a long time since he'd felt such immediate attraction.

Christ, she's a stunner...

She sent him another glance from beneath thick dark lashes. Once again, her lips taunted him with a teasing smile. Knowing he shouldn't, but unable to resist, he climbed off his stool and drew closer. He seated himself on the empty stool beside her.

"Hi. I'm Grayson."

She inclined her head. "Charlotte."

She was even more beautiful up close. Flawless olive-toned skin. Eyes of a deep blue, their almond shape accentuated by her makeup. Her dark brown, wavy hair flowed like chocolate, rich and glossy past her shoulders. She moved to re-cross her legs and he caught a whiff of her perfume. A warm and heady hint of something exotic...

"Do you come here often, Grayson?"

Her husky tone ignited a fire in his groin. Desire coursed through him. He struggled to remember what she'd asked.

"Um. No. Yes. Sometimes. After work. To blow off steam, you know?" He laughed, silently cursing his awkwardness. He couldn't remember the last time he'd flirted with a woman and never one as beautiful as this.

She took another sip of her wine, seemingly unfazed. "What do you do?" she asked.

"I'm a lawyer. I work in the city."

She pulled a face and this time, his laugh was genuine.

"I know, right?" He winked.

She chuckled. "Well, now I know why you need to blow off steam."

He caught the eye of the bartender and signaled for another drink before returning his attention to Charlotte.

"So, how about you? I take it you're not a lawyer?" he teased.

She chuckled again and the husky sound of it shivered across his skin. "God no! I'm a cop."

This time it was his turn to pull a face. "A cop? You don't look like a cop."

She stared down at her wineglass, but a secret smile turned up her lips, sending another rush of heated blood to his cock. And then she turned to him with one perfect shapely dark brow arched upwards.

"What do I look like then?"

Their gazes caught and held. His heart thumped. The air around them grew charged. He leaned closer. "You look like someone who wants a fuck."

Her eyes flared wide. He heard her sharp intake of breath. A pulse fluttered under the smooth skin of her neck. He waited for her rebuke, or maybe even a slap across the face, but neither were forthcoming. Instead, she drew in a deep breath and smiled.

"You sound very confident of that."

He continued to hold her gaze. "I am."

She turned away abruptly and took refuge in her wine. A definite retreat from their brief repartee, but he was reluctant to leave it there. His beer arrived and he thanked the bartender and handed the man some money. Grayson returned his attention to the woman.

Charlotte...

"So... Shall we?"

She frowned and moved slightly away. "Shall we what?"

"Shall we dance?"

The lines on her forehead cleared. She smiled. "Oh. I thought you were going to suggest..."

Her voice faded away. Twin spots of color appeared on her cheeks. Her embarrassment touched something inside him. She looked younger than he'd first guessed and even more beautiful.

He gave her a wicked smile. "Suggest what? That we get the hell out of here and do what we've both been wanting to do the moment we set eyes on each other?" He ran the tip of his finger down her bare arm. Her eyes flared wide with awareness. He smiled with satisfaction and added, "Don't worry, we're going to do that too. But first, let's dance."

With that, he took her by the hand and led her confidently toward the dance floor.

Chapter Two

With one hand on Grayson's shoulder and the other grasped firmly in his big hand, Charlotte couldn't help but admire the confident way he led her around the dance floor. The music had changed to something slow and Grayson pulled her in close. His body was hard and muscular. Her breasts brushed his chest and she gasped. Her nipples immediately pebbled. He shot her a knowing look.

She averted her gaze and stared at his jacket. He wore a charcoal-gray suit that fit him like it had been made for him. And perhaps it had. Lawyers who worked in the city were usually paid well, especially if they were good. He moved and the firm muscles in his shoulder bunched beneath her hand.

Her heart skipped a beat. The smell of his expensive cologne filled her nostrils. Her chest went tight on a wave of desire. She looked up at him and caught the glint of amusement in his eyes.

"Don't look at me like that," he drawled.

"Like what?" She cursed silently at the breathless sound of her voice.

"Like you want to eat me all up."

The heat of embarrassment washed over her cheeks. She ducked her head and then brought it back up again to stare him boldly in the face. She'd come out tonight to have some fun, to throw caution to the wind. And yes, to take somebody home for the night. She'd never had a one night stand before, but somewhere between when she'd left her unit and walked through the door of the Brass Monkey, she'd made up her mind to do something completely out of character.

After having her boyfriend wound her with a parting shot about her lack of flair in the bedroom, she needed something to boost her self-esteem and to restore her faith in her attractiveness as a woman. What better way to do that than to pick up a willing man? Engage in some no-strings-attached sex. Experience an orgasm free from emotional entanglements. Yes. That sounded exactly like what she needed.

She'd noticed Grayson the minute she'd stepped up to the bar. He'd been seated alone, drinking. She'd taken a seat further down the bar and waited for him to notice her. It hadn't taken long.

His short blond hair, the color of ripened wheat, was mussed, like he'd run his hands through it more than once. His cheeks and jaw were rough with a five o'clock shadow. He was tall and his shoulders were broad. He looked like he worked out. Best of all, he wore no wedding ring.

She might have been prepared to set aside most of her morals for the night, but she drew the line at sleeping with married men. Of course, she was well aware a lack of wedding ring didn't necessarily indicate he wasn't married. There were plenty of men who went without that significant piece of jewelry, not always because they were being deceitful.

Some of them worked with their hands, or in dangerous jobs where wearing any kind of jewelry had the potential to cause serious injury. This guy had already told her he was a lawyer. Hardly a workplace where the wearing of a wedding ring would give rise to physical injury. The only way to know for sure if he were married was to ask him.

"So, tell me a little more about yourself, Grayson. Are you married?"

He stumbled slightly, but recovered quickly. "Does it matter?"

She merely offered him a shrug. "It does to me."

He compressed his lips. "I'm...recently separated."

She acknowledged his response with a brief nod and a surreptitious sigh of relief. Though she'd been hoping for a different answer, at least she didn't have to feel guilty about potentially breaking up a marriage.

They were dancing so close she could feel the heat from his body. He released her hand and cupped her ass with both of his hands, pulling her even closer. The unmistakable bulge of his erection pressed insistently against her belly. The obvious evidence of his desire left her feeling weak with need. Her stomach filled with butterflies.

The music came to an end and the DJ swung into another round of upbeat music. Grayson led her off the dance floor and returned her to her seat. She picked up her wineglass and emptied it. He did the same with his beer. Once again, he reached for her hand.

"Ready?" he asked.

She ignored the rush of protests on the tip of her tongue and forced herself to remember what this night was all about. With a determined intake of breath, she nodded. "Let's do it."

They walked out hand in hand. Outside on the footpath, Grayson drew her in close and kissed her. His lips were soft and firm and sensuous and boy did he know how to use them. Her arms slid around his neck and she kissed him back. His tongue pressed against her lips. She opened them, granting him access. The kiss deepened. She clung to his shoulders. When she finally lifted her head, she was breathless.

"Wow." She laughed nervously.

He gave a lopsided grin. "That was just for starters."

He grabbed her hand and pulled her along the footpath, keeping an eye out for a taxi. "Do you live close by?" he asked.

She felt a moment of hesitation. What she was about to do was fraught with danger. Any sane woman would never take a man she'd just met home. Anything could happen. He might be a serial killer, a drug dealer, a thief. And even though her gut was confident he was none of those things, he already knew too much about her. She sure as hell didn't want him knowing where she lived.

He regarded her expectantly, waiting for her answer. She smiled. "There's a hotel not far from here. How about we go there?"

He gave her a knowing look. "You don't trust me."

"Don't take it personally. I'm a cop. I don't trust anyone."

He grinned, flashing even, white teeth. "Fair enough."

Grayson pulled the woman in close beside him as she leaned back against the seat of the taxi. Night had settled in and they were cocooned in a seductive blanket of darkness. She checked her phone and gave the driver the address and then snuggled against him. She lay her head on his chest. He tightened his hold.

He thought about Lydia and was filled with guilt, but then remembering what he'd found out that day, he thrust those feelings away. Their marriage was over. He'd known it for months. He just hadn't wanted to acknowledge it, to say it out loud. To say it would make it real. Mean he had to do something about it. Dividing property, refinancing debts. Thank God they didn't have any kids.

Charlotte's hand stole over his lap and her fingers caressed him through his suit pants. His cock immediately sprang back to life. She pressed and fondled and squeezed and it was all he could do not to take her there and then. But he wanted more from her than a quick toss in the back of a taxi. He wanted her beneath him, clinging to him, her shapely legs around his hips, crying out his name.

His chest tightened on a surge of desire and he was relieved when the taxi pulled up to the curb a few minutes later. He fished in his back pocket for his wallet and handed the driver more than enough money to cover the fare. Taking Charlotte by the hand, he opened the door and together they slid across the seat and climbed out. She stumbled slightly in her high heels and he grabbed her around the waist to steady her. He wasn't sure how much she'd had to drink. She didn't appear inebriated, but he didn't want to take advantage of her.

"Are you all right?" he asked.

"Yes. Of course. Why?"

"I just want to make sure you still want to do this."

In response, she draped her arms around his neck and pulled him close. She tilted her head backwards and then came up on her tiptoes and pressed her lips to his. Just the feel of her soft lips against his filled him with another hot rush of desire.

"Does that answer your question?" she asked.

Her voice was husky with need. Her eyes were filled with desire. She smiled slowly and then winked. His gut somersaulted. Blood pounded in his cock.

"I guess so," he murmured.

With his arm around her shoulders, they walked past the doorman and into the plush hotel lobby. Grayson murmured for her to stay right there and then went up to the front desk.

In short order, he secured a room and came back brandishing a room card.

"Tenth floor. Ocean view."

Once again, she wrapped her arms around him and gave him a passionate kiss. "I think we're going to be too busy to appreciate an ocean view."

Grayson's control slipped. He walked her over to the bank of lifts and pressed the button. He pulled her close against him while they waited. Finally the lift arrived and he followed her in. He was relieved it was empty. As the doors closed silently behind them, he couldn't wait a moment longer to kiss her again.

Pushing her up against the wall of the lift, he held her immobile with his body. His head came down and he claimed her lips, kissing her urgently, filled with pent-up passion. They stayed that way, lips locked together, until the slide of the lift doors opening at their floor registered in his mind. He pulled back with reluctance, pleased that she looked as dazed as he felt.

He took her hand and led her halfway down a long corridor, coming to a halt outside a door that had the number "18" stenciled in fancy silver numerals. He pushed the keycard into the slot. The light flashed green; he turned the latch and opened the door. With her hand still in his, he drew her inside and immediately took her in his arms again.

Their lips met in another heated kiss, this one more frantic than the last. It was as if they'd both come to the decision that now they were in the privacy of a hotel room, they were free to explore the powerful desire they'd both felt the moment they'd laid eyes on each other. Grayson cupped her face in his hands and kissed her over and over again. His body was on fire. He burned to feel every inch of her, skin to skin, buried deep inside her.

With that objective in mind, he backed her up toward the bed, his lips fused with hers. Wild desire pulsed through him. He felt like he might explode. It had been months since he'd had sex with Lydia. His balls were heavy and tight. But this wasn't just about that. He'd never felt so turned on by a woman. Not even during his university days when he'd slept with more women than he cared to remember.

This is madness… I don't even know this woman… How can she drive me so wild?

This had started out as revenge for his wife's betrayal and affirmation of his attractiveness to women, but it had turned into something so much more. Feelings of lust he'd never before experienced. It was exhilarating, heady, unbelievable… Also a little scary.

Slowly, he pulled away so that he could catch his breath. He was pleased to see Charlotte's chest heaved, too. He moved to switch on one of the bedside lamps and flooded the room with soft, golden light. Glancing around him, he took note of the spacious hotel room. Like the girl behind the counter had told him, it boasted sensational ocean views.

Decorative street lights illuminated the wide, sandy-white beach. Night had stolen all but the slightest glimmer of moonlight on the water. They could be looking at a desert for all they could see. Not that the view mattered. He couldn't care less what was outside the window. His entire focus was on the woman in the room.

She reached for his tie and began loosening it, smiling softly to herself as she did so. Holding his gaze, she slid the tie from around his neck, flung it over her shoulder and then started in on the buttons on his shirt. Emboldened by her eagerness to get him naked, he reached out and took hold of the tab on her zipper.

Their gazes meshed. The heat of desire that burned in her eyes nearly did him in. He inched the zipper halfway down, slowly exposing her large round breasts. They were encased in a scrap of sexy black lace. His breath caught. He was desperately trying to go slow, but it was all he could do not to fling her on the bed and fuck her.

With an effort, he held onto his self-control, his breath hissing through clenched teeth. Seemingly oblivious to his inner struggle, she made a sound of impatience and pulled the tail of his shirt out of his suit pants. She pushed the soft cotton off his shoulders, pulled it down his arms and tossed it to the floor. She stared at his naked chest as if mesmerized. He knew exactly how she felt. He was having a hard time dragging his gaze away from her breasts.

Reaching out, he eased the zipper of her dress lower. The leather parted, exposing more and more of her skin. Grayson's breath caught. She was even more beautiful in the gentle glow of the lamplight. With her dress half undone and her black lace-encased breasts overflowing the opening, he was filled with the need to touch her. He stepped forward at the same time she did and they came together with a passion that left him breathless.

Frantic now, he reached for the zipper tab and pulled it all the way down. Her dress separated into two pieces of shiny leather. She shrugged out of it and dropped it to the floor. He stared at her in amazement. She was the most perfectly formed woman he'd ever seen.

She barely came up to his shoulder, even in her extra high heels. Petite in stature, yet curvy in all the right places. Her generous breasts, the flare of her hips, the slim, shapely thighs and calves. He was overawed by her beauty. And then her hands went to his waist and she started in on his belt. Her fingers brushed his cock and he sucked in his breath.

The smile she gave him was filled with satisfaction. Her eyes teased him, along with her fingers. And then his button popped and the zipper of his pants went down. He shucked them off his hips and kicked them aside. She put her hand inside his boxers and encircled his cock. He barely suppressed a moan.

"You like that?" she asked, her voice husky with need.

"I like it a lot," he managed.

She looked at him, her eyes intense. "I want to see you naked."

Charlotte heard the words fall out of her mouth and could hardly believe she'd said them. She was hardly experienced when it came to sexual partners. Especially when it came to taking the lead. Before Keith, she'd only had one other lover. But somehow, with Grayson it seemed natural. She felt so feminine, so powerful, like she was the one calling the shots. She saw the way he looked at her, the heat, the desire in his eyes: like he'd die if he didn't have her. That was a heady feeling.

The soft light from the bedside lamp illuminated his pectorals. They were tanned and toned and well-defined. His washboard stomach drew her gaze. She reached out and raked her fingernails across it. She heard him suck in his breath and smiled to herself, loving the fact she could elicit such an involuntary response from him. His muscles were as hard and firm as they looked. Unable to help herself, she then traced the line of dark hair that went from his belly button and disappeared into the top of his boxers.

He stopped her hand before she had a chance to caress his erection once again and placed her hand palm-down on his chest. She could feel the pounding of his heart and it matched the rhythm of her own.

"Can you feel that? Can you feel what you do to me? I'm desperate to fuck you, Charlotte."

His coarse language excited her. Her nipples tightened in response. Grayson noticed. His lips parted on a silent intake of breath. His eyes darkened with desire.

His reaction sent another wave of need coursing through her and all of a sudden she was impatient to feel his skin against hers. She reached around and unclasped her bra and let the scrap of lace fall to the floor. Grayson's eyes flared wide. She held his gaze as she slowly stepped out of her panties.

"God, you're so beautiful."

She basked in his obvious admiration and then reached out for his boxers. He helped her remove them and then stood while she looked her fill. He was fully aroused and every bit as beautiful as she'd imagined. Broad shoulders. Narrow hips. Long, muscular legs. Everything about him turned her on.

"Fuck me," she breathed and was gratified by his husky growl.

He took her in his arms and kissed her roughly, almost savagely, as if his control had finally snapped. Bending low, he picked her up in his arms and carried her to the bed. He lowered her to the mattress and followed her down, covering her body with his. Hardness melded against softness. He kissed her mouth, her cheeks and eyes and then made his way down to her breasts. He suckled one nipple and then the other and she writhed against him.

Desire burned in her core. She stirred restlessly against him, urging him on with small moans of encouragement. And then reality reared its head. She flushed with embarrassment, unable to believe that though her purpose was to find a man for the night, she'd forgotten all about protection. Averting her gaze, she pushed gently against him.

He frowned down at her. "Charlotte? Is something wrong?"

She uttered the solitary word. "Condom."

Relief passed over his face. He moved off her and reached into his suit pants. He pulled out a small packet and quickly sheathed himself. He rejoined her on the bed and once again kissed her deeply, thoroughly, flooding her with desire. As his hand moved down, in search of his ultimate target, he enjoyed the satiny softness of her belly. He was relieved to find her hot and wet.

"Are we okay?" he asked as he settled himself between her thighs.

Her legs fell open in silent assent. His cock nudged at her entrance. He lifted her thigh high and in one swift thrust, he was inside her. She gasped from the strength of his sudden entry.

He felt huge and hard and hot, filling her like no other had. She clung to his shoulders as his hips moved in a powerful rhythm. The desire inside her built. He whispered hot words of encouragement, his breath harsh in her ear. And then she was suddenly there, at the precipice.

Her fingernails dug into his shoulders. Her inner muscles clenched and contracted. With a gasp, she cried out her relief, her pleasure sharp and hot. She crashed over the other side. Grayson thrust harder, faster, deeper and a few seconds later he stiffened above her as he groaned out his own release. He collapsed on top of her for a moment or two, panting harshly.

And then he rolled off her and she was left thinking about how wonderful it had been. If this was how one-night stands felt, she was all for them. In fact, she looked forward to doing it all over again with him.

Chapter Three

The sound of her phone ringing dragged Charlotte from a deep sleep. She opened her eyes and blinked, feeling disorientated. She squinted through the dimness at the unfamiliar room. The light was all wrong. It was too dark. A faint headache made itself known. She closed her eyes against it, wanting nothing more than to escape back into sleep.

And then memories from last night hit her in a rush. Her eyes flew open and her gaze went to the other side of the bed. It was empty.

He's gone.

The mess of the bedsheets, her scattered clothes and the pleasant soreness in her thigh muscles were the only reminders of what had happened. Struggling to sit up, she reached for the light switch. The illuminated numbers on the clock radio told her it was a little past four in the morning.

"Ugh!" she groaned.

The phone kept ringing from somewhere far away. Her thoughts immediately went to her family. While her parents were only in their sixties, it was always possible that something had happened to them. A heart attack. A stroke. A car accident. Or maybe it was one of her brothers or sisters?

Get a grip, Charlotte. For goodness sake! Answer the damn phone!

Climbing out of bed, she found her evening bag on the floor. She avoided looking at her crumpled pile of underwear as she picked up the bag and pulled out her phone. She checked the screen.

Wendell Boney.

Shit. Her boss. Pushing back what felt like a bad case of bed hair, Charlotte sat down on the bed. She drew in a deep breath and tried to sound authoritative as she answered the phone.

"Good morning, sir. What's going on?"

"Sorry to call you so early, Charlotte, but there's been a murder. I thought you might want to ride along. Tony's lead investigator, of course, but you could—"

"Yes! Yes!" Charlotte shouted, coming fully awake. "Of course I want to ride along."

"Well, okay. I'll text you the details. You can catch up with Tony at the scene."

Tossing the phone on the bed, Charlotte threw on her underwear and the leather dress. She wasted another few moments searching for her stilettos and then grabbed her evening bag, tossed her phone back inside, and headed for the door. She thought fleetingly of the sexy lawyer who'd shown her such a good time, but there was no time to think any more on that now.

Pulling the door closed behind her, she headed for the lift. Excitement and apprehension coursed through her. Her first homicide. Better not mess it up.

By the time Charlotte arrived at the crime scene, the sun had peeked its head over the horizon. The rush of catching a taxi home, a quick shower and change before heading out again had her adrenaline pumping, along with the slightly scary knowledge she was about to front up to her very first murder scene. She found herself in an upmarket Cronulla neighborhood, a couple of miles from the beach. In fact, it wasn't all that far from her unit. The realization was slightly disconcerting.

Climbing out of her car, she observed a large freestanding home—a circa mid-2000s, rendered pale gray brick structure, with white trim and a black tile roof. It was of a similar style and age to all the other houses in the street. The wooden front door was painted charcoal and currently stood wide open. Uniformed officers traipsed in and out of the house. Charlotte hoped someone had secured the scene.

Blue-and-white checked police tape cordoned off the front yard. Charlotte ducked under the tape and flashed her newly minted homicide credentials to the general duties cops who were gathered on the lawn.

"Is Sabattini here yet?" she asked.

"Tony? Haven't seen him," one of the cops said.

The other cop snickered. "No doubt he's sleeping off another hangover. Surely you know what he's like."

Charlotte bit down on a surge of irritation. Her partner might very well be the joke of her department, but it annoyed her to see two junior officers blatantly disrespecting him. She pulled out her phone and dialed Tony's number, praying the officers were wrong. To her relief, he answered on the third ring.

"Barrington, what the hell? It's half-past five in the morning. This better be good."

She swallowed a sigh. "I'm sorry, Tony. Didn't Wendell call you?"

There was a pause and then Tony spoke again. "Looks like I might have missed his calls," he mumbled. "What's going on?"

Charlotte swallowed another sigh. "We have a situation. I've been called out to a homicide. I thought you might want to tag along."

He grunted in response. "Mind what you're saying, Barrington. I'm the senior detective here. You're nothing but a—"

"Okay, okay. That was a joke. But you know what, I'm here and you're not. If you want to hold my hand and guide me through the murder scene, I suggest you get over here fast."

With that she ended the call and then texted him the address. She was relieved when he sent her a thumbs up in response. Though she didn't doubt her investigative abilities, the pressure to do things right was enormous. She'd be pleased for some support, even if it was in the form of Tony Sabattini. Tony was a cop with an enviable success record in his day, but who'd seen too much in his time as a homicide detective and was now jaded, careless and well overdue for retirement.

Knowing he was on his way over, Charlotte gave instructions for the uniformed officers to canvass the neighborhood for witnesses and then waited for Sabattini before entering the house. Drunk or not, she'd feel much more confident with Tony, the veteran homicide cop, taking the lead. She was a newbie. She wasn't arrogant enough to assume she had the knowledge to navigate the complexities of a homicide on her own. Someone's wife, daughter, mother or sister was lying dead inside. They deserved answers. They deserved to have the perpetrator caught and they deserved to have someone with the experience to give them the best chance of achieving those things.

Sabattini arrived in his beat-up old Ford about fifteen minutes later. It ground to a halt in a cloud of exhaust smoke. So much for pollution... He climbed out and slowly made his way up the path. It took him a couple of attempts to duck under the police tape. He drew closer and Charlotte's heart sank. She could smell alcohol on his breath.

"Thanks for coming," she murmured, deliberately ignoring his level of intoxication. Even with a few drinks under his belt, she had no doubt Sabattini was still much better at this than she was.

He grunted a response and then cleared his throat and turned his head. He hawked up a lump of phlegm and spat it out. Charlotte ignored him. Together, they walked over to the uniforms.

"What do we have?" Sabattini rasped.

The oldest officer cleared his throat. "Female victim. Caucasian, mid to late twenties. Has suffered multiple stab wounds. We're still waiting for the guys from the morgue to arrive, but it appears our vic's been dead several hours. She's cool to the touch and rigor mortis has set in."

"Who found her?" Sabattini asked.

"The husband. Mr. Thorpe. Says he arrived home around four this morning and found her dead on the living room floor."

"Where is he?" Charlotte asked.

"Over there." The cop indicated a tall, broad-shouldered man who stood in the front yard with his back to her. Short wheat-colored hair. Tall, athletic. He certainly looked strong enough to overpower a woman. In the dawn light, something about him looked familiar. She was almost afraid to approach him.

Charlotte returned her attention to the uniforms. "Has anyone spoken to him yet?"

"No. We were waiting for you guys to arrive."

She and Tony walked over to the man whose shoulders were hunched as if trying to ward off the encroaching dawn.

"Mr Thorpe, I'm Detective Sabattini and this is Detective Barrington. Would you mind answering a few questions?"

The husband turned slowly to face them. Charlotte gasped in shock.

Oh, God... It's him... Grayson... The man from the bar... The man I spent the night with...

He looked just as shocked as she felt. She'd told him she was a cop. She hadn't told him she worked in homicide. Green eyes that were clouded with pain and confusion stared back at her, filled with questions neither of them could ask. Even so, she felt a familiar kick of attraction. Her mind was filled with flashbacks of her running her hands over his chiseled jaw, his biceps, the toned planes of his stomach...

He still wore the same charcoal-gray suit, though the tie was missing. She cataloged each of his features, her mind in turmoil. Her heart thumped. Her chest went tight. All of a sudden she couldn't breathe. And then one thought dominated everything else.

I need to tell Sabattini...

Oblivious to Charlotte's turmoil, Tony pulled out his notebook and a pen. "Can you think of anyone who'd want to do this to your wife?" Sabattini asked, his gaze fixed on Thorpe's face.

Grayson looked pained. "I don't know. No. I... I can't think of anyone."

"What do you do for a living, Mr Thorpe?" Sabattini asked.

"I'm a lawyer. I specialize in probate law and litigation. I mainly represent disgruntled beneficiaries who want to challenge a will."

Sabattini snorted. "Sounds like that could get ugly."

Thorpe shrugged. "I guess. From time to time. No one likes to lose, especially when there's money involved."

"Could this have something to do with you being a lawyer?" Sabattini asked. "Did you piss anyone off lately?"

Thorpe paled and looked visibly shaken. "Oh, God. I hope not."

Charlotte finally found her voice. "So there could be someone with that kind of anger against you?"

Thorpe frowned and then slowly shook his head. "No, surely not. No, I've put some people offside from time to time, but I don't believe any of them would be capable of murder."

"Are you thinking of anyone in particular?" Charlotte asked.

"Maybe. My latest case. The judgment was handed down last week. We... We won. There was a lot of money at stake. Ten million. I represented two of three siblings who were unhappy with their share. It got pretty nasty."

"How did the loser fare?" Sabattini asked.

"Not so good. The judgment was in the sum of seven million dollars, plus costs. That's going to come out of the losing party's share."

"That's enough to make anyone angry," Sabattini observed. "Why are you so sure the disgruntled relative couldn't be responsible for your wife's murder?"

Grayson scrubbed at his hair. "Well, he knows nothing about me, for one! I'm just another lawyer. And he sure as hell knows nothing about Lydia! I work for Sydney Legal. It's a large law firm in the city. Lydia rarely comes into the city. I think she's been to my office all of three times over the five years I've worked there."

He told me he was separated...

Once again, Charlotte was bombarded with images of them naked. With an effort, she forced them aside.

"How long have you two been married?" she asked stiffly.

"Four years. We've dated since university and married a year after I graduated. I was studying law. She was studying medicine."

"So she's a doctor?" Sabattini asked.

"No. She switched to psychology about two years into her medical degree."

"Where did your wife work?" Sabattini asked.

"She has...had her own counseling practice in Cronulla Plaza. She opened the doors a couple of years ago."

"Did she ever mention any patients she was having trouble with?" Charlotte asked.

"No, she never talked about her work. Patient confidentiality and all that. It was the same for me."

"Was there anything unusual about your wife's behavior in recent times?" Sabattini asked.

"What do you mean?"

"You know, strange phone calls, hang-ups? Did she act like something was troubling her? Did you ever hear her arguing with anyone over the phone?"

He averted his gaze and stared at the grass. "No, nothing like that."

Charlotte frowned. There was a subtle change in Thorpe's demeanor. A new tension around his mouth and his body had a tautness that hadn't been in evidence before. Charlotte flicked a glance toward her partner. The surreptitious movement of Tony's head reassured her he'd also noticed.

"Are you sure?" Charlotte asked.

Thorpe looked at her. "Yes, of course."

"What about the two of you?" Sabattini asked. "Any problems in your marriage?"

Charlotte's stomach somersaulted. She held her breath, waiting for Thorpe's response. He glanced at her briefly and then averted his gaze.

"Actually, we hadn't been getting on so well lately. Nothing I could put my finger on. She just seemed kind of...distant. We hadn't been intimate for months."

Charlotte eased out her breath, but she couldn't afford to relax. Until they had a time of death, she had to treat him like any other potential suspect. "Did the two of you fight?"

Thorpe shrugged. "I guess. Sometimes. Everyone fights."

"How often?" she asked.

"Not often."

"Did it ever get physical?" she asked.

His eyes flared with anger. "Never."

"What did you fight about?" Sabattini asked.

"I don't know. The usual stuff."

"Such as?" Sabattini persisted.

"Work, mainly."

"You said you didn't talk about your work with each other," Charlotte said.

"We didn't. What I meant was, we argued about how much time I spent at the office. That kind of thing." And then he looked at Sabattini, his eyes hard. "Am I a suspect, Detective?"

"Everyone's a suspect Mr Thorpe," Sabattini replied smoothly. "Surely you know those closest to the victim are the first ones we look at."

Thorpe gave a half-shrug in response.

"Do you have any children, Mr Thorpe?" Charlotte asked.

"No."

"Can't have any? Don't want any?"

"Neither. We... We haven't...hadn't gotten around to having that discussion, yet."

Charlotte blinked in surprise. "I'm sorry, how long did you say you've been married?"

"Four years."

"Right. Four years. And in all that time you've never had a conversation with your wife about whether or not you want kids?"

Once again, his only response was a non-committal shrug.

"What time did you leave for work yesterday?" Sabattini asked.

"I was out the door by six o'clock. Same as every other day."

"You told one of our officers you arrived home about four this morning. Is that right?" Sabattini asked.

Thorpe drew in a deep breath and then released it on a sigh. "Yes."

Charlotte fixed her gaze on the ground, unable to look at Grayson. She braced herself for Sabattini's inevitable next line of questioning.

"That's a hell of a long day, Mr Thorpe. What time did you finish work?"

A flush stained Grayson's cheeks. "I... I left early. Just after three."

"I see. And where did you go?"

"I went to a bar."

"Until four this morning?"

"No. I'm not sure what time it was when I left the bar."

"Closing time?" Sabattini asked.

"No. Not that late. Maybe seven or eight. I don't really remember."

"Where did you go then?" Sabattini asked.

Charlotte's breath caught in her throat.

I have to tell Sabattini... I have to come clean...

She tensed, waiting for Grayson's response.

"I met a woman in the bar. We went to a hotel. Afterwards, I went back to the bar and retrieved my car and drove home. That's when I found Lydia."

"Does this woman have a name?"

Grayson's gaze glanced off hers. Once again, Charlotte held her breath.

Grayson looked back at Sabattini and shook his head. "I guess. But we didn't exchange personal details."

Charlotte slowly eased out her breath and was immediately overcome with guilt.

I have to tell him... But I can hardly do it here...

"What about earlier? Where were you before you went to the bar?" Sabattini asked.

"I was at work."

"All day?"

"Well, I went out for lunch. About twelve. I got back to the office at two."

Charlotte forced herself back into the conversation before Sabattini wondered what was amiss. "That's a rather long lunch break," she said.

Grayson glanced again in her direction. "I had a few errands to run."

"Where did you go?" Sabattini asked.

Thorpe shrugged. "Does it matter?"

Sabattini gave him a hard look. "Don't piss me off, Mr Thorpe. Your wife's dead. Everything matters."

A look of impatience crossed Grayson's face. Once again, he looked at Charlotte and then refocused his attention on her partner. "You're wasting your time with all these questions. I didn't do it."

"Until we have a definitive time of death, we need to cover all bases," Charlotte replied.

Thorpe sighed. "I went to the mayor's office."

"In the city?" she asked.

"No. In...Sutherland."

"Your local council? You planning on doing some renovations?" Sabattini asked.

Thorpe flushed. "No. My meeting with Mayor Matthews was...of a personal nature."

"He a friend of yours?" Sabattini asked.

Thorpe's flush deepened. Charlotte caught a flash of anger in his eyes.

"No. We're not friends."

"What did you do afterwards?" Charlotte asked.

"I had a two o'clock appointment with a client in my office. I left again right afterwards. A bit after three. Ask my executive assistant. She'll confirm what I say."

"Oh, don't worry. We will." Sabattini shot him another hard look. "What time did you arrive at the bar last night?"

"About half past three. I drove there straight from work."

"Three seems awfully early for a lawyer to be leaving work. Were you meeting someone?"

"No. I... I had a lot on my mind. I needed to get away for a while, to think."

"So you went to a bar. Does this bar have a name?" Sabattini asked.

"The Brass Monkey. It's downstairs in the Cronulla Plaza."

Sabattini's eyes narrowed. "Your wife had her office in the Cronulla Plaza, didn't she?"

Grayson's gaze remained steady on Sabattini's face. "Yes. So?"

"Nothing. Just a little curious you'd go somewhere so close to where your wife works. Especially when you were on the prowl for a little something on the side."

Anger flashed across Grayson's face. He glared at Sabattini. "First of all, it was half past three when I got there. My wife's office closes at five. She normally does a Pilates class straight after work and then goes home. There was no chance of running into her. Secondly, I didn't go there to pick up a woman, Detective. I went there to escape. Like I said, my wife had grown more and more distant and I didn't know what to do about it. I had a few drinks. Then I got talking to a woman. We had another drink. We danced. I didn't plan on sleeping with her, but it happened."

"I assume the bartender at the Brass Monkey will verify this?"

Grayson shrugged. "I don't know if he paid much attention to us, but he should certainly remember I was there. He served me several times."

Charlotte took down the pertinent details, including Grayson's contact numbers. Then she handed him her business card. "We'll be in touch, Mr Thorpe. No doubt we'll have more questions. In the meantime, if you think of anything else, call me. By the way, we'll need you to stop by the station and make a formal statement. Sometime later today would be good. Oh, and don't go planning any trips out of town without telling us. Until we have an exact time of death and we've checked out alibis, we can't rule anyone out."

Grayson gave her an unreadable look and then slowly tucked the small piece of white cardboard into the pocket of his shirt. His eyes were still dazed with shock. Charlotte wished she could offer him some sympathy, but the truth was, she was also in a spin. Hell, for all she knew she was Grayson's alibi. Or not. Until they knew the time of death, anything was possible. She definitely needed to come clean with Sabattini. Now.

She turned toward her partner and braced herself for what she was about to say. Sabattini appeared oblivious to her inner turmoil. With casual movements, he tucked his notebook and pen back into his shirt pocket. Before she could open her mouth, he turned on his heel and headed toward the house. Charlotte's teeth snapped shut.

He didn't even bother to check if I was following him! Talk about rude and insufferable! We're meant to be partners...

Swallowing her irritation, she hurried after the senior detective. "Tony? Wait up. Tony? Could I have a word?"

To her consternation, he ignored her. Either that, or he didn't hear her. He continued past two more officers and then into the house. Panting slightly from exertion, Charlotte came to a halt in the entryway.

The house was clean and modern. The overall color scheme was pale gray, including the tiled floor and soft furnishings. A massive wide-screen TV was mounted on one wall of the living room, complete with an impressive surround sound system. Whoever lived there liked watching movies, or sport, or whatever. Or else they were just plain showing off. The screen was big enough that it would almost feel like you were there on the set, or in the game.

The kitchen was a mixture of pale marble countertops and white cupboards. Like the rest of the house, it was also scrupulously clean. And then some of the uniformed officers moved aside and Charlotte caught a glimpse of the body.

Her stomach clenched. Her breath came fast. With an effort, she kept herself calm. If she wanted to succeed as a homicide detective, she'd better get used to the sight of corpses.

Lydia Thorpe lay in a pool of blood on the tiles, not far from a large sectional sofa that took up a decent amount of the open plan living room. She was fully dressed in a tailored navy-blue suit and a pale pink silk blouse. The flash of a lightbulb startled Charlotte. She blinked.

The police photographer took another photo of the body and then moved a few steps away and took another one. Being careful not to step in any of the blood spatter, he continued to move cautiously around the perimeter of the crime scene snapping pictures, preserving the gruesome images on his camera.

A number of crime scene technicians were also there processing the scene. Checking the place for fingerprints, bagging evidence and searching for pieces of the puzzle that would eventually come together to form a picture of what had happened there and who might be responsible. Charlotte caught sight of her partner talking to one of the uniforms.

"Any signs of forced entry?" Sabattini asked.

"No."

"Do we know if anything's missing?"

"I'm not sure. We haven't spoken to the husband about that yet, but the place is as neat as a pin. No cupboards left open. Nothing looks to be rummaged through. This doesn't look like a robbery to me."

Charlotte compressed her lips and stood there in silence. No signs of forced entry. No signs of a robbery. Whoever it was, it appeared Lydia Thorpe had invited the killer into her home, had possibly even known them.

"Have you found the murder weapon?" Sabattini asked the uniform.

"No. And there's nothing missing from the knife block we found in the kitchen."

Tony scratched at the bristles on his chin. "So the killer might very well have come prepared. That indicates premeditation."

"Certainly looks that way," the uniform replied.

A disturbance in the front doorway snagged Charlotte's attention. She turned around in time to see Doctor Samantha Wolfe, the state's chief forensic pathologist, enter the room, along with two morgue technicians who had a stretcher and body bag in tow. Samantha greeted those assembled with a brief smile and a wave and then went straight over to where Lydia lay. The photographer had finished and now took a step back to allow Samantha access to the body. She opened her black medical bag and began her examination.

Charlotte glanced at Sabattini. The uniform had since moved away. She couldn't put it off a moment longer. Dragging in a quick breath, she pulled Sabattini aside. Her stomach churned with nerves.

Sabattini frowned. "What is it, Barrington? You're looking a little queasy. Don't tell me you're going to lose it at your first homicide?"

With an effort, Charlotte forced herself to speak. "Of course not. It's nothing like that."

"Then what's the problem?"

She licked her dry lips and averted her gaze.

"Come on, Barrington. I don't have time for this. Spit it out."

He went to turn away and she reached out and grabbed his arm, stopping him. He frowned again.

"Tony... I'm sorry, but... I know him. Grayson Thorpe."

Tony's bushy eyebrows shot upwards. "You know him?"

Charlotte pulled a face. "Well, I don't know him.... The thing is, I..." She licked her lips again, and looked away, this time in embarrassment. "It was me. I was the woman he met in the Brass Monkey last night. I was the woman who went to a hotel with him."

Sabattini's eyes widened in shock. "Holy crap. You're kidding me?"

"I wish I was."

"So that's your thing, is it? Having sex with strangers?"

Charlotte tensed. "Not that it's any of your business, but no. It's not. I... I've never done that before."

Sabattini blew his breath out on a heavy sigh. "Hell. This complicates matters."

Charlotte grimaced. "You're telling me."

"We'll have to tell the boss. You won't be able to work this case."

Her shoulders slumped on a sigh. "I thought you might say that."

He gave her an impatient look "What did you expect? It can't be any other way. You're off the case. As soon as we get back to the station, I'll bring Wendell up to speed. You can stay for now, but don't touch anything. I mean it. Stay the hell out of the way and for fuck's sake, don't go talking to anyone. Got it?"

His voice had turned as hard as his eyes. Charlotte nodded reluctantly. Inwardly, she cursed.

My first homicide case and I've managed to mess it up... Damn it!

Charlotte stood back and watched in silence as the morgue technicians zipped up a body bag around the corpse. They then lifted the body onto the stretcher and wheeled it away. With a sigh, she found a spot out of the way and tried to get ahold of her disappointment.

Her first homicide and she was relegated to the bench.

Damn it!

Chapter Four

Charlotte dragged her feet as she followed Sabattini into the Cronulla Police Station later that morning. She'd chafed at every minute she'd been forced into the role of observer at her first homicide crime scene and she was even more nervous about the upcoming confrontation with her boss. The moment they entered the squad room, Sabattini made a beeline for the bathroom. Charlotte swallowed a sigh and went to her desk. She could see Wendell through the wall of glass that partitioned his office from the rest of the squad room.

Detective Superintendent Wendell Boney was a veteran cop with more than thirty years in the service. He was highly respected in the ranks, both as an astute investigator and an all-round good bloke. Her mouth went dry at the thought of speaking with him. The possibility that if she didn't get up the courage to speak with him now, Sabattini would beat her to it, was enough impetus to bring her to her feet.

She pushed away from her desk and straightened her skirt. Nerves churned in her stomach. Dragging in a fortifying breath, she squared her shoulders and strode to Boney's office. She tapped on his open door.

"Um, sir? Do you have a moment?"

He looked up from the stack of papers he'd been reading. The light from his desk lamp illuminated his caramel-colored skin. His dark brown eyes and wide flat nose were further evidence of his aboriginal heritage.

"Charlotte. How'd you go with your first homicide? I hope Tony showed you the ropes."

A fresh wave of nerves rushed through her. It was obvious Tony hadn't phoned their boss ahead of time and given him a heads-up about what had happened. She ought to be grateful for that. After all, her new partner owed her no favors. She clenched her hands into fists and drew in a deep breath.

"Um... It was great. Exciting... So much to learn..." She glanced up at him, feeling panicky. "The thing is sir, I screwed up," she blurted.

Wendell's eyes went wide. "You screwed up? Already? How'd you manage to do that?"

In stilted sentences and feeling more embarrassed than she'd ever felt in her life, Charlotte outlined the circumstances of what had happened. Her boss remained silent throughout. After she was finished, she stared at the floor, awaiting his response.

Wendell took so long to reply, the waiting nearly drove her insane. She tried to relax her fists, but the tension in her body wouldn't let her. Her mouth was dry. Her heart hammered. By the time he finally spoke, her nerves had reached a fever pitch. To her surprise, his tone was both measured and calm.

"I must confess, Charlotte. When I first received your application to apply for the detective's position in my department, I was dubious. You're the daughter of a billionaire. No doubt rich, spoiled and pampered. You were the last person I wanted on my team. But I took the liberty of speaking with some of your previous supervisors. They all spoke highly of your work ethic, your instincts and your willingness to get your hands dirty and not give up. I'm willing to admit I was surprised. So, I decided to give you a chance."

Charlotte stared at him in disbelief, her mind racing. She'd had no idea he'd initially wanted to overlook her for the position. She was quietly relieved her former supervisors had spoken out in support of her promotion, but Wendell's reticence to employ her also made her all the more determined to prove to him she was exactly the kind of cop he needed on his team.

She eyed him somberly. "I'm sorry, sir. But with all due respect, how was I to know that the following morning the man I had been with the night before would be questioned for murder. I swear, I had no idea who Thorpe was until we approached him for questioning."

Feeling awkward, Charlotte tried for some levity "The thing is, sir, I don't usually pick up men in bars. The fact my first bar hookup could potentially be a murderer is a clanger of a first time, to say the least!"

There wasn't so much as a flicker of amusement in Wendell's eyes. "I don't care what you do in your personal life, Barrington. That's your business. But I do care about the integrity of this murder investigation. Your connection with the victim's husband, however fleeting, is a conflict of interest. I'm removing you from the case."

Everything inside her wanted to protest, but Wendell was right. There was no way she could risk bringing the investigation into question. She wanted to believe the man she'd given herself to so passionately and with such complete abandon wasn't a cold-hearted killer, but until Grayson was cleared she had no choice but to consider him a suspect, along with everyone else.

"It's not my place to judge you, Charlotte. As I said, I don't give a toss about your personal life. My decision is based purely on what's best for the investigation." He paused and then added, "I take it Tony knows?"

"Yes, of course. I told him at the scene."

He nodded with approval. "Very good, Barrington. It reflects well on you that you came forward with this. You could have kept it to yourself and risked jeopardizing the entire investigation. You chose not to do that, even when it has come at some considerable personal and professional cost."

Wendell eyed her solemnly. "So, I commend you for your courage. You've only been here a month, but so far, I like what I see. Though your first homicide investigation didn't get off the ground, my gut tells me I made the right decision when I hired you on my team. My gut's rarely wrong about people. There will be other cases. Pick up your ass and focus on that and if Tony needs help with any of his other cases, feel free to pick up the slack."

Charlotte was flooded with relief. "I will, sir. No problem, sir. Consider it done. I will work harder than any detective here."

Her boss chuckled. "I have no doubt you mean every word of that."

He returned his attention to the paperwork on his desk, effectively dismissing her. She turned on her heel and left. With her head lowered, she crossed the squad room and flung herself down in her chair. Sabattini glanced up from where he was seated behind his desk a short distance away.

"You talk to Wendell?"

"Yep."

"He pulled you from the investigation?"

She sighed. "Yep."

"He had no choice. You know that, right?"

"Right."

"Listen, kiddo. Cheer up. There's sure to be another homicide sooner or later. The next one that comes across our desk is yours, okay?"

Charlotte breathed out and nodded. "Okay."

"Besides," Sabattini added, "this one looks pretty cut and dried. That kind of rage, coupled with the husband admitting to marriage problems... I don't think we have to look too far for our killer."

Charlotte sat up straighter in her seat and stared at him. "You can't be serious? We have no evidence Grayson was involved."

Sabattini smirked. "Not yet. But you wait and see. I've been in this game a long time and the stats support it. It's always the husband."

"Not always," Charlotte felt the need to point out.

Sabattini turned belligerent. "Okay, not always, but most of the time. It's obvious their marriage was on the rocks. He already admitted to cheating. Hell, he spent the night with you. The uniforms who canvassed the neighborhood confirmed they'd heard the couple arguing on several occasions. It seemed the arguments had grown in volume and intensity in recent weeks."

He yawned and stretched his arms up over his head. "If you ask me, this was a pressure-cooker situation just waiting for the right time to explode." He glanced at his watch and frowned. "Shit. Another six hours before I can have a drink. Are you a rum drinker, Barrington?"

Charlotte deliberately ignored his question. Instead, she focused her response on his earlier statements. "Couples argue all the time. Surely you're not going to tell me each and every one of those fights have the potential to lead to murder?"

Sabattini shot her a surly look. "Why are you busting my balls about this, Barrington? Remind me again how many homicides you've solved. Oh, that's right. Zero. This was your first case. And you managed to fuck it up before you even got your foot inside the door. Don't you dare tell me what might or might not set some people off. You know nothing."

Charlotte bit back the sharp retort teetering on the tip of her tongue. Pissing Sabattini off would get her nowhere. They were partners. Like Detective Superintendent Wendell Boney said, there would be other cases. She and Sabattini needed to learn to work together.

She sighed. "I guess we'll find out if the husband did it once the forensic pathologist has determined time of death. When can we expect the autopsy report?"

Sabattini eyed her balefully. "We're not expecting anything. You're off this case, remember?"

Charlotte opened her mouth instinctively to protest and then closed it again. With another sigh, she turned away and focused on the pile of files on her desk. At least she now had time to catch up on her paperwork.

From the corner of her eye, she saw a breaking news story flash across the TV that was mounted on the office wall across from her desk. A picture of Grayson Thorpe dressed in a fresh tailored suit and tie filled the screen. Charlotte's breath caught in her throat. She strained to hear against the hum of conversation in the squad room.

"In breaking news, Lydia Thorpe, the wife of well-respected Sydney Legal probate lawyer, Grayson Thorpe, was murdered last night in their family home in the seaside suburb of Cronulla. Doctor Lydia Thorpe was a psychologist who ran her own local practice. Police are conducting enquires. If you have any information concerning the murder, please come forward."

Grayson's handsome face filled the screen. Charlotte could hardly look at him. At least he hadn't lied about his occupation. She hoped that meant he might also have been honest about the other things he'd said. It didn't help that Sabattini was convinced Grayson was guilty. All she could hope was that the veteran cop would look below the surface and keep an open mind. She hated the fact that the lead investigator cared more about losing himself in a bottle than putting the right person behind bars, but there was nothing she could do about that. Like he said, she was off the case.

The door to the squad room opened. Charlotte saw a uniformed cop walk over to Sabattini.

"There's a Grayson Thorpe waiting downstairs with his lawyer. He's here to make a formal statement."

Charlotte looked at Sabattini. She was desperate to sit in on the interview, but she had very little hope that would happen. As if he could read her mind, Sabattini looked at her and shook his head.

"Not a chance, Barrington." With that he pushed away from his desk and left.

Charlotte poured herself another glass of wine and tried to put the day's events behind her. Raoul jumped up and made himself comfortable on her lap. She stroked him absentmindedly, her thoughts still consumed by Grayson and the murder and everything else that had happened that day.

Has it really only been a day?

It felt like a lifetime ago since she'd dressed to kill and had left the house in search of a good time. Boy, had that backfired. Okay, so she'd had a good time with Grayson— scratch that. She'd had the best sex ever! Hot and passionate. A mind-blowing orgasm. He'd seemed to enjoy it as much as she had. He'd definitely obliterated memories of Keith and his parting words about her lack of sexual prowess.

It was what had come afterwards that had her stomach churning with knots. She was still upset about being taken off the case. Of course, she understood the decision, but for heaven's sake! Of all the weird coincidences! And on her very first homicide investigation! And her very first one night stand... It was like something out of a B-grade movie. The final insult would be for her sexy and passionate lover to turn out to be a murderer.

"Ugh!" She groaned at the thought.

Picking up the TV remote, she pressed the power button. Grayson's image immediately filled the screen. He stood beside his lawyer outside the Cronulla Police Station. From what the reporter was saying, the footage had been taken after his record of interview. Though the lawyer did all the talking, Grayson remained calm and steady beside him. The only indication that he was troubled was the fear that clouded his eyes.

What's he afraid of? That we'll discover the truth?

Or was it merely the trauma of attending the police station to give an account of his whereabouts at the time his wife was being brutally murdered that had upset him? He was a probate lawyer. They didn't tend to be familiar with the workings of a police investigation. She wondered how he'd done in his interview and wished she had the right to call Sabattini and ask for an update.

Of all the men in Cronulla to sleep with... Why did I have to choose him?

Of course, she knew the answer. She'd been attracted to him right away. He'd exuded a tantalizing charisma she hadn't been able to resist. His charm, his good looks, his honesty. They'd come together to form an irresistible combination she hadn't been able to walk away from. Even now, after everything that had happened, flashbacks of their night together continued to flood her mind.

The combustible heat between them, the passion, the intensity... The frenetic energy that had them going at each other like they couldn't survive without the other. They'd had sex twice more after that first time and it had been just as good each time. He'd also been a caring and considerate lover. Sex had never been like that before.

But now she couldn't get those erotic images, those hot and heavy feelings, out of her mind and they were driving her insane. The sexy stranger who'd turned into her passionate lover was now squarely at the center of a murder investigation. Why? How? She couldn't equate the amazing, considerate lover with a killer. It was doing her head in. She needed to quit thinking about him. Starting now.

The sound of her phone ringing provided a welcome distraction. Setting Raoul aside, she climbed off the couch and padded barefoot to the kitchen counter where she'd left her phone on the charger. She checked the number on the screen, but it was unfamiliar. She considered letting it go through to voicemail, but at the last moment she answered the call.

"Charlotte Barrington."

"Charlotte. It's Grayson."

Charlotte's heart skipped a beat and then adrenaline kicked in. She gulped. "How did you get my number?"

"Your business card, remember?"

Shit.

"I can't talk to you," she said. "You're a suspect in a murder investigation."

"Please don't hang up!" His voice was tinged with desperation. "You have to tell them you were with me. Out of respect for you, I've kept your name out of it for now, but you have to—"

"I have. I told them. And now I'm off the case."

"I didn't do it, Charlotte. I didn't kill my wife."

"That's not for me to decide, Grayson. Please don't call me again." With that, she ended the call.

Setting her phone back on the counter, she buried her face in her hands. Drawing in a few shaky breaths, she fought hard to reestablish her equilibrium. She'd handed over her business card without thinking. It was standard procedure when interviewing potential witnesses. Though this was her first homicide, she'd spent years investigating other types of crime. You could never tell when someone would remember something significant. It was important they had a way to get in contact.

But that courtesy couldn't extend to Grayson Thorpe. At least, not with her. She'd make sure to tell Sabattini to reach out to Grayson and provide him with Tony's contact number, if he hadn't already.

God, what a mess! I can't believe I'm in this situation! I've led such a cautious, predictable life! I never do anything without looking at it from every side, almost to the point where I hamstring my ability to make a decision. And now, when I finally find the courage to do something spontaneous, it's turned into a disaster of epic proportions.

Feeling despondent, she picked up her phone and made her way back to the couch. Scrolling through her contacts, she stopped when she got to Trace. Her brother was a cop in the small rural town of Broken. Along with her and Molly, he was also one of the triplets. The three of them were closer than close. As a fellow cop, Trace also had personal insights into the job and the particular stresses that came with it.

Raoul jumped back up into her lap. Absently, she reached out and scratched between his ears as she listened to the phone dial out.

"Charlotte! What's happening?"

Trace's cheerful voice brought an involuntary smile to her lips. He sounded upbeat.

"Well, I've had better days, but it sounds like you've had a good day."

"Yeah, you could say that. I've been off a couple of days. Played a few rounds of golf. Had some drinks with friends. Now I'm kicking back, eating Chinese takeaway and watching football on TV."

"Sounds like the perfect night in," she replied with a smile.

"So, why is it that you've had better days? What's happened?" Trace asked around a mouthful of food.

With a heavy sigh, Charlotte told him about Grayson Thorpe. She left nothing out. She wasn't worried about Trace judging her. They loved and respected each other too much for that. The thing is, she needed his advice. She also needed to air her concerns with someone who'd understand.

"I've been partnered with Tony Sabattini."

"Sabattini? He's been around a long time. You could do worse than to be partnered with him. He's forgotten more than the rest of us will ever know."

"True. Have you seen him lately?"

"No."

"He's..." Charlotte hesitated. "He's not quite the man he used to be. I'm not sure if something happened in his personal life or whether it's just the cop life taking its toll, but he seems more interested in losing himself in a bottle of rum than he does in solving this latest case. He turned up at the crime scene this morning drunk."

Trace gasped in surprise. "You're kidding!"

"I'm afraid not. He wasn't falling-down drunk, but he reeked of alcohol. The thing I'm most concerned about is that he appears to have already made up his mind about Grayson's guilt."

"How do you mean?"

"He told me quite succinctly that the case is pretty well cut and dried. More often than not it's the husband, he told me. I'm afraid he's going to railroad Grayson and not bother to look at anyone else."

"The guy's a lawyer, isn't he? I'm sure he can look after himself."

"That's true, but a probate lawyer... and still... Do you think you can get hold of the autopsy report for me?"

"You know I can't do that, Charlotte."

She closed her eyes briefly against a surge of irritation. "Trace, I'm not asking you to reveal any specific details. I just need to know the time of death."

"The answer's still no, Charlotte. You're off the case, remember? And even if you weren't, I can't call the morgue and request access to a report from a case I have nothing to do with."

Charlotte's chest went tight on a surge of panic. "Please, Trace. If the time of death lines up with when I was with Grayson, I'll know for sure he's not the perp. Please. I need to know. For the sake of my sanity."

"I'm sorry you feel that way, but it's still a no from me. And please don't go bugging Zac," he said, referring to their younger brother who was also a cop. "You know he can't refuse you anything. It isn't fair, Charlotte. Not only that, it's against the rules. Do you want to get all of us in trouble? I'm going to pretend we never had this conversation."

Charlotte opened her mouth, intent on making another attempt to persuade him, but then guilt seeped in and squashed any further thoughts of asking either of her siblings to do something they weren't comfortable doing. She closed her mouth, deflated. There would be no help from either quarter and she shouldn't have expected that from them. She'd just have to live with the unknown awhile longer and hope Sabattini was more forthcoming with information.

Chapter Five

Grayson did his best to focus on the typed statement in front of him, but it was proving difficult. The case was due in court in a few weeks and he was falling behind in his preparation. Thank goodness for his paralegal who'd included detailed notes alongside the statement. Still it would be Grayson on his feet before the judge, arguing his client's case.

The problem was, he wasn't sleeping. No surprise there. Three days earlier, his entire life had been turned upside down. It wasn't just the fact his wife had been brutally murdered and the police were doing their best to pin it on him, but he hadn't been allowed in the house. Now that he had permission, he didn't want to return home.

He'd spent the past two nights in a hotel room. Not the same hotel he'd been to with Charlotte. God, he couldn't bear that kind of torment. A few hours ago, the police had informed him his house was no longer considered a crime scene, but there was no way he could bring himself to return. The shock of finding his wife's murdered body was still too fresh. He'd forced himself inside only long enough to pack a bag with some essentials and had hightailed it away from there as quickly as he could.

Crime scene tape still cordoned off his front yard. The detritus of a forensic investigation was still spread all over his house. Fingerprint dust lay on every available surface. Drawers had been opened and the contents photographed. Every room of his house had been picked over, searched, poked and prodded as police tried to come up with various scenarios to explain how his wife had ended up lying in a pool of blood on his living room floor. Stabbed to death!

It had been a hell of a shock finding her. Accompanying that was an overwhelming sense of guilt. If he hadn't gone to a bar after work... If he hadn't spent the night with Charlotte... If he'd been home like he should have been, was it possible his wife might still be alive...? It was no wonder he couldn't stay focused on something as normal and mundane as his work or get a decent night's sleep.

He had so many questions. So many regrets for not trying harder. Why was my wife seeing someone else? What happened that went so wrong? One shock after another and on top of that, Charlotte Barrington had been tossed into the mix. All on the very same night.

Thoughts of the beautiful detective flooded his mind. Charlotte Barrington. Their night together had been amazing. She'd made him feel things he hadn't felt for a long time. Desirable, attractive, wanted. Like she couldn't get enough of him. He couldn't remember the last time he'd received even a modicum of passion from his wife.

Grayson immediately felt guilty. Lydia was dead. She deserved better. He had no idea who was responsible. One thing he knew: It sure as hell wasn't him.

His thoughts slid to the Mayor of Sutherland Shire and then skittered away again. The first shocking discovery Grayson had made that fateful day was that his wife had been having an affair with Simon Matthews.

The joke's on me... I should have seen it coming... I should have known...

Grayson still couldn't believe how obtuse he'd been. It hadn't even occurred to him that Lydia had been cheating. He'd thought her distant attitude had stemmed from the fact he'd been working long hours and it had been way too long since they'd taken time out to reconnect and breathe life back into their relationship.

Is Matthews responsible for Lydia's death?

What if Matthews had gone to Grayson's home straight after their meeting and he and Lydia had gotten into a fight? Grayson didn't know enough about the mayor to say whether the man was capable of that kind of violence, but what if he were?

I should have told Detective Sabattini about Lydia's affair... What if Matthews killed her?

At the time, all he'd been able to focus on was that his wife was dead. Thinking about where he'd been during the final hours of his wife's death had filled him with guilt. The last thing he'd wanted to do was besmirch Lydia's memory by sharing with the detectives her infidelity and the fact she'd been having an affair with their mayor.

But that had probably been a mistake. They'd asked him if he could think of anyone who might have wanted to kill his wife and he'd told them no. He'd lied. To save Lydia's reputation, but also to deflect blame from himself. They'd think he, as a husband who'd just discovered his wife of four years was cheating, could be angry, upset, unpredictable. Someone in that situation might even turn violent...

The same could be said for the mayor. After Grayson's surprise visit, Simon Matthews was under no delusions: He knew the game was up. It was just as possible he'd been as upset and angry and unpredictable as the cuckolded husband. At the very least, Grayson should have told the detectives about the affair so they could speak with the mayor and verify his alibi.

What Grayson really wanted to do was speak to Charlotte again. He wanted to hear her voice. He wanted to remember their night of passion, the way she'd made him feel. Most of all, he wanted her to know he wasn't a killer, that he could never do something like that. Lydia's infidelity might have been shocking and it had certainly hurt, but nothing would have driven him to murder, despite what the police might think.

He'd turned up at the station and provided a formal statement like they'd requested, but that hadn't put an end to the harassment. Already there had been two further phone calls from the police. Purporting to be for the purposes of follow up questions, they were full of thinly veiled accusations. He was weary, tired of it.

There was also the possibility that Lydia had been murdered while he was with Charlotte. No doubt Charlotte was appalled by the thought she might have to provide his alibi, but as far as he was concerned, it would be a wonderful stroke of luck if the times lined up. What better way to convince the police of his innocence than to offer up another cop as his alibi.

He clung to the thought. It might be his only hope.

Trying to look busy had to be one of the most challenging things to do, Charlotte decided as she read over yet another witness statement from a cold case that might or might not ever be re-opened. Sabattini had suggested it would be a good way to hone her investigative skills and being a rookie in the homicide department, she needed all the help she could get. But even the detectives who'd investigated these cases in real time hadn't been able to solve them. She was pretty sure she had no hope of making a breakthrough. Especially when her mind was full of the Thorpe investigation and whether or not she would actually be Grayson's alibi.

It had been three days since the murder and she hadn't even gotten a basic update from Sabattini. In an effort to get the conversation started, she'd told him about Grayson's phone call.

"Why the hell would he call you?" Sabattini growled. "He knows I'm the officer in charge of the case. I made that clear when he came in for the record of interview. He knows how to reach me."

The look Tony leveled on her was full of suspicion. It took all of Charlotte's self-control not to squirm. She had nothing to feel guilty about. She'd done nothing wrong.

She eyed him steadily. "I don't know why he called me. I... I gave him my card back at the crime scene as is standard procedure. Maybe mine was the first one he found? Who knows?"

Sabattini's expression turned hard. "You're off the case, Barrington. You seem to have difficulty remembering that. If he calls you again, you put him through to me. Got it."

She nodded and lowered her gaze. She wanted so much to ask him if he'd received the autopsy report, but he'd already left the room. Besides, now wasn't the time. For now, Sabattini was annoyed about Grayson's phone call. There was no way he'd pass on any information about the case.

Swallowing a sigh, she returned to the cold case statements and made an effort to read. After an interminable twenty minutes had passed and she was still on the same page, she set aside the statement and pushed away from her desk. She needed some air. Maybe a strong coffee. A brisk walk to clear her head.

Muttering words to that effect in Sabattini's direction, she grabbed her jacket from the back of her chair and slipped it on. The unseasonably warm April weather they'd been experiencing of late seemed to have dissipated. A cool gust of wind blew in from over the ocean and sent goosebumps pebbling along her skin, reminding her that winter was on its way. She shivered and pulled her jacket closer.

Striding away from the police station, she headed in the direction of her favorite coffee van. A double shot espresso might be just what she needed to lift herself out of her funk. She was halfway there when her phone rang. She glanced down at the screen. Once again, it was a number she didn't recognize. Her thoughts immediately went to Grayson, but she dismissed the idea almost as quickly. She'd made it clear to him she was off the case. There was nothing she could do to help him. She'd made it equally clear he wasn't to call her.

With a soft sigh, she answered the call. "Charlotte Barrington."

"Charlotte. It's Grayson."

Anger ignited inside her. "Grayson! I already told you—"

"I know. I know. But I can't help it. I don't have anyone else to talk to. I'm going crazy. That detective has spoken to me again. I can tell he thinks I did it. I can hear it in his voice. The endless, repetitive questions, the sly innuendos... What's his name? Detective Sabattini? He's not even trying to look for someone else. Please, he is one of your colleagues. Surely there's something you can do?"

Charlotte clenched her teeth and kept walking. "I've already told you, Grayson. I've been taken off the case. There's nothing I can do. And until you're cleared as a suspect, I can't talk to you. Now, if you don't mind—"

"Please! Don't hang up!"

He sounded so desperate, she paused. "Grayson..."

"My wife was having an affair," he blurted. "With the Mayor of Sutherland Shire. That's why I went to see him that day. I'd only just found out..."

Charlotte frowned. "Wait. Lydia was having an affair?"

"Yes. I don't know why I didn't guess, but the truth is, it never occurred to me. Apparently it had been going on for months. Right under my nose."

"How did you find out?"

"One of my neighbors. She'd seen enough of their comings and goings to work out the truth of it. She felt sorry for me. So she told me."

"What's your neighbor's name?"

"Cindy Blenheim."

Charlotte typed the name into a note in her phone. "Thanks for the information. I'll be sure to pass it on to the detectives working the case. In the meantime, if you think of anything else, you need to speak with Detective Sabattini. This is his case. Either that or get your lawyer to pass on the information. Don't call me again. Got it?"

She heard his heavy sigh.

"Got it."

"Good." With that, she ended the call.

After purchasing a double-shot espresso, Charlotte returned to the office. She took a seat at her desk, her head buzzing. Sabattini sat at his desk a short distance away with a cup of coffee in hand. Charlotte looked across at him and then drew in a deep breath.

"I just had another call from Grayson Thorpe."

Sabattini's eyes widened with shock. "What the hell? Didn't I just warn you about that?"

Charlotte's face went hot. "You did, but he called me while I was out."

"You shouldn't have answered." Sabattini's face twisted with disgust. "What the hell's wrong with you Barrington?"

Charlotte clenched her teeth and drew in a calming breath. "In my defense, I didn't know it was him. Although you might find this surprising, Grayson Thorpe isn't in my phone contacts."

"You should have told him you've been removed from the case."

"I did. He doesn't seem to be listening."

Sabattini glared at her. "It's your job to make him listen."

"Okay," Charlotte replied. "But he called with some information."

Sabattini frowned. "What information?"

"He told me his wife was having an affair with the Mayor of Sutherland Shire."

Sabattini's face registered his surprise. "No wonder he said they weren't friends."

"Yes. Of course, we need to check his story against what the mayor has to say."

Sabattini was already shaking his head. "You have a short memory, Barrington. There's no we on this."

Charlotte barely managed to stop herself from rolling her eyes. "Okay, Tony. I get it. When are you going to interview the mayor?"

Sabattini gave her an infuriating shrug. "When I get round to it."

Charlotte bit her lip and silently counted to five. "Have you received the autopsy report yet?"

"Not yet. And what does it matter to you? You're off this case, remember?"

She threw her hands up in the air, unable to contain her frustration. "Okay! You don't need to keep rubbing it in! I'm just curious. I was kind of involved in it for a little while, remember?"

"Oh, yeah. Now I remember. You showed the perp a good time right before he topped his wife."

Charlotte held onto her temper with the greatest of effort. "We don't know that yet. Until you have a time of death, nothing can be ruled in...or out. Right now we have no evidence to charge him with anything."

Sabattini dismissed her comment with a wave of his hand. "Yeah, yeah, yeah. Look, when you've been around for as long as I have, you get to know how this game works. Nine times out of ten, the husband's the culprit. And for all

Thorpe's posturing and claims of innocence, my money's still on him being our man. Marriage problems, cheating and bam! They argue. He snaps. Takes her out."

Sabattini leaned back against his seat and stretched his arms above his head. "Of course, I still like to be thorough, so I'm gonna talk to the mayor and check out Thorpe's alibi, but I'll do it in my own sweet time. Got it?"

Charlotte stared at him, feeling more and more apprehensive. It seemed clear to her that Sabattini intended to only look for evidence that supported his theory that Lydia Thorpe was murdered by her husband.

I can't let him do it... I can't let his preconceptions about guilt and innocence potentially ruin a man's life...

There was nothing for it. Though she was potentially putting her job on the line, she had no choice. She wouldn't sit by and let a man who might very well be innocent be railroaded into being charged with a crime he didn't commit. Somehow she would find a way to talk to the mayor herself.

Taking a punt that Sabattini wouldn't head out to interview the mayor that very same day, Charlotte set aside her feelings of guilt, offered him another vague excuse for her absence and headed in her BMW toward Sutherland. Thirty minutes later, she was shown into a nicely furnished waiting room outside the office of the Mayor of Sutherland Shire and left to her own devices.

The girl who sat behind the reception desk was busy answering phone calls and tapping away on a keyboard. Every now and then she glanced in Charlotte's direction, but didn't attempt to engage her in conversation.

Charlotte wished she'd been able to flash her police credentials. That would have gotten the girl's attention. But Charlotte wasn't a complete idiot. She didn't want the whole world to know she was there and there was no way she wanted to risk news of her visit getting back to her superiors. She was risking enough as it was.

Twenty minutes crawled by with not so much as an apology or an offer to fetch a cup of coffee. Charlotte sat with her arms crossed over her chest and tried to contain her irritation. There were certain privileges she'd gotten used to, being a cop. One of them was that she was hardly ever kept waiting.

Another ten minutes passed. The receptionist remained immersed in her work. With a loud sigh, Charlotte stood and walked over to the girl's desk.

Plastering a smile across her face, she eyed the woman. "How much longer do you think Mr Matthews will be?"

"It's hard to say," the girl replied, barely taking the time to glance up at Charlotte. "He's a very busy man. You should have called ahead and made an appointment."

With that, the girl returned to tapping on her keyboard. Charlotte gritted her teeth against a sharp retort and returned to her seat. She picked up her phone and began scrolling through her social media accounts. They were filled with mindless drivel from people she hardly knew and that did nothing to calm her increasing irritation.

Just when she didn't think she could stand the waiting a moment longer, a door opened further along the corridor and a man came striding out. As he got closer, he offered her a smile.

Charlotte froze.

Chapter Six

The mayor held out his hand toward her. In a daze, Charlotte shook it.

"Ms Barrington. I'm Simon Matthews. Sorry to keep you waiting."

He looked freakily similar to Grayson Thorpe. Tall, broad-shouldered, blond. At first glance they could be brothers. But unlike her first meeting with Grayson, she felt no attraction to this man. Not even a glimmer of a spark.

Then Charlotte noticed other things about him: his weak chin and the sulkiness around his mouth. A slight paunch hung over his belt. There was a softness about him that made her think he'd turn and run, rather than fight and would probably become difficult if he didn't get his own way. She wondered what Lydia Thorpe had seen in him.

Matthews showed her into his office and offered her a seat. He sat in the chair behind his desk and leaned back, crossing one leg over the other.

"So, Ms Barrington. What can I do for you?"

There was no way the man would confide his secrets to her voluntarily. She had no choice. She had to let him think this was a formal visit and hope like hell he didn't complain to her superiors. Reaching into the pocket of her jacket, she pulled out her police credentials and flashed them before him.

The mayor's face turned pale. His eyes widened in shock. "You're a detective?"

"Yes. I didn't say anything to your secretary because I thought you might want to keep this quiet for as long as you can. I want to ask you a few questions about Lydia Thorpe."

Matthews shook his head slowly back and forth, looking dazed. "Poor Lydia. I heard it on the news. I can't believe someone did this to her."

Charlotte eyed him steadily. "So you knew her?"

Matthews looked away. "Yes."

"How well did you know her?"

Once again, the mayor kept his gaze averted. "Well enough. We were...lovers."

Charlotte was surprised by his candidness. "Did her husband know?"

"Yes."

"Is that why he came to see you the day of her murder?"

"Yes."

So Grayson told me the truth about that...

Without a time of death, there was no point asking Matthews for an alibi, but she could find out a bit more about how he'd spent the day in question and who he'd been with.

"Talk me through the day Lydia died. Where were you?"

"Please, I had nothing to do with her death."

Charlotte eyed him steadily. "Just answer the question."

Matthews blew out his breath on a heavy sigh. "I arrived at work at nine. I was here for most of the day. I met with Grayson Thorpe at half-past twelve. The meeting didn't last long."

"How long?"

"I don't know. Ten minutes or so."

"What did you talk about?"

"We didn't talk. He shouted. I said very little."

"He was upset about you and his wife?"

"Yes."

"What did he say?"

"He barged in here and started shouting at me about how I was to stay the hell away from Lydia."

"What else did he say?"

Matthews looked uncomfortable. "This sounds terrible given what's happened, but he said... He said if I didn't stay away from his wife he'd kill me."

Charlotte blinked in surprise. "He said he'd kill you?"

"Yes."

"Do you think he meant it?"

"He looked mad enough to kill."

"So he was angry when he left here?"

"Yes."

"Do you think he's capable of murdering his wife?"

Matthews sighed again and looked away. "I... I don't know. To tell you the truth, that was the first time I'd met him."

"Did Lydia ever say anything to you about being afraid of him?"

"No. I mean, she was unhappy in her marriage—bored, dissatisfied. She complained he was always at work and never had enough time for her, but I didn't get the sense she was frightened of him."

"How did you and Lydia meet?" Charlotte asked.

"She's my therapist. Of course, she stopped seeing me in a professional capacity when we...became involved."

"How long had the affair been going on?"

"Six months, but it had almost burned itself out."

"You'd lost interest?"

"No, not me. But I think Lydia had. Our meetings were becoming less frequent and when we were together, she seemed distracted. I got the impression she was only going through the motions."

"How did that make you feel?" Charlotte asked.

Matthews narrowed his eyes at her. "If you're asking was I upset enough to want to do her harm, the answer's no." He heaved out another weary sigh. "The thing is, I liked Lydia. She was a lot of fun. We had some good times. But I can't say I was upset about the end of our affair. These things are only meant to be short term. It had run its natural course."

"I thought you said she was the one to lose interest? You seem awfully accepting that things had come to an end."

He shrugged. "I don't know what you want me to say, Detective. While I enjoyed our physical encounters, I wasn't in love with her."

His voice choked on the last words. Though he looked visibly upset, Charlotte's gaze remained steady on his face. She'd interviewed plenty of witnesses. She was constantly amazed by some people's excellent acting ability. She didn't know Matthews well enough to discern at this point in time whether he was one of them.

"How did Grayson find out about the affair?" she asked in a flat voice.

Matthews sniffed. "I think one of the neighbors might have seen us... We weren't exactly discreet. That was part of the appeal... Part of the excitement. More so for Lydia than me. Perhaps the neighbor said something to Lydia's husband..."

That fit in with what Grayson had told her. Charlotte made a mental note to ask Sabattini to canvass the neighbors again. She'd have to do it discreetly and with due respect. She didn't want him to think she was telling him what to do or how to run his investigation.

Matthews made a sound in the back of his throat, drawing her attention back to him.

"It's ironic," he said. "Grayson found out right when it was more or less over..." He shook his head, his expression filled with bewilderment. "I still can't believe she's gone..."

Charlotte arrived at work the next day bursting to confer with Sabattini about the case and, in particular, whether he'd made any progress, but she forced herself to play things cool. Tony would be furious she'd spoken to the mayor and besides, what information had she gained, apart from the fact Matthews had said he'd been in his office for most of the day in question and that he'd backed up what she'd already been told by Grayson. Until they had a definitive cause of death, they couldn't pin anything on anyone.

She should have stayed out of it, like Wendell and Sabattini had ordered. The only thing she'd achieved was that she felt a bit better about Grayson. It was possible he was telling the truth.

She wondered if Tony planned to interview Matthews that day. She felt slightly queasy at the thought the mayor might mention her visit of the day before, but there was nothing she could do about that if he did. She'd deal with the fallout if and when it came to that. In the meantime, she was keen to speak with her partner and prise out of him an update on the case.

Charlotte dropped her handbag on her desk and looked over to where Sabattini usually sat. His desk was vacant. Neither was he in the tearoom. She had a sudden rush of apprehension that he might have already left to interview the mayor. With her heart beating fast, she sidled up to Wendell in his office.

"Where's Tony?" she asked as casually as she could.

"He called in sick."

She frowned. "Sick? What, with the flu or something? He seemed fine yesterday."

"Let's just say his illness is self-inflicted."

Comprehension dawned. Charlotte rolled her eyes and looked at her boss with disbelief. "You mean he's hung over?"

Wendell merely shrugged. "After all he's been through, he's entitled to a mental health day every now and then."

"Sir, with all due respect, he's an alcoholic! I mean, I don't know him well, but I've smelled alcohol on his breath every day I've worked with him." And then her frustration with her partner boiled over.

"Do you know if Sabattini has received the autopsy report for Lydia Thorpe yet? The waiting is driving me crazy! He knows how important the time of death is. He hasn't even asked me to clarify the hours I was with Grayson Thorpe. I'm wondering if he ever will. Then there's Grayson's alibi for earlier in the day. Tony told me yesterday he still hadn't checked into that." She scrubbed at her hair. "I mean, why is he still here?"

Wendell's expression turned somber. "Take a seat, Barrington. There's something you need to know."

Charlotte swallowed a sigh and did as she was directed. Wendell drew in a deep breath.

"You've only been here a month, so I'm going to overlook that little outburst. What you don't know is that Tony's been to hell and back this past year. His wife lost her long battle with cancer. Then a few weeks after he buried her, his only child was killed in a car accident."

Charlotte gasped in horror. "Oh, my God!"

Wendell nodded grimly. "Yes. He took time off, of course. I insisted upon it. But after a month he begged me to let him come back. Said work was his only solace. The only way he could find a reason to climb out of bed."

Wendell sighed. "He's a good cop. Been around a lot of years. Solved an impressive number of homicides too." He held up his hands in a sign of surrender. "What choice did I have? I understood his need to work. I'd feel that way too. So

I let him come back. First on light duties, mainly desk work, then on more meaty stuff. This is his first homicide since he returned."

Charlotte shook her head, still trying to process all she'd heard. "I'm sorry," she whispered. "I had no idea."

"Of course you didn't. Why would you? You haven't been here long enough to get the low-down on everyone in the office. And not too many people around here know. Tony didn't want them to feel sorry for him." Wendell leaned closer. "The reason I'm telling you is because he's your partner and I want you to go easy on him. I understand your frustration that he might not be moving as fast as you'd like, but trust me, he'll get there. I also have full confidence that he'll do a first class job. Okay?"

Charlotte nodded in agreement, feeling guilty over her earlier outburst. "Okay."

"When he gets back, I'll talk to him. Make sure he's still on track," Wendell quietly assured her.

Still feeling appalled and embarrassed by her outburst, she mumbled more apologies, nodded her thanks and left.

Tony tilted the highball glass to his lips and drank the last of his whiskey. His head thumped, indicating he'd had way too much already and it wasn't even midday. But ignoring the silent warning, he reached for the bottle that stood on a small table beside his elbow and refilled his glass. Every now and then he had a day like this one, where he felt like he was drowning in the abyss.

Every room of his house was devoid of life. Not a whisper of sound, not a hint of laughter... Nothing to stop the memories from crowding in and overwhelming him.

He stared at the blank TV screen. Some nights he switched it on. It helped to fill the silence, brought life to his dead house. It had been that way since the only two people he'd ever cared about had been taken from him way too soon. Angelica had only been fifty. Katerina, not even twenty-three.

How am I supposed to go on without them?

They had been his life. Now he was expected to keep climbing out of bed each morning to face each new day when his only reason for living was gone. His only salvation was his work, but even that was suffering. He'd pleaded with his boss to let him return from leave, but since he'd been back he'd done little to earn his keep.

Now he'd been partnered with a woman who was barely older than his daughter. She was all keen and eager and no doubt brilliant. Full of questions, unbridled enthusiasm and ideas. Charlotte Barrington. And every time he looked at her, he was reminded of his daughter.

Yes. Charlotte Barrington.

He remembered being just like her in the beginning, and even later, before life had dealt him a double heavy blow.

He should cut her some slack. It wasn't her fault he was this way. She was just trying to do her job. And good on her. It couldn't have been easy to discover she was caught up in a murder investigation in a way she could never have imagined. To be taken off her very first homicide as a result. That had to hurt. He knew how he would have felt were he in the same circumstance.

Of course it was the only choice open to Wendell. There was no way they could jeopardize the investigation by letting Charlotte participate. Defense lawyers lived for little discrepancies such as this. Anything to muddy the waters with a jury and secure a not guilty verdict.

He thought about Charlotte's frustration that he wasn't moving fast enough. He understood her reaction. Still, he wasn't going to be told what to do by a whippersnapper like Barrington.

He'd smooth things over with her in the morning. He'd interview the mayor and see if Thorpe's alibi checked out. But first he'd call the morgue and chase up the autopsy report. They'd told him there was a backlog of cases and he'd just have to wait. But he'd waited four days already. That was enough. Until they had a definitive time of death, interviewing potential suspects for the purposes of nailing down alibis was nothing but a waste of time.

Chapter Seven

Tony flashed his credentials at the girl who sat behind the desk at the Lidcombe Morgue. The ninety-one million-dollar state-of-the-art complex had been opened in December 2018 and was home to both the Forensic Medicine Department and the state Coroner's Court. Tony was a frequent enough visitor that the receptionist glanced at him briefly and then waved him on. He continued through the double doors that led out back.

Pain stabbed behind his eyes. He winced at the headache that had made itself known the instant he'd opened his eyes that morning. He'd already popped some painkillers, but they'd barely taken the edge off. Once again, he only had himself to blame.

I've got to stop this shit... Got to quit the drinking... Waking up like this, over and over... It's killing me.

Doctor Samantha Wolfe was already gowned up. Her face was covered in a mask, her hands protected by latex gloves. She stood looking at x-rays that were pinned to an illuminated panel fixed to one wall of the autopsy suite. The naked body of Lydia Thorpe lay on a stainless steel gurney beside her. The forensic pathologist glanced up as he approached.

"How are you doing, Tony? You look terrible."

He merely grunted in response. Trust Sam to tell it like it was. They'd known each other professionally a long time. She was probably one of his closest friends. Which went to say how fucked up his social life was that he numbered, among his besties, a forensic pathologist who spent her days working with the dead.

Still, Tony was relieved Sam was conducting the autopsy. As chief forensic pathologist, she was by far the best in her field. She had a reputation for being professional and thorough and she didn't put up with any nonsense. He and some of his colleagues had been concerned when she married Detective Rohan Coleridge that she might give up her work for domestic life, but that hadn't happened and Tony, for one, was relieved.

"Find anything exciting?" he asked, nodding toward the x-rays.

"No evidence of bullet wounds and that's confirmed by the x-ray. No fractures, apart from nicks in two of her ribs. They were caused by the knife blade."

"What else can you tell me?"

'There's no evidence of sexual assault. There're a number of defensive wounds on the victim's hands."

"So she put up a good fight."

"Yes. I've taken scrapings from underneath her fingernails, from her mouth and vagina. I'll send them to the lab for testing. Hopefully we might find someone else's DNA."

Tony glanced at the body. "What's your official cause of death?"

Samantha pursed her lips. "Lydia Thorpe suffered from thirty-seven stab wounds, two of which penetrated her heart. Either one of them was sufficient to be considered the death blow."

Tony let out a low whistle. 'Thirty-seven stab wounds? Talk about overkill."

Sam nodded in agreement. "That's what I thought."

"She was found by the husband," he offered.

"A crime of passion?"

"Maybe. He admitted to marriage problems and that she was cheating. He'd just found out. Maybe they got into an argument and she came off worst?"

"She's not a small woman. Eighty-five kilograms. Plenty of muscle, like she worked out regularly. Strong and fit. How big is the husband?"

"Big enough. Definitely capable of inflicting this kind of damage. There were no signs of forced entry. Nothing was missing."

"So you don't think this was a random attack, or a robbery gone wrong?"

Tony compressed his lips and shook his head. "No. Thirty-seven stab wounds? This was personal." He turned and gazed down at the ravaged body of Lydia Thorpe. "What can you tell me about the knife?"

"The wounds were all made by a knife with a straight-edged blade somewhere in the vicinity of ten or twelve inches long."

"So the kind you might find in someone's butcher block?"

"Yes."

Samantha pulled off her gloves and began washing her hands in the nearby sink. "I've estimated time of death between midday and six that evening. I hope that narrows down the suspect list."

Tony shot Sam a grateful smile. "Everything helps. Thanks, Sam. I really appreciate you doing this one. My new partner —Charlotte Barrington—has kind of gotten herself caught up unintentionally in this one. We can't afford any mistakes."

Sam looked mildly curious. "How so?"

Tony sighed. "She met the husband in a bar the same day his wife was killed. They spent the night together."

Sam's eyes widened with surprise. "Wow. That complicates things."

Tony nodded grimly. "Yeah. Now that we have a time of death, we can narrow things down a bit."

Sam's expression looked troubled. "Do you know what time they hooked up?"

"Not yet. I wanted to wait for the time of death before I asked too many questions."

"Of course. I hope for both of your sakes she's not his alibi."

Tony's gut clenched. "So do I."

Tony's next stop was Sydney Legal. Now that he had a time of death, his questions could get more pointed. Grayson Thorpe had given them an accounting of his movements the day his wife had been murdered. The best person to verify that information was Thorpe's secretary. After giving his name to the man who sat behind the reception desk in the impressive foyer of Sydney Legal, Tony waited impatiently while the man phoned through to Thorpe's office.

The marble tile under Tony's feet shone like it had been polished. Priceless artworks lined the walls, including a massive abstract sculpture that stood opposite the bank of lifts. The place reeked of opulence, money and success. No doubt they billed their clients to match.

The ding of the lift snagged his attention. He looked across and saw a woman striding toward him. She looked about as young as his late daughter, shoulder-length brown hair, tall, slim. Blue eyes. Good skin. Nice smile. Kind of girl next door. In her hand she carried a laptop.

"Detective Sabattini? I'm Anne Howarth. I work for Grayson Thorpe."

Tony shook the outstretched hand. "Is there somewhere we can talk?"

"Of course. Follow me."

She took him into a small but tastefully furnished interview room not far from the bank of lifts. She seated herself at the empty table. Tony sat down opposite.

"So, Ms Howarth. What do you do for Grayson Thorpe? Are you his secretary?"

She gave Tony a tight smile. "His executive assistant."

Tony frowned with irritation. "What the hell is an executive assistant? Do you keep his appointments, or not?"

"Yes. Mr Thorpe has a digital calendar. I keep it updated with all of his court obligations, client appointments and other important dates."

Tony gave her a brief nod. "Good. Then I guess you're the one I need to speak with." He took out a notebook and pen.

The woman's forehead furrowed. "Do you mind if I ask what this is about?"

Tony looked at her. "I assume you know Grayson Thorpe's wife was found murdered five days ago."

"Yes," she replied, turning pale. "Grayson called to tell us. He's not in the office, of course. Taking some time off. We're all still in shock."

"How well did you know Lydia Thorpe?"

The EA compressed her lips. "I didn't. Not really. We'd been introduced at a staff function, but to tell you the truth, I rarely saw Mrs Thorpe at the office. I think I've seen her twice in all the time I've worked for her husband."

"And how long has that been?"

"Five years. I've been with him since he started here."

"What about phone calls? How often did Mrs Thorpe call her husband?"

"I never took a call from her. Of course, she could have been calling him directly on his mobile."

"What can you tell me about that day? Did Mr Thorpe come into work?"

"Yes, of course."

"What time did he arrive?"

She smiled. "He always gets here before me, so I can't tell you when he arrived, but he was in his office when I got here at nine o'clock."

"Did he see any clients that day?"

"Yes. He had back-to-back appointments all morning. I can show you if you like."

With that, she opened the laptop and tapped on the keyboard. Moving to stand beside her, Tony watched the screen fill with what looked like some kind of calendar.

The woman pointed to the screen. "You can see here...in these red boxes, Mr Thorpe had meetings with clients. This green box is where he had a court appearance. One of his cases came before the court. He was gone about thirty-five minutes."

"Did he take a lunch break?"

"Yes. Often he orders in a sandwich from the deli right down the street and eats it at his desk but that day he went out."

"What time did he leave?"

"Midday."

"Do you know what time he returned?"

"Yes. He had a two o'clock appointment with a client. He called me to tell me he was caught up in traffic and might be a few minutes late."

"Was he?"

"No. He got here right on two."

Tony nodded. "What time did he leave that day?"

For the first time, the woman looked troubled. Lines once again furrowed her brow.

"Most afternoons he doesn't leave until late. Never before five."

"But this day was different, wasn't it?" Tony murmured.

The EA bit her lip and sighed. "Yes."

"What time did he leave work?"

"Right after his two o'clock appointment."

"What time was that?"

"A bit after three. I remember it clearly because he never leaves that early. I was surprised. I even wondered if he were sick. And he had other afternoon appointments. He asked me to cancel them. That in itself was very strange. He never does that. He's one of the hardest-working lawyers I know. I remember thinking at the time that something must be wrong."

"Did he seem different to you that afternoon, when he arrived back from lunch?"

The woman slowly nodded. "Yes. I hate to say it, but he looked...rattled. Like something had happened and he didn't know what to do about it. I had to remind him twice about his two o'clock appointment and even then he seemed a bit confused about why they were there."

"I thought you said he'd called you to tell you he might be running late for that appointment?"

"Yes. That's another reason why this was all so strange. He'd called me only twenty minutes earlier about that. By the time he arrived at the office, it was as if he'd forgotten all about it."

"Did you talk to him about it? Ask him if there was something going on?"

She shook her head. "No. He's my boss. We don't have that kind of relationship."

"Fair enough." Tony paused as a stab of pain reminded him his headache was very much still around. He forced himself to continue. "What kind of boss is he?"

She smiled. "He's a great boss. Hard working, conscientious, a perfectionist."

"Isn't that hard on you? To work for someone with such high standards?"

She shook her head. "No. Not at all. I always strive to do my best. I like to be challenged. I also like it when my efforts are recognized."

"Thorpe did that, did he? Recognize your efforts?"

"Yes. He's always been very generous with his compliments. He regards all of his support staff as a vital part of his team. We succeed off the efforts of all of us."

"So he's not your typical hotshot lawyer with an ego the size of the Opera House?"

"No, not at all. Quite the opposite. He's a decent guy and a great boss. I'm so sad for him. When I think about what happened to his wife... It's just so terrible."

The girl looked like she might be ready to cry. Tony handed her his card. "Thank you for your time, Ms Howarth. If you think of anything else, give me a call."

She took the card and pushed back from the desk. She stood and offered her hand for another brief handshake.

As Tony made his way outside the building, he thought about what he'd learned. According to the EA, Thorpe was a top bloke. He'd gone to lunch at twelve. His first appointment after lunch had been at two, just like he'd said. It was a thirty minute drive out to Sutherland. Unless he'd lied about his meeting with the mayor, he didn't have a lot of time to kill his wife, clean up and then return to work. At least, not during his lunch break.

Of course, he could have done it later that afternoon. After all, the time of death was estimated between twelve and six. Charlotte Barrington had told him she'd met Thorpe in a bar that very same night. He hadn't asked her for more details. Until they knew the time of death, it hadn't been relevant.

Now they were. Thorpe had told them he'd left work and gone to the Brass Monkey, a bar in Cronulla. The journey to Cronulla from the city took about as long as it did to get to the Sutherland Shire council chambers. Thirty minutes. That meant Thorpe had been at the bar from half-past three. Or thereabouts. If he'd been telling the truth.

Had Barrington been with him from that time? If so, she might very well be his alibi. He hoped for her sake it wasn't so. The last thing she needed as a rookie detective was to be caught up on the wrong side of a homicide.

A wave of agony centered in Tony's forehead. He winced and rubbed his hand against it in an effort to ease the pain. Reaching into his suit jacket, he pulled out a packet of painkillers and swallowed two more of them dry.

I really need to get off the booze. It's not good for anyone... Least of all, me.

Chapter Eight

It was mid-afternoon and Charlotte was bored and wired with way too much caffeine. Sabattini still hadn't made an appearance in the squad room and his absence was driving her slowly mad. With a sigh, she stared at the witness statement in front of her and tried to concentrate. She'd read the last paragraph at least three times already and its contents still hadn't registered.

The problem was, her thoughts were consumed with the Thorpe investigation and more particularly, Grayson. She was desperate to know where it was heading. Had Tony spoken to any other witnesses? Had he made a breakthrough? Did he have anyone other than Grayson in his sights?

Grayson...

Her dreams the night before had been filled with him. Touching her, teasing her, kissing her. Looming above her, naked and aroused. And then the images had shifted and a shaft of light had glinted off a knife he held in his hand. His sexy smile had turned into a snarl. He lifted his arm in a high arc and then came swinging down toward her.

She tried to get out of the way, but she was stuck. Something was holding her down. She'd come awake with her heart racing, panting, cold with fear. Her legs were twisted in the sheets. It had taken more than half an hour for her to regain her calm.

She'd told Grayson in no uncertain terms to stop contacting her, but it wasn't that easy to eradicate her memories. Her night with him had been magical. Like nothing she'd ever experienced. It was weird. She never imagined a one night stand could be so good. In her mind, they were nothing more than a wham, bam, thank you ma'am kind of occasion and, for her that had been part of the appeal.

But things had been so comfortable between her and Grayson. Right from the start there had been a physical connection. Then, as they'd flirted and danced and later, had sex, she'd felt a tangible emotional connection. She was sure he'd felt it too. In fact, if they hadn't walked smack bang into a murder investigation, she would have definitely hooked up with him again.

And therein lies the problem...

Leaning her hand on her chin, she sighed again. With a decided lack of enthusiasm, she returned her attention to the cold case statement just as the door to the squad room opened and Tony walked in. Charlotte's heart skipped a beat and then began pumping fast. She stared at the papers in front of her and did her best to get her pulse under control. When she thought it was safe to speak, she lifted her head and gave him a casual wave.

"How's it going?" she asked, proud of the way she managed to sound so offhand.

Tony ignored her question. "What time did you meet Grayson Thorpe in that bar?"

She blinked and quickly recalibrated. "It was a little past five. We were there until around eight-thirty. Why?"

"I spoke with his secretary, or his EA or whoever the hell she is. She told me he went to lunch at twelve and returned at two. He left the office again a bit past three."

Charlotte looked at him with surprise. "You spoke to Grayson's secretary?"

Sabattini gave her an exaggerated eye roll. "Yes, Barrington. Despite what you think, I've been working hard on this case. I'll have you know I met up with Samantha Wolfe at the morgue before I stopped by Sydney Legal."

Excitement and anticipation quickened Charlotte's pulse. "You have the autopsy report?"

"Yes. Well, an oral one at least. It will take a week to get the written report. That won't include toxicology or DNA results."

Charlotte's heart skipped a beat. Adrenaline surged through her veins. She flashed to her meeting a couple of days before and was flooded with guilt. She'd carried out the illicit interview because she'd lost faith in Sabattini's objectivity and willingness to conduct a thorough investigation. And all along he'd been working his butt off. It was all she could do not to confess her indiscretion and blurt out an apology.

Instead, she listened intently as he summarized Samantha Wolfe's findings. Afterwards Charlotte was quiet. She felt strangely let down. The six-hour window of opportunity meant they couldn't yet rule Grayson out. Equally disappointing was the knowledge she was Grayson's alibi for at least part of that time. Her night with him would now become part of the official record. Embarrassment burned through her.

"I'm sorry," Tony said, looking like he really meant it. "I know how hard you were wishing you'd be kept out of this case. It seems like it's not meant to be."

Charlotte managed a tight smile. "Thank you. And you're right. I can't imagine what it's going to be like if I have to give evidence about my connection to this matter. Definitely not the way I wanted to start off my career in homicide."

"Don't sweat it. Things will work out."

"You don't know that."

Sabattini grinned. It took years off his weathered face. "Oh, but I do. There's always another tragedy to distract people from what's happening today."

She appreciated his effort to reassure her and wished she shared his confidence. "Keep me in the loop?" she asked hopefully.

"I'll see what I can do."

It was more than she'd expected. She turned back to her computer screen and pulled her keyboard toward her. She'd been stood down from the investigation, but that didn't mean she couldn't do a little off-the-record digging. Starting with the police database.

She tapped on the keys and opened a search screen. No doubt Tony had already done background checks on both Grayson and his wife, but then again, maybe not. Though Charlotte had more sympathy for her partner now she'd been made aware of Tony's sad history, that didn't mean she wasn't still chaffing at his go-slow approach. He might have spent the day on the case, but his overall attitude toward the investigation lacked the urgency that pounded through her veins. The inner conflict and turmoil was doing her head in.

In an effort to force herself to relax, she drew in a deep breath and eased it out. With a quiet sigh, she entered Grayson's details and pressed "enter" and then waited for the results to load. A couple of traffic tickets. No criminal record. Not surprising for a lawyer. Criminals didn't tend to get hired in firms with reputations like Sydney Legal's.

She also ran a background check on the victim. Lydia Thorpe was also clean. On impulse, Charlotte searched under the mayor's name. Again, there was nothing of significance. Not that she'd expected the Mayor of Sutherland Shire to have a criminal record. He wouldn't have risen so high in the ranks if that had been the case.

A shadow fell across her desk. Charlotte looked up and saw Tony. His gaze was fixed on her monitor. Her face flamed with guilt. There was no point in minimizing her screen. He'd already seen the damning evidence.

"You're off the case, Barrington. Don't you know what that means?"

Tony's voice was gruff, but there was no underlying anger in his tone. She ducked her head in embarrassment and nodded.

"Of course. I'm sorry. It's just that..." She gave him a shrug, helpless to explain.

He perched on the edge of her desk. "I understand. I really do. I was young and eager like you once."

He must have seen the dubiousness she felt on her face. He gave a self-deprecating laugh. "It might be hard for you to believe, but it's true. And I was a damned fine investigator. I put away my fair share of the bad guys." He sighed. "But you can't be involved in this one, Barrington. We can't afford to hand the defense any opportunity to get off whoever did this. You know the rules. At least, I hope you do."

"Of course I do. But I want to help. Even unofficially. There must be something I can do."

"Like interviewing the mayor?"

Charlotte stared at him in shock. Her belly took a nosedive. She couldn't bring herself to look at him.

"H-how...?"

"The mayor called me to complain about a detective who'd showed up the day before yesterday unannounced at his office. Lucky for you, he couldn't remember your name." Sabattini shook his head. Anger and disappointment filled his face. "I can't believe you did something so stupid, Barrington. You might have put the whole investigation at risk."

Charlotte gasped. Her face burned. "I'm sorry! I...I..."

Tony's expression softened. "Hey, I get it. But I can't have you going rogue like this. What the hell would Wendell do? He'd fire your ass, that's what he'd do and you could say goodbye to your career in homicide before it's even started. Is that what you want?"

"No! Of course not! Being a homicide detective is all I've ever wanted!"

"Then you better start treating your position here with some respect. And that goes for the direct order from your boss that you remove yourself from this case." Sabattini paused to draw in a breath. "Now, I'm prepared to keep this between the two of us. But let this be your one and only warning. Don't go inserting yourself into this investigation again. At least not where you can be identified by members of the public. Got it?"

Charlotte nodded. "Yes, sir. I understand. I'm sorry. And... thank you... For keeping this between us."

Sabattini gave a brief nod. "You might as well tell me if the mayor said anything of interest. I haven't gotten around to interviewing him yet."

Charlotte swiveled in her chair and gave Tony her full attention. She recounted what she'd learned from the mayor, including the fact he'd confessed to having an affair with Lydia Thorpe and had also confirmed the meeting he'd had with Grayson around half-past twelve on the day Lydia had been murdered.

"So it seems Thorpe was at least telling the truth about that," Sabattini mused. He scratched at the three-day growth on his chin. "We have a six-hour window of opportunity. From what the mayor said, Thorpe was only with him for a short period of time. We can rule out the fact Thorpe murdered his wife in the half hour beforehand because we know he left his office at twelve and it would have taken him at least that long to get to Sutherland from the city, but what about afterwards? You didn't see him in the Brass Monkey until around five o'clock."

Charlotte nodded. "You're right, but you're forgetting he was back in his office at two. The trip from Sutherland back to the city would have taken at least thirty minutes at that time of day. Doesn't leave much time for him to drive home to Cronulla, murder his wife, clean up and then be back in his office by two."

"I agree. It's tight. And seeing as it appears the mayor corroborates at least that part of Thorpe's alibi, I think we can safely assume he didn't kill his wife between the hours of twelve and three. Which leaves the time between three and five when you saw him in the bar."

"He said he went straight to the bar from his office. Got there about half-past three. It would have taken him about thirty minutes to get there from his office."

Sabattini pursed his lips. "Yes, that's what he said, but he wouldn't be the first suspect to lie to the police. We need to speak to the bartender at the Brass Monkey."

Charlotte started in surprise. A smile started to form on her lips. Tony saw her reaction and then grimaced and shook his head.

"Sorry, force of habit. I mean I will speak to the bartender. You'll stay here and deal with that paperwork."

He pointed to a pile of files that were stacked high on his desk. Charlotte opened her mouth to protest and then slowly closed it again. Sabattini had been far more forthcoming than she had a right to expect. It would do her good to remember that. Especially if she wanted him to continue to share his insights and information about the case with her.

The door to the squad room opened. A uniformed officer ducked his head in. His gaze searched the room and landed on Charlotte and Sabattini.

"There's someone downstairs wanting to talk to the detective in charge of the Lydia Thorpe homicide."

Charlotte's heart skipped a beat. She looked pleadingly up to Sabattini.

"Don't look at me like that, Barrington. You know I can't let you sit in on this interview."

"Please, Tony. I promise I won't say a word."

"Do you want to get both of us fired?"

"Of course not. I just—"

"I'll let you sit in the observation room, behind the one-way glass. That's my best offer."

Charlotte almost threw her arms around him. She restrained herself just in time. Instead, she gave him a wide smile.

"Thank you, Tony," she gushed. "I really mean it. Thank you."

He merely grumbled and moved away. Charlotte sprang up from her chair and hurried to the room they used to observe witnesses in secret. A few moments later, Sabattini entered the room, followed by a woman about Charlotte's age.

The woman identified herself as Melissa Robinson. She was short and stocky, with spiky dark hair. She wore a bright orange, high-visibility work shirt and navy-blue work pants, along with steel-capped boots. The sleeves of her shirt were rolled up to her elbows, exposing an impressive amount of ink.

Sabattini started the interview and ascertained the woman lived in the northern suburb of Hornsby and worked in construction, mostly in the northern suburbs.

"How do you know Lydia Thorpe?"

"She's my best friend."

The announcement took Charlotte completely by surprise. Melissa Robinson was a blue collar construction worker. From what Charlotte had seen and been told about Grayson's wife, Lydia Thorpe was the epitome of a stylish, well-educated professional. The two women were chalk and cheese.

Perhaps they'd been friends from before? Maybe they'd known each other from school? There were any number of possibilities for the unusual coupling. Charlotte set her thoughts aside and focused on the interview.

"Do you have information about the case?" Sabattini asked.

"Yes." Robinson crossed her arms over her chest and looked away, her expression one of deep reluctance.

"Would you care to share it with me?" Sabattini prompted.

Charlotte heard the faint trace of irritation in his voice.

Robinson looked back at him.

"Detective, I want you to know this isn't easy. I've gone back and forth about coming forward with this. I don't know if it's relevant, but I kept seeing those news stories, asking for people to come forward if they had anything that might help with the investigation."

She blew out a shaky breath. "Lydia was my best friend. She deserves justice. That's why I'm here."

"Okay," Sabattini replied, giving Robinson an encouraging smile.

"I saw Grayson Thorpe leaving the house around one o'clock the same day Lydia was murdered," she blurted out.

Sabattini looked startled. "You were there? At Lydia's house?"

"Yes. We were meant to have lunch together. We'd arranged to meet there."

"Was Lydia home?"

"No. I knocked on the door, but there was no answer. I called her mobile, but it went straight to voicemail."

"Did you leave her a message?"

"Yes. But she never called back." The woman's voice choked with emotion. She buried her face in her hands. Sabattini gave her a few moments to collect herself.

"What did you do then?" he asked when she looked up at him.

"I climbed back into my car and went to leave."

"Is that when you saw Grayson Thorpe?"

"Yes. I was already in my car when the front door opened. Grayson Thorpe came out and started heading toward his car."

"And you're certain it was Grayson Thorpe?"

Robinson eyed Sabattini steadily. "Dead certain."

"What kind of car was he driving?"

"A navy-blue BMW."

Charlotte blinked fast, trying to come to terms with what she'd just heard. Her stomach was clenched, her belly filled with a hard, cold block of dread. She'd almost convinced herself Grayson couldn't be responsible for his wife's death. The timeline was simply too tight. But according to Lydia's best friend, Grayson had found time to stop by his house after his meeting with Matthews. Charlotte wondered what Sabattini made of all this.

She watched as Tony thanked the witness for her time, gave her one of his cards and saw her out. A few minutes later, he returned to the squad room. Charlotte scrambled out of the observation room and strode up to Tony.

"Do you believe her?" she asked without preamble.

Sabattini eyed her calmly. "At this stage, I have no reason to suspect she's lying. Do you?"

"No."

"I'd come to the same conclusion you had: Thorpe didn't have time to carry out the murder between his meeting with the mayor and his arrival back at work. But what if he did? What if he was so angry after discovering his wife was having an affair with the mayor that he broke all speed records to get home? He found his wife there and just started laying into her. He could have had a quick shower, changed his clothes and gotten back to work in time for his two o'clock appointment."

Sabattini's breath came fast. "We know he left the office an hour later. He could have returned home to the crime scene that afternoon and finished cleaning up and still have been in the Brass Monkey by five. It's possible."

Charlotte's stomach tightened. Ice weighed down her veins. Sabatttini was right. It was possible. She looked at him. "Did Thorpe's EA mention anything about a change of clothes? Surely that's something she would have noticed?"

"I don't know. I didn't ask her. She did say he acted strangely upon his return. Rattled, I think was the word she used."

The dread increased inside Charlotte's stomach. She eyed Sabattini steadily. "You need to talk to the bartender at the Brass Monkey. Let's hope Thorpe arrived there when he said he did. Even better, that his arrival was recorded on CCTV."

Chapter Nine

Grayson nodded encouragingly toward the client who sat opposite him. He even attempted to take notes, but it was difficult. It had been more than a week since he'd discovered his wife's lifeless body.

There had been so much blood!

He'd taken a week's leave to get his head sorted and for the media frenzy die down, but now he wondered if he shouldn't have taken more time off. He couldn't stay focused. Between the horrible images parading through his head and thoughts of the woman he'd been with the same night his wife had been brutally slain, his concentration was shot.

The client droned on about the unfair and unforgivable division of assets under her late father's will. The entire estate was worth less than a million dollars and as far as Grayson could tell, there were at least half a dozen beneficiaries with a potential claim against the estate. By the time the legal bills were paid, they'd be fighting over pennies.

Old man Johnson had seen fit to cut out his whole family and had left his entire estate to charity. Grayson couldn't help but wonder about the kind of man who could do that.

Either that, or his family had done him over something fierce during his lifetime and this was his way of getting back. Grayson didn't have all the details yet and today wasn't going to be the day of his enlightenment. With a quick glance at his watch, he shot his client a look of apology.

"I'm really sorry, Maxine, but I'm going to have to cut this short. I have an urgent matter before the court and any moment the registrar might call requesting my presence. It's bad timing for you, but unfortunately, the judges don't run to my schedule. Please accept my apologies. See my assistant, Anne, on the way out. She'll help you make another appointment."

The woman blinked in surprise and quickly gathered herself. "Oh, all right. Well, I guess we'll pick this up another time."

Grayson managed a smile. "Of course. I look forward to hearing more about your predicament as soon as possible. Rest assured, we'll do something about rectifying this gross oversight."

Maxine beamed. "I knew you were the right lawyer for this case. I did a lot of research on the Internet in the weeks before I decided to come here. You have amazing reviews. I can see they're completely justified. I look forward to meeting with you again."

Grayson muttered a suitable response. He was glad the woman didn't keep up to date with the news. He'd been bracing himself for the inevitable morbid curiosity. If she'd gotten wind he was a potential suspect in a murder investigation, she might not be so keen to have him dealing with her case.

After showing Maxine out and urging Anne to book her in for another appointment, Grayson returned to his office. He glanced at the suit jacket that hung on the coat rack. It was looking decidedly rumpled. He never spent a week in the same jacket. Normally it would be off to the drycleaners after two or three days. But that wasn't an option at the moment. He didn't have any other clothes.

Though he'd thrown together a few things before getting the hell out of his house, it hadn't included spare suits. The truth was, he needed to go home and get more clothes. His own pillow might also help.

He hadn't been sleeping well. And no wonder... His wife had been murdered. His life had been turned upside down. But he had to face his demons sometime. He couldn't live out of hotels indefinitely. He was a senior associate at Sydney Legal. He had a reputation to uphold. At least he had to look the part, even if he was falling apart on the inside.

I have to go back... I have to return to my house... The scene of the crime... God help me...

Dragging in a deep breath, Grayson braced himself for what he was about to do. He only hoped the contract cleaners had already stopped by and done their thing. The last thing he needed was to come face to face again with the stark reminder of what had happened on the marble tiles of his living room.

Charlotte flicked on her indicator and turned the unmarked police car into Grayson's street. She glanced at Sabattini who sat in the passenger seat next to her. It had been more than a week since they'd been there. The written autopsy report had arrived, confirming what Tony had already been told. So had the toxicology results. Zero for alcohol and illegal drugs. Same for prescription meds. It seemed Lydia Thorpe lived a clean life.

They were still waiting for the DNA results. It was a long shot, but for someone who'd fought her assailant as fiercely as Lydia had, there was always a chance the killer had left something of themselves behind. They could only hope.

After warning her once again to stay out of the investigation, Sabattini had then asked her to drive him to Cronulla so he could interview Grayson's neighbors. Though Charlotte had been taken by surprise by the request, she didn't question him or ask him if he'd cleared it with Wendell. She was just pleased she'd been allowed to tag along. But now she shot Tony a look of concern. He'd been silent and withdrawn on their way down to Cronulla. His skin had a sickly pallor to it that didn't bode well. He kept swiping at sweat that gathered on his forehead.

"Are you all right?" she asked.

He grunted. "I'm fine. A bit under the weather. It's nothing. Just a headache, but I don't feel up to driving." Then he shot her a ferocious frown. "Keep this to yourself, Barrington. And don't you forget, you're here as an observer only. I ask the questions. All of the questions. I don't want to hear so much as a peep out of you. Got it?"

She nodded. She would have agreed to accompany him on any terms. Grayson's neighbors had been canvassed by the uniforms the night of the murder, but apparently no one had seen or heard anything suspicious in the hours beforehand. Most had been at work during the relevant time frame. But according to Melissa Robinson, Grayson had come home that afternoon. Then there was the mayor who thought a neighbor might have seen him with the victim. It was worth following up, if only to confirm Robinson's story.

Charlotte pulled the car into the curb and turned to Sabattini. "How do you want to do this?"

"I'm going to do a door knock. Cover all the houses in the street. You're going to stay put."

"But—"

Sabattini held up a hand to cut her off. Before he could speak, his face crumpled with pain.

Charlotte frowned with concern. "Tony? Are you all right?"

"My head," he groaned. "It's killing me."

"Do you want a painkiller?"

"I've already taken two, but yeah... Give me some more."

"Are you sure?"

"Yes." He groaned.

Charlotte scrambled around in her handbag. Eventually she came up with a packet of painkillers. "Here," she said, offering it to him.

He took them with a grateful look and swallowed two tablets dry. A few moments later, he drew in a deep breath.

"Okay, you can come with me, but only to lend me credibility. People watch too much TV. Too many of them get confused with fiction over reality. They expect detectives to work in pairs. That's how it is on Law and Order, right?"

He gave her a tight smile that was more like a grimace. "They're more likely to open up with you beside me. But you're to keep your mouth shut, okay? I'm the one asking all the questions. Got it?" He gave her a hard look.

Charlotte held his gaze. "Got it."

Sabattini sighed. "Good. Let's get this over with."

The neighbor to the left of the Thorpe house wasn't home. Sabattini slipped a business card under the door and then moved to the house on the right. This time they had more success. The door was opened by a woman about Charlotte's age. True to her word, Charlotte didn't utter a sound.

"Hi. I'm Detective Sabattini and this is Detective Barrington."

"Oh, you must be here about the murder. That poor woman! I can't believe something like that happened on my street!"

Sabattini made a murmured sound of agreement. "We're canvassing people in the neighborhood who might have seen something that day. Were you home the day Lydia Thorpe was murdered?"

The woman nodded. Her light brown hair fell forward, concealing part of her face. "Yes, I was. Well, at least for part of that time."

"What's your name?" Sabattini asked.

"Cindy Blenheim."

Charlotte frowned. She remembered Grayson mentioning that name.

"What do you do for a living, Cindy?" Sabattini asked.

"I-I'm a nurse at Sutherland Hospital. But right now I'm on maternity leave. I have a four-month-old."

Sabattini scribbled in his notebook. "How long have you lived next to the Thorpes?"

"They were here before me. I've been their neighbor for three years."

"Did you know Lydia Thorpe?"

"Yes, of course. We didn't socialize or anything, but we were neighborly."

"What does that mean?" Sabattini asked.

"You know, we'd say hi to each other if we happened to be out in the front yard at the same time. Talk about the weather. That kind of thing."

"What about her husband? Do you have anything to do with him?"

"Not often. He works long hours. He's a lawyer for one of those swanky firms in the city. Occasionally I see him in the yard on the weekend. Mostly mowing the lawn. We wave hello to each other. Sometimes we stop for a chat. He's always been pleasant. He helped me out with a legal matter once. I was very grateful for that. He asks after Aleah all the time. That's my baby. I've often wondered why he doesn't have any kids. He seems to like them well enough."

"What can you tell us about Lydia?" Sabattini asked.

The woman frowned. "She was perfectly pleasant, too. Not over the top cordial or friendly like Grayson, but polite and courteous. She was always dressed in designer suits and sky-high stilettos." Cindy looked down at her feet that were shod in fluffy slippers in the shape of rabbits. "I don't know how she walked in those things."

"Did the Thorpes have many visitors?" Sabattini asked.

"No, not really. They seem to be too busy to entertain. Of course the mayor visited regularly, but he was only there for Lydia."

The woman blushed and averted her gaze. Charlotte looked at Sabattini. He gave her an imperceptible nod.

"You're referring to the Mayor of Sutherland Shire? Simon Matthews?" Sabattini asked.

"Yes."

"What can you tell us about him?"

Cindy's blush deepened. She squirmed uncomfortably. Sabattini was quick to reassure her.

"We're not here to pass judgment on your neighbor, or anyone else for that matter. We're just here to get answers. Were Lydia and Simon Matthews having an affair?"

The woman stared at the ground and nodded. "Yes."

"How long do you think it had been going on?" Sabattini asked.

Cindy shrugged. "I'm not sure. At least four months. I've only been home since the birth of Aleah. Before that, I worked fulltime. Shiftwork. My roster was all over the place. It's only since I've been on maternity leave that I've paid any attention to what happens on my street."

"What led you to think they were having an affair?"

Another uncomfortable shrug. "He was at her house almost every day. Sometimes she'd meet him at the front door wearing only lingerie. It was obvious what was going on. They were quite open about it. Kissing goodbye in the front yard. They didn't seem to care who saw them. Granted, most everyone in this street is at work during the day. The chances of someone seeing them together were pretty low."

"Did Lydia know you were home?"

"I'm not sure. I assume so. Then again, I always park in the garage. It's possible she thought I was still working."

"Did you say anything to Grayson Thorpe about your suspicions?" Sabattini asked.

Cindy flushed guiltily. "Yes. I mean, I wouldn't normally interfere, but... Grayson has been so good to me. I'm a single mom. He helped force my ex to pay child support. It's not his area of specialty, but when he found out what was going on, he wanted to help out. I could never afford the services of a lawyer like Grayson... He offered to do it pro bono. When I realized what was going on with Lydia... I felt I had to do the right thing by him. So I told him."

"How did he react?"

"Shocked. Devastated. I don't think he had any idea."

"How long ago was this?"

"The same morning Lydia was murdered."

Sabattini looked as surprised as Charlotte felt. "You waited all that time?"

The woman's flush deepened. "I... They were serious accusations. I wanted to be sure. Besides, it wasn't always easy to catch Grayson. Like I said, he worked long hours. It was often after ten when he got home."

"You were keeping tabs on him?" Sabattini asked.

Cindy pouted. "No, of course not! He's my neighbor. His garage wall is only a few yards from my bedroom. Plus, I'm often up late with Aleah. She's not exactly the perfect sleeper."

"Sorry to hear that. It must be tough trying to cope with a young baby all on your own," Sabattini sympathized.

The woman sniffed. "Yes, it is. But I'm fine. We're both fine."

"I'm sure you are."

"Grayson Thorpe and Simon Matthews look quite similar, don't you think?" Charlotte asked.

The question fell out of her mouth before she realized she'd spoken. She clamped her mouth shut, horrified. Sabattini glared at her. Cindy didn't appear to notice the sudden tension between the two detectives.

"Yes," she said slowly. "I noticed that, too. I guess Lydia has...had a type."

"Did Lydia ever bring anyone else home?" Sabattini asked.

"Like, another man?"

"Yes."

"No. I only saw her with the mayor. And her girlfriend, of course. She often called in."

"You mean Melissa Robinson?" Sabattini asked.

Cindy shrugged. "I don't know her name. Short, stocky, spiky dark hair."

"Sounds like Melissa," Sabattini agreed.

"She drives an old beat up Toyota Land Cruiser. It always looks a bit out of place in this neighborhood."

"Did you see anyone around the day of the murder? Melissa, perhaps?" Sabattini asked.

"No. I'm sorry. An officer already asked me this the other night. I had an appointment with the community nurse that day. Aleah was due for her vaccinations. We left a bit after eleven for a midday appointment. The nurse was late and then our appointment ran overtime. We went to the mall afterwards and I did some shopping. We didn't get home until about four that afternoon."

"Did you ever hear Grayson and Lydia arguing? As you say, your houses aren't too far away from each other."

Cindy shrugged again and looked away. "I guess."

"You did hear them arguing?" Sabattini persisted.

"Yes, of course. From time to time."

"How loud did it get?"

"Pretty loud, especially recently."

Sabattini frowned. "They argued worse lately?"

"Yes."

"Do you know what they were arguing about?"

The woman shook her head. "No. At the time, I wondered if it was about Lydia's affair, but the way Grayson reacted when I told him... He appeared genuinely blindsided... I honestly think he didn't know."

From the corner of her eye, Charlotte saw a navy-blue BMW pull up next door. Her heart skipped a beat. Grayson Thorpe sat behind the wheel. He climbed out and straightened to his full height. His brow was furrowed, as if in thought. He hadn't seen them yet.

Drawn to him like a magnet and against her better judgment, Charlotte looked her fill. Tall, broad shouldered, sexy. Attraction slammed into her, nearly leaving her breathless. She steeled herself in case she had to come up close and personal to him once again.

Chapter Ten

Grayson stared at the house he and Lydia had purchased four years ago and tried to find the courage to step inside. They'd spent their first night as a married couple snuggled up under the covers of their brand new king-sized bed. Grayson had even carried Lydia over the threshold. They'd giggled like teenagers. It felt like yesterday.

Where did it go all wrong? When did we start growing apart? When did she begin looking elsewhere for companionship, for love?

He was flooded with guilt. He couldn't deny he had to take some responsibility for the breakdown of their marriage. Okay, so Lydia had been the first to break her marriage vows, but he'd done the same with Charlotte that night. And he hadn't helped matters by devoting so much time to his career. They'd often argued about that. He'd learned to block her arguments out, put his head down and keep working. Which only served to infuriate her further. It was a vicious cycle that had seemed never ending. Now Lydia was dead.

From the corner of his eye he caught sight of a movement. He turned his head and saw Charlotte and the other detective talking to his neighbor. His stomach dropped.

This can't be good...

Charlotte looked stunning in a tailored cream-colored pantsuit. She'd teamed it with sensible low-heeled shoes. It reminded him how petite she was. Even from this distance, she exuded sex appeal. She might not be much taller than the average thirteen-year-old, but she sure packed a punch in her tiny frame.

Rather than hanging loose around her shoulders, her thick brown hair was pulled back into a bun, but even the severe hairstyle couldn't take away from her natural beauty. He was suddenly bombarded with images of her silky, tanned limbs entwined with his, her mouth moving over every inch of him.

He forced the erotic thoughts from his mind and swallowed a regretful sigh. As much as he'd wished to repeat the experience, that was never going to happen. Her partner was investigating his wife's murder and it looked like she might be back on the case, too. And he was on the suspect list. Probably at the top of it. He'd seen enough at Sydney Legal to know the husband was always the prime suspect. The older detective had said as much at the scene.

Grayson's gaze slid to Cindy. She looked stressed and tired. Raising a young baby on her own must be difficult. At least he'd been able to get her no-good boyfriend to pay child support. The bastard had left her the moment she'd given him the news about the baby. As if Cindy was the only one responsible for the fact she was pregnant. The asshole. Grayson had no time for fathers who tried to skip out on paying child support.

He looked at Cindy again. Her gaze was fixed on the ground and a blush had filled her cheeks with color. She looks guilty... Realization struck him. She's told the detective about Lydia's affair... That was the only explanation. Not that it mattered. He had nothing to hide. And he'd already told Charlotte who had no doubt shared the information with her partner.

He headed toward his house, determined to ignore them. From the corner of his eye, he saw Charlotte and the older detective excuse themselves and walk toward him.

Shit.

"Mr Thorpe. Wait up," the older detective—Sabattini—called out.

Grayson stopped and waited for them to approach. His gaze lingered on Charlotte. "I thought you'd been taken off the case," he stated.

She glanced at her partner and inclined her head. "You're right. Detective Sabattini is in charge of this investigation. I'm merely tagging along."

Sabattini narrowed his eyes at him. "Why didn't you tell us you came home that day, after your meeting with the mayor?"

Grayson tensed. He glanced toward Cindy, wondering what the hell she'd told them. She avoided his gaze. He looked back at the grizzled detective. "I don't know where you got your information, but it's wrong. I didn't come home. After I left the mayor, I drove straight back to the office."

"We have a witness who says they saw you here that day," Sabattini insisted.

A renewed wave of anger and frustration washed over Grayson. He scrubbed at the whiskers on his face.

"So. We're back to that again. I told you, I didn't kill my wife. I also didn't come anywhere near my house once I left for work that day. After my meeting with Matthews, I returned to my office in the city. Then I went out for a drink. You both know what happened after that."

He stared at Charlotte and addressed the rest of his answer to her. "I left the hotel in the early hours of the morning, collected my car from the Brass Monkey and went home." He returned his attention to Sabattini. "That's when I found Lydia and I immediately called the police. Whoever this witness is, they're wrong."

Sabattini glared at him. "We only have your word you went straight back to the office after your meeting with Matthews. You could have easily swung by your home, murdered your wife, cleaned up and then gone back to work."

This time Grayson's frustration swelled over. He made a sound of disgust in the back of his throat. "For fuck's sake! How many times do I have to tell you? I didn't murder my wife! You know what? I shouldn't even be talking to you without my lawyer present, but I have nothing to hide."

He dragged in a breath in an effort to control his temper. It would do him no good to give the detectives evidence of the anger he felt inside at being unjustly accused.

He eyed Charlotte steadily. "Let me explain again. I met with Simon Matthews during my lunch break. He confirmed he and my wife were having an affair. I wanted to go and confront her there and then, but I was furious. I was on the verge of losing control. I knew I had to give myself time to get ahold of myself. Besides, as far as I was aware, Lydia was at her office. I could hardly confront her about her cheating in front of a client."

"So what did you do?" Sabattini asked.

"Like I said, I went back to my office. I had clients to see, work to attend to. It was the best thing I could have done. By the time I was ready to leave, I'd managed to calm down. I realized my marriage was over. It hurt like hell that my wife was cheating on me. I wasn't going to kiss and make up and forgive her again. It was hard enough the first time. I didn't have it in me to go through all that again."

Charlotte went still. Sabattini also came alert. He sought clarification. "This wasn't the first time your wife had cheated?"

Grayson's shoulders slumped on a weary sigh. He was tired of all the questions, tired of going round in circles. Tired that the police only seemed to have their sights on him. He might as well come clean.

"No, it wasn't," he said quietly. "A couple of years ago, there was someone else. Someone who worked near her office. She told me she felt neglected and that she wished she'd never done it. She told me she loved me and swore it would never happen again."

"And you believed her?" Sabattini asked.

"Yes."

"You told us that first night your wife had been distant of late, but there was no mention of any cheating. How do you explain that?" Sabattini asked.

Grayson hung his head and blew out his breath. "I'm sorry. I probably should have been more upfront with you."

Sabattini's expression turned belligerent. "Yes, you should have. In my experience, someone who lies to the police has something to hide."

Grayson glared at the older detective. "Look, you and I both know in this kind of situation the husband's always the prime suspect. If I'd told you that morning my wife was having an affair, you'd have taken me away in handcuffs. Am I right?"

Sabattini's tone was as dry as the desert. "You watch too much TV, Mr Thorpe. Yes, that kind of information would certainly have gotten our attention, but I'd like to think we would have waited until we had more evidence of your guilt before locking you up."

Grayson didn't so much as crack a smile. "Do you have a time of death?"

The detective waited a heartbeat before answering. "Yes. The forensic pathologist estimates your wife was murdered somewhere between midday and six that night."

Grayson breathed out a sigh of relief. "Then I'm in the clear."

"Not so fast. I'm not completely convinced you didn't come back here and do away with your wife after your meeting with the mayor. Besides, we still haven't spoken to the bartender at the Brass Monkey."

Grayson made a sound of frustration in the back of his throat. "Then what the hell are you waiting for?"

The older detective merely looked at him.

Anger and frustration coursed through Grayson. "While you're in go-slow mode, my life's being put through the wringer. And no one seems to care. I didn't kill my wife! How many times do I have to tell you!" he shouted. Then he looked at Charlotte. "Do you honestly think I'm capable of something like that?"

She glanced at her partner and then looked back at him. "I hardly know you. Besides, you're asking the wrong person. You wouldn't believe the things we've seen, and from people you'd least suspect."

"You've already proven you can be deceitful," Sabattini said, his eyes hard. "Cheating on your wife, for one."

"You're right and I'm sorry for that." He turned to Charlotte. "And I shouldn't have lied to you about being separated. The thing is, in my mind, I already was. My marriage had been over for some time. I'd just refused to acknowledge it. And ever since our night together..."

"Stop!" she cried on a sharp intake of breath.

Her face was flushed with anger or embarrassment—he couldn't tell which. Maybe both? Without thinking, he reached out to her, wanting to reassure her. His fingers brushed the soft skin of her cheek moments before she stepped out of reach.

"Charlotte...?" he beseeched her.

She shot him a panicked look and then spun around and strode away from them, headed in the direction of the unmarked police car that was parked at the curb. Grayson took a step in that direction. Sabattini cursed. Grayson turned back to face him.

With his hands on his hips, the older detective stared him down, his expression hard. "I wouldn't if I were you."

Chastened, Grayson stayed where he was, but that didn't mean he wasn't filled with a yearning so overwhelming it left him feeling weak.

Why did we have to meet in such fucked-up circumstances? If only…

Sabattini continued to glare at him. "You said you weren't prepared to forgive your wife her indiscretion a second time. Does that mean you'd planned to tell her your marriage was over?"

Grayson sighed. "Yes. I'd had enough. Her affair with Matthews was the final straw."

"Did you call ahead to warn her?"

"No. I didn't want to give her time to formulate her arguments, to hit me with all the reasons why I should let her stay. I wanted to catch her off guard. That's one of the reasons I left work so early. On a normal day, I wouldn't get home until much later—sometimes as late as nine or ten at night. I know working that late wasn't fair to Lydia, but I thought she understood. I was doing this for us. I wanted to make junior partner. The only way to do that was to work harder than anyone else. I'd explained this to her many times before. She wasn't exactly happy about it, but I thought she understood." He dragged in a ragged breath.

"I was going to confront her that night, but first, I needed a drink, something to fortify me while I dug up the courage I needed to bring the ax down on my marriage."

His shoulders slumped. He was so tired of all the questions, having to regurgitate the sorry details of their lives over and over again, but he was also determined to make the detective see. Then perhaps the man would stop focusing his investigation on the wrong person.

"And then I met Charlotte," he continued. "My plans were sent awry. I hadn't planned it that way. It just happened." He paused, his thoughts conjuring up those marvelous hours spent in Charlotte's arms.

"It had rained late the previous afternoon," he continued. "A heavy downpour. The streets were slick and wet. My mind was in turmoil. I'd just come from the bed of a woman who'd made me feel things I'm not sure I've ever felt in my life." He glanced sideways at Sabattini, but the detective's expression remained closed and unreadable.

"I remember driving home after leaving the hotel and thinking about what an asshole I was. I'd forgotten to text Lydia. She didn't have a clue where I was. On top of that, I'd just betrayed my wedding vows. I'm such an asshole I tried to justify my behavior by reminding myself Lydia had cheated first. As if that made a difference."

He pulled a face, disgusted to admit he'd even thought that. But it was true and he was trying to be as open and honest as he could be.

"I remember thinking about the storm that had passed and hoping the leak I'd repaired, in the roof had held. I arrived home just before four in the morning. I parked in the driveway. I grabbed my briefcase off the back seat and went inside. It was dark and quiet. I assumed Lydia was asleep. I switched on a light so I wouldn't bump into anything and walked into the living room... That's where I found her...." His voice faded away as the memories crashed into him. "It's a sight I'll never forget."

His voice cracked with emotion. His chest was tight with pain. He dragged in another ragged breath and prayed for the nightmare to be over.

Sabattini's expression remained unreadable, his eyes had turned hard. "Someone saw you here that afternoon, Grayson. Leaving your house."

Grayson glared back at him. "They're mistaken."

"Do you have any proof of that?"

"No. See, I wasn't thinking about needing to have an alibi for the murder of my wife. I left my office, drove to Sutherland, saw the mayor and came back."

Sabattini continued to watch him closely. "Oh, yes. The mayor who was having an affair with your wife. How did that make you feel?"

Anger surged up inside Grayson before he could stop it. "How the hell do you think that made me feel?"

"I thought you told us your marriage was in trouble?"

"Even knowing that, it still felt like a kick in the guts to hear Lydia was cheating on me. Again."

"So, you were angry?"

"Of course I was. I was furious."

"You threatened to kill Matthews."

Grayson paused and then slowly nodded. "Yes."

"Later that same afternoon, your wife was murdered."

His eyes narrowed to angry slits. "It wasn't like that! I didn't do it, Detective. No matter what you might think. Do you really think I could butcher my wife, change my clothes and then head back to work as if nothing happened? You've talked to my executive assistant. You know I came back from lunch and dealt with another appointment."

"You said you parked in the driveway when you arrived home in the early hours of that morning. Why didn't you park in the garage? There's room enough for two vehicles."

"Except there isn't."

Sabattini frowned. His gaze darted toward the roller doors in front of the double-car garage and then came back to him. He lifted a single bushy eyebrow in silent query. "It looks like a double garage to me."

"You're right. But Lydia has always parked her car in there and I store a ski boat on the other side."

Sabattini nodded. "Okay, I get that. What I don't understand is why someone would say they'd seen you here around one o'clock on the afternoon of Lydia's murder."

He made a sound of frustration in the back of his throat. "For God's sake! How many times do I have to tell you! I didn't come home that day! Who said I did?"

"I can't say."

"The hell you can't. What you mean is, you won't."

"Can't. Won't. The outcome's the same."

"Words matter, Detective."

"Fair enough. But I'm not going to apologize. This is my investigation. I'm going to run it any way I see fit. I'm trying to find out who murdered your wife. I would have thought you'd have a vested interest in that outcome."

"Of course I do. I might have been planning on ending my marriage, but I didn't wish Lydia any harm."

"Well, someone sure as hell did."

Chapter Eleven

Charlotte stared through the driver's side window of the unmarked police car and waited for Sabattini to finish with Grayson. She'd tried hard to remain indifferent when he'd mentioned their intimate encounter in front of her partner, but in the end it had been beyond her. She'd taken refuge in the car.

She still couldn't believe she was connected with a murder investigation, even on the periphery. Who would have guessed the very man she'd chosen to have a one night stand with would turn up on a murder suspect list the very next day? It was ludicrous. Unfortunately, it was true and wishing things were different would get her nowhere.

While Grayson had been answering Sabattini's questions, she'd watched him closely, gauging his every reaction. At one point, his face appeared ravaged with anger and pain. If he was faking it, he was doing a darn good job.

She'd interviewed her fair share of criminals. Most couldn't keep up that level of deceit for long, especially when faced with such pointed questions from an experienced detective looking to make an arrest. And to be honest, Grayson's window of opportunity to commit the murder was narrowing fast. If the bartender confirmed he'd arrived there around half-past three, like Grayson said, then that would be the end of it. He'd no longer be a suspect.

To her relief, Sabattini started heading toward the squad car. From the corner of her eye, she saw Grayson walk toward his house. Sabattini opened the car door and climbed in. She shot him a sideways glance.

"Find out anything new?"

"Not really. He's sticking to his story."

"You think he's lying?"

"Probably not, but it's my job to keep up the pressure. That way he might slip up."

"I think you need to talk to Melissa Robinson again," Charlotte said as she started the ignition. "Robinson's certain she saw Grayson leaving the Thorpe house. But what if she was mistaken? What if the man she saw was Simon Matthews?"

Sabattini narrowed his eyes at her. "Good detective work, Barrington. I'm so glad you came along."

The sarcasm in his voice was unmistakable. Charlotte flushed. "I'm sorry. I overstepped. Of course you've already thought of that."

Anger glinted in Tony's eyes. "I told you to keep your mouth shut. I told you not to say a word. You're an observer, Barrington. I thought I made that clear."

Her embarrassment deepened. She checked over her shoulder and pulled out onto the road.

"I'm sorry Tony," she said again. "I didn't mean to question Cindy. It's just that, I've seen Simon Matthews. His similarity to Grayson Thorpe is striking. I don't think it's beyond ridiculous to consider Melissa Robinson could very well have been mistaken about who she saw that day."

"It wasn't just Cindy. You involved yourself in the conversation with Grayson, too."

Charlotte didn't know what to say. She'd opened her mouth when she'd specifically promised she wouldn't.

Sabattini had every right to be mad.

He glared at her for a few moments, waiting for her response. When she didn't, he cursed under his breath and turned to stare out the window. They drove the next ten minutes in silence. Then he slapped his thigh and sighed.

"Seeing as we're already out here, you might as well sit in on my interview with the bartender. The Brass Monkey's only a couple of blocks from here."

Charlotte nodded, barely daring to speak. It was more than she deserved. Once again, she tried to smooth things over.

"Listen, Tony. I'm really sorry about what happened back there. I had no idea Grayson was going to arrive home and I didn't initiate the conversation between us. It just...sort of happened. It's no excuse, but... You were there. The guy addressed me directly. What was I supposed to do without looking like a fool?"

She tossed a glance in his direction. His jaw remained clenched, his expression closed. She took hold of her courage and forged on. "To tell you the truth, I'm feeling pretty confident he's not our guy. The timeline's just too tight and if the bartender confirms Grayson arrived around half-past three, then that only supports the theory he can't be the perp."

Sabattini glared at her. "Are you finished?"

Charlotte nodded.

"Don't eliminate any potential suspect until you have irrefutable proof they're not involved. That's the first rule of any investigation."

"Yes sir," she mumbled, once again feeling suitably chastened.

They traveled the rest of the way in tense silence. When they pulled up outside the Cronulla Plaza, Sabattini turned to her and held up a forefinger, his expression fierce. "Now, I'm warning you. Not a word. You're here as an observer only. I'm the only one asking the questions. Got it?"

"Got it."

They climbed out of the car and made their way downstairs and through the doors that led into the Brass Monkey. Sabattini had called ahead to check that the bartender who'd been working the night Lydia died was on duty. Someone on the other end of the phone had confirmed he was.

Charlotte recognized Phillip Carr as the bartender who'd served her and Grayson. Carr had short dark hair, dark eyes and was good looking enough to attract both men and women alike. Tony introduced them and flashed his credentials. Carr invited them to follow him into a back office where they could talk in private.

The bartender shot a curious glance in Charlotte's direction. "Have we met before? You look familiar."

Fire burned a path across Charlotte's face. She muttered something unintelligible and averted her gaze.

"We want to talk to you about Grayson Thorpe," Sabattini said, deliberately ignoring the exchange. "He was here the other night. In fact, he told us he arrived at half-past three."

Sabattini reached into the pocket of his suit jacket and produced a photograph of Grayson. It looked like the kind of photo taken by the HR department.

"This is Grayson Thorpe," Sabattini continued, showing Carr the photo.

The bartender took the photo and looked at it. "Yeah, he comes in here every now and then. What day are you interested in?"

"Last Tuesday afternoon."

"It's hard for me to say for sure if he was here then. Your best bet is to review the CCTV footage."

Charlotte's heart skipped a beat. Sabattini smiled. "Now we're talking. Do you mind running the tapes?"

"No problem," Carr replied. "We keep a thirty-day backup on site."

The bartender disappeared into a small storage room and returned with a DVD. He slipped it into a DVD player and switched on a TV screen with a remote. Grainy black-and-white images filled the screen. Carr fast-forwarded through the footage until they reached the day in question. Both Charlotte and Sabattini leaned forward. Charlotte held her breath.

"Stop!" Sabattini shouted.

Charlotte's stomach somersaulted with nerves. In the camera positioned over the entrance, Grayson could be seen arriving at the bar. The time on the footage showed it was a little after half-past three. Another camera showed Grayson seated at the bar, drinking.

"Let's fast-forward a bit more," Sabattini said.

Carr did as he was asked. The footage continued to show Grayson at the bar, drinking alone. He didn't seem to be paying any attention to the people around him, or the international game of cricket that was playing on a widescreen TV. At a little past five, the door opened and the cameras captured Charlotte as she stepped inside.

Her pulse took off at a gallop. She watched herself on the screen as she perched on a barstool not far away from Grayson. After a few moments, he looked across at her. She saw Sabattini taking note of her tight leather dress. Her face flamed with embarrassment. To her relief, his expression didn't change. Neither did he make a comment.

The footage continued to roll. Charlotte watched as Grayson moved and came to sit beside her. She remembered their conversation and her face burned hotter. Then they climbed off their stools and headed for the dance floor. By the time the camera captured their departure, the time on the footage read half-past eight.

Sabattini asked Carr to email him a copy of the footage. Then he thanked the bartender for his time. Charlotte and Tony returned to the car in silence. Charlotte's mind worked furiously. Unless Grayson had managed to get home and murder his wife in the short time after his meeting with the mayor and when he arrived back at his office, he was in the clear. The only sticking point was the evidence from the witness who was certain she'd seen Grayson outside his house.

As Charlotte switched on the ignition and headed the car in the direction of the station, Sabattini turned to her and sighed.

"I'll call Melissa Robinson first thing when we get back to the station and get her in for another interview."

After spending an inordinate amount of time staring at his closed front door, Grayson eventually found the courage to go inside his house. Fortunately, the cleaning crew had removed all evidence of his wife's violent end. He could still see the scene in his mind's eye, but it wasn't quite the same as having to pass by the blood and gore where it lay spattered across his living room floor.

He walked into the kitchen and opened the fridge. He felt like he was a sleepwalker, merely going through the motions. He couldn't remember the last time he'd had something decent to eat.

The contents of the fridge were completely uninspiring. Milk going sour. Leftovers from more than a week ago. A wilted head of lettuce. Two wrinkled apples. Not that he felt hungry. It was more that he was looking for a distraction, something—anything—to take his mind off what had happened right here in his house.

He wished he had a clue pointing to who could have done something so shocking, so disgusting, so evil. Neither of them had any enemies, at least, not that he knew of. They were an ordinary couple living in the suburbs, going to work, getting on with their lives. Okay, so their lives weren't perfect and if he were honest, he'd admit he'd been as unhappy in their marriage as Lydia had obviously been.

Still, he'd never wished her harm. He'd been as shocked and devastated as anyone to discover his wife had been murdered. He understood the nature of the detective's questions. He was the most likely suspect, after all. But he sure as hell hadn't butchered his wife. Which meant the killer was still out there. Might even be watching him now.

What if the killer isn't finished? What if he has a vendetta against both of us? What if the job's only half done?

He shuddered on a sudden wave of apprehension and glanced instinctively toward the front windows. The blinds were still open. No doubt they'd been open that fateful night he'd arrived home in the early hours of the morning. Lydia normally closed them when she got home. She always made it home before he did, even on those rare occasions when he left work early. He had at least a thirty-minute commute during peak hour.

Arriving home that morning after spending those magical hours in Charlotte's arms, he hadn't even noticed the blinds were still open. Probably because his head was filled with what had just happened and what he planned to say to Lydia about bringing their marriage to an end. Anger and hurt from her betrayal with the mayor had also been on his mind.

Grayson sighed. He needed to try harder to convince the police he was innocent. They were wasting precious time questioning him. Sabattini had asked him if he had any proof he didn't go home that day and he'd told the detective no. But now he realized he did. He'd stopped to fill his car with fuel on his way back to the city. He couldn't remember the time, but it was well after his meeting with the mayor. He fished in his pocket for Charlotte's business card.

Charlotte.

He knew he should call Sabattini, but he wanted to talk to Charlotte again. He didn't care that she was angry with him. He just wanted to hear her voice.

God, how he wished things were different! Of all the women in Sydney, he had to come across a little firecracker that set his heart racing and made him feel things he'd never felt before. He'd been drawn to her right from the beginning. Had wanted to know her name. Then she'd encouraged his attentions and it had ended in the way both of them had wanted. It had been the best night of his life... And the following morning, in those early hours, it became the worst.

With a groan, he buried his face in his hands. The house felt empty and cold without Lydia. They might have been at odds in recent months, but that didn't mean he'd stopped caring about her. His indiscretion with Charlotte was never meant to be anything more than a one night stand. A way to deal with the pain of what felt like his inevitable marriage break-up.

The fact that Charlotte had blown his world in a way he could never have imagined was something he hadn't factored in. Along with coming home to a murdered wife. Now any hope of repeating the experience he'd had with Charlotte had been smashed to smithereens.

But that didn't stop him from thinking about the beautiful detective. He thought about her way too much. He wished they didn't have a history between them that made it impossible to look at her and not see her naked beneath him. He had to make her see he wasn't the killer she and her partner were looking for.

With that thought in mind, he dialed her number and waited for her to pick up. To his relief, she answered right away.

"Detective Barrington."

"Detective, it's Grayson Thorpe."

"Mr Thorpe. If this is about the investigation, you need to speak with Detective Sabattini."

Her voice was cool, clipped, detached. He pushed past it. "I remembered something."

"Yes?" Her tone was only marginally warmer.

"Your partner asked me if I had any proof I didn't return home the day Lydia was murdered. I told him no. But I was wrong. I pulled into a Shell service station on Botany Road to fill up my car. I didn't keep the receipt and I don't know the exact time, but it was probably a bit past one o'clock. There would be CCTV footage, wouldn't there? You'd be able to see me on it."

"I'll pass the information on to Detective Sabattini. He'll be in touch." She ended the call.

Grayson sat there a moment holding the phone, longing for something that seemed impossible.

Charlotte set her phone back on her desk and stared at the blank screen. She couldn't believe Grayson had called her again. He knew she wasn't part of the investigation. He knew there was nothing she could do. And yet he continued to contact her to impart important information.

She supposed she ought to be flattered that he wanted to remain in contact with her. She couldn't deny a secret part of her was thrilled. Her attraction to him hadn't waned because he was now caught up in a murder investigation. It was ludicrous, but that's just the way she felt. Her continued feelings for him were partly attributable to the fact she'd always felt, deep down, that he was innocent of his wife's death. And now it looked like he might have the proof he needed to clear his name.

She glanced across at Sabattini's desk, but it was unoccupied. Pushing back her chair, she stood and made her way to the tearoom. To her relief, she found Tony refilling his coffee mug. He glanced over his shoulder as she approached.

"What is it now, Barrington?"

His tone was caustic and filled with impatience. She refused to be deterred.

"I just had a call from Grayson."

Tony's face turned red. "What the hell? What is it with him and you? He knows you're off this investigation. How many times does he have to be told?"

Charlotte held her hand up in an effort to placate him. "I know, Tony. Believe me, I know. But hear me out. Grayson stopped to fuel up on his way back to town that afternoon. He has proof he wasn't the man Robinson says she saw outside the Thorpe house."

Some of the anger in Tony's face eased. "Keep talking," he said in a much more reasonable voice.

Charlotte filled him in on what she knew. Tony's expression shifted from disgruntled to showing mild interest.

"Call the service station and put in a request for the footage," Sabattini said.

"I'll get on it right away."

A uniformed officer walked into the tearoom. He looked at Sabattini. "There's a Melissa Robinson waiting for you downstairs."

Charlotte kept her gaze fixed on the floor. She knew better than to hope Sabattini would let her sit in on another interview, especially one being conducted right under the nose of their boss. Tony murmured thanks to the uniform and turned to leave the room, coffee mug in hand.

"I think you'll find the observation room's empty at the moment," he muttered as he passed by her.

Charlotte's pulse leaped into overdrive. She stumbled in her hurry to reach the observation room. She took a seat behind the two-way glass and tried to get ahold of her emotions. Her heart thumped. Her palms were cold. She couldn't wait to hear what Robinson said when Tony put it to her that she'd been mistaken about seeing Grayson that afternoon.

While she waited for Sabattini to appear with his witness, she pulled out her phone and dialed one of the general duties cops who worked in the offices below.

"Ryan. It's Charlotte. I need a favor."

Giving him the details of the Shell service station on Botany Road, she asked him to call the owner and request a copy of the CCTV footage taken on the day of the murder.

"I'll get right on it," Ryan assured her.

"Thank you. I need it like...yesterday."

"Got it."

The door to the interview room opened and Sabattini followed Melissa inside. She wore the same kind of clothing as the last time. High visibility shirt, work pants, steel-capped boots. She took a seat at the table. Tony sat down opposite. Her body language was relaxed. If she had anything to hide, she certainly didn't appear nervous about it.

Tony started by recapping what she'd told him the first time. Once again, she repeated her certainty that she'd seen Grayson Thorpe leaving his home about one o'clock the day his wife had been murdered.

"What made you think it was Grayson Thorpe?" Sabattini asked.

Melissa shrugged. "I knew what he looked like. I was parked at the curb. I had a clear view. It was him."

"Have you ever met Lydia's husband?"

"No. But I've seen plenty of photos of him around her house."

"What kind of photos?"

"Wedding pictures, mostly."

"From several years ago."

"Yes, I guess."

"People change over time. Are you sure it was Grayson you saw?"

Her gaze remained steady on Sabattini's. "Yes. I'm sure."

Sabattini sat back in his chair. "Tell me, Melissa. Have you ever met the Mayor of Sutherland Shire?"

"No."

"His name is Simon Matthews. Do you know what he looks like?"

"No."

Sabattini showed her a picture. Melissa expressed surprise.

"He looks a lot like Grayson Thorpe, doesn't he?" asked Sabattini.

She shrugged. "Maybe. Not really. The hair, maybe."

"Do you think it's possible this was the man you saw leaving Lydia Thorpe's house that day?"

"No. It was Grayson Thorpe. I'm certain of it."

"And you say this was about one o'clock?"

"Yes."

"Are you certain it was that time?"

"Yes. I checked my phone right after I pulled up outside Lydia's house. We'd arranged to meet at one. I like to be punctual."

"Mr Thorpe said his wife was working that day. Do you know why she agreed to meet you at her home?"

"Yes. She texted me to say she needed to go home and collect a patient file. She'd forgotten to take it with her that morning."

"What was Mr Thorpe wearing?"

"I don't remember. A suit and tie, I think. White business shirt. I didn't pay that much attention."

"Did he look disheveled in any way? Like he'd been in a fight?"

"I don't remember. I don't think so, but I only saw him for a few seconds and then he climbed into his car and drove away."

"Right. A navy-blue BMW."

"Yes. I couldn't tell you the model. I'm not that good with cars."

"But you're certain you saw Grayson Thorpe leave his house and drive away in his car."

"Yes."

"Okay, thank you Ms Robinson. By the way, how long have you known Lydia Thorpe?"

"Oh, we went to high school together. We were in the same class. We've been best friends for years."

"And yet you've never met her husband?"

Melissa's confidence faltered momentarily, but she quickly recovered. "We lost touch for a few years."

"I see."

"Did Lydia ever talk to you about her marriage?"

Melissa nodded. "Yes."

"Did she talk about anything in particular?"

Melissa shrugged. "Just that she was unhappy."

"She told you that?"

"Many times."

"Why didn't she leave?"

"How do you know she wasn't planning to?"

Tony's gaze remained steady on Melissa's face. "Was she?"

"As a matter of fact, yes. That's what makes this so hard. Someone killed her before she got the chance."

"You talked about her leaving?"

"Yes."

Charlotte could tell Sabattini was trying hard to hide his surprise. "How long ago?"

"The last time was only a few days before she died."

"Really? Did she have a plan?"

"Yes. We were going to head north to Brisbane."

"We?"

Melissa flushed. "Yes. We were going to leave together."

"I see. Did Grayson know?"

"She was supposed to tell him that night. That was the plan. Only...she was murdered."

"Why didn't you tell me this before? When you came in the first time?"

The woman shrugged. "I didn't think about it then."

"I see. Do you think perhaps Lydia told him about her plans to leave earlier than expected? Could that have been the reason Grayson came home that afternoon?"

Melissa eyed Sabattini steadily. "That would be my guess."

Chapter Twelve

Charlotte returned to her desk and waited for Sabattini to see Melissa out. He returned a few moments later.

"She must be mistaken," Charlotte said the moment Tony appeared.

"Whoa! Slow down! Don't go getting ahead of yourself. We only have Grayson's word he stopped to fuel up. Until we have irrefutable proof of that, he stays on the suspect list."

"But—"

Tony stared her down. "What did I tell you, Barrington? Don't rule anyone out without proper justification and that means irrefutable evidence. You'll never be a decent detective if you don't learn that lesson and apply it to every single investigation."

"Of course. I'm sorry," Charlotte replied, dutifully chastened.

Tony was right, but it was hard for her to continue to view Grayson as a suspect. Right from the outset, her gut had told her he wasn't capable of murder and her instincts had never let her down. What she needed was the irrefutable evidence of Grayson's innocence. Tony kept harping on about that and with that thought in mind, she picked up the phone.

"Ryan. How are you doing with that CCTV footage from the service station?"

"Good. I just received it. I'll email the file to you."

Charlotte thanked him and ended the call. She turned to Sabattini. "We have the CCTV footage."

With her heart thumping and adrenaline surging through her veins, Charlotte tapped on her keyboard and accessed her email. A moment later, the file from the service station popped up in her inbox. With a hand that wasn't quite steady, she clicked on the file and waited for it to load.

Sabattini stood by her shoulder. It seemed to take forever, but finally grainy black-and-white images appeared on the screen. Charlotte used the mouse to advance the footage.

"Grayson said he was there a bit past one o'clock," she said.

Stopping the footage at one, Charlotte let it roll slowly forward. They both watched the screen intently, searching for a dark colored BMW.

"There!" Tony said and pointed to the screen.

Charlotte's heart skipped a beat. They both watched in silence as the car came to a stop beside a fuel pump. Charlotte held her breath. Grayson climbed out of the car and started fueling up. Charlotte's shoulders slumped on a sigh. The time stamp was one-thirteen.

Sabattini whistled low under his breath. "Seems like our boy was telling the truth about his movements that day."

Charlotte leaned back against her chair, weak with relief. "It can't be him. We know he met with the mayor around half-past twelve. Matthews said Grayson wasn't there long. Ten minutes or so. Let's say he left there by twelve forty-five. There was no way he could be four suburbs away in Botany by one-thirteen if he'd made a detour to his house in Cronulla, got into a fight with his wife and stabbed her thirty-seven times."

Tony nodded. "Don't forget he also had to have taken time to clean himself up. You're right. Grayson Thorpe didn't murder his wife."

"Then who the hell did Melissa Robinson see leaving the Thorpe house?"

Tony compressed his lips. "Either she's mistaken about that and it was in fact the mayor, or she saw no one and she lied about that." He paused and his expression turned grim. "We need to check out Matthews' alibi. We also need to look deeper into Melissa Robinson. I find it curious that a woman Lydia had been best friends with since her school days wasn't invited to her wedding."

Charlotte kept her expression blank, but it was difficult. Though she knew it was only a slip of the tongue, she rejoiced inside at Tony's use of the word "we."

She nodded slowly. "I get that the mayor might have had motivation. After all, we only have his word that he was okay about the affair coming to an end. Who knows? He might have been upset that Lydia was moving on. Then he had the visit from Grayson. Maybe that was the spark that ignited the fire?"

"But was he enraged enough to stab the woman thirty-seven times?" Sabattini mused.

Charlotte shrugged. "Who knows?"

"There's only one way to find out. We need to shake his tree a little harder."

Once again, Tony had used the word "we." This time, he pulled himself up on it. "What I meant was...I... Um, I shouldn't have said "we." There is no "we." Even though it looks like Thorpe's in the clear, we both know what the boss said." His cheeks turned red.

Charlotte took pity on him. "It's fine, Tony. I understand. I appreciate all that you've shared with me so far. You've taken a risk keeping me in the loop. I don't take that kind of courage lightly."

He made a non-committal sound and turned away. "I guess I'd better go and talk to the mayor." Before he got to the door, he glanced at her over his shoulder. "I can feel another headache coming on. Would you mind driving me out to Sutherland?"

Charlotte frowned. "You look all right to me."

Tony shot her a look filled with exasperation. "Do I have to spell it out? Do you want to tag along or not, Barrington?"

Charlotte's heart leaped with excitement. She grabbed her handbag and joined him at the door.

Tony gave her a fierce look. "Just remember, I'm the one asking questions."

"Deal."

Grayson tilted the beer glass toward his lips and swallowed. He was perched on a barstool at the Brass Monkey and was well on the way to getting drunk. It was only four in the afternoon and already he was drinking. He should have still been at work, slogging away at his cases, putting in enough billable hours that his dreams of making junior partner might actually come true. That's if his bosses could overlook the fact he was caught up in a murder investigation.

The problem was Charlotte. He couldn't stop thinking about her. She'd ruined his concentration. He couldn't focus. She consumed his every waking moment and tantalized him in his dreams.

Not that he'd been sleeping lately. Between the sudden end of his marriage and the murder of his wife, his life had been turned upside down. To top it off, erotic thoughts of the bewitching little detective were slowly driving him mad.

He cursed under his breath and scrubbed at his hair, trying to block out the memories.

I have to forget about her. This thing between us... It was over before it started...

Still that didn't stop him from wishing things were different.

A bartender he didn't recognize appeared and Grayson ordered another drink. He swiveled on his barstool, picturing the night he'd seen Charlotte perched on the stool not far from him. She'd looked like sex on legs in that short, tight leather dress, in search of a good time. And boy, had he been willing to help her out.

His body reacted instinctively. Blood rushed to his cock. He focused on the woman seated a few yards away and realized he was staring. He quickly lowered his gaze as his body calmed and then slowly looked back at her again.

She was about his age, maybe a little older. Her blond hair looked like it had come out of a bottle. Still, she was attractive enough. Big breasts, showcased in a tight red dress, spilled generously over the top of the bodice. Her curvy hips and long, toned legs completed a tidy package.

She smiled, her teeth showing white against the bright red lipstick that outlined her generous mouth. The open invitation in her eyes was meant to entice him and maybe a couple of weeks ago it would have.

He let his gaze slide over her from head to toe, taking his time. His body didn't react. In fact, he didn't feel the slightest surge of attraction. He cursed under his breath.

This is ridiculous! It's all Charlotte's fault! She's ruined me for anyone else...

Turning away, he buried his irritation in another drink.

It was late in the afternoon when Charlotte and Tony pulled up outside the Sutherland Shire Council Chambers. They hadn't called ahead, preferring to surprise the mayor. They didn't want him to have time to think about his responses, or plan a hasty exit. Besides, this time Tony could use his badge to get them inside the dark paneled walls of Matthews' office without having to cool their heels outside.

The young woman who sat behind the reception desk was the same one Charlotte had seen before. When Tony stated their business and showed her his badge, the woman was startled. She was much more amendable to their request for a few minutes with her boss and buzzed him in right away.

"Mr Matthews has asked me to show you to his office," she said as she hung up the phone a few moments later.

The woman stood and sashayed her way down the corridor. She knocked briefly on the closed door and then opened it. Stepping aside, she indicated for them to enter.

Charlotte and Tony walked into Matthews' office. He was seated behind his desk. This time, he looked nervous. Not that Charlotte read too much into that. A lot of people felt nervous when they were being interviewed by the police.

Tony made the introductions, deliberately ignoring the fact Charlotte had been there before. They both took a seat across from him. As agreed, Tony did all the talking.

"We want to take you back to the day Lydia Thorpe was murdered. Give us a rundown of your movements that day."

"I already spoke to that other detective about this." His gaze shifted to Charlotte. "It was you, wasn't it?"

Before she could respond, Tony smoothly interjected. "We want to hear it again. Humor us."

Matthews huffed out a sigh, but told them he'd arrived at work at nine and had met with Grayson Thorpe at twelve-thirty.

"What happened after Mr Thorpe's departure?"

"I... I was upset. I'd just been confronted by an angry husband. I needed some time to think."

"Did you go anywhere?" Sabattini demanded.

The mayor looked down at his desk. "Yes. I left my office shortly after Grayson."

"How long were you gone?" Tony asked.

Matthews' gaze darted around the room. "A little while."

Tony's gaze bored into his. "How long?"

"A couple of hours." Sweat had popped out on the mayor's forehead. He swiped at it with the back of his hand.

"You have to understand, Detective. I was upset about the confrontation with Lydia's husband. It made things all the more real. I've had affairs in the past. Dalliances that barely lasted a few months. I never got found out. The husbands remained oblivious. No one got hurt. The two of us had some fun and then things petered out. I expected it to be the same way with Lydia. Only Grayson did find out and he was far from happy about it."

Matthews' shoulders slumped. "The afternoon he stormed into my office, I was completely taken aback. Lydia had told me her marriage was in trouble. She assured me there was nothing left worth saving. But I could tell from her husband's reaction that she was wrong.

"He was angry and he was hurting. I was overwhelmed with guilt. After all, it was just as he said. I'd been sleeping with his wife. He put the allegations to me and I didn't deny it. I think that made him even more upset. He came there looking for a fight, but I capitulated right out of the blocks. He shouted for a while, but when he got no argument from me, he left."

He gave an uneasy chuckle. "It's hard to carry on an argument with someone who's not arguing back."

Charlotte and Tony merely glared at him in silence. Matthews hurriedly spoke again. "I... I was shaken up. I needed some time to think. I told Sally I was going out."

"Sally?" Sabattini asked.

"My EA. She's the one who showed you in here."

Sabattini acknowledged Matthews' comment with a nod. "Where did you go?"

Matthews sighed wearily. "I drove around for a while, trying to get my thoughts straight. All I could see was Thorpe's face, angry and upset. Shocked. Hurt."

"Did you call Lydia and tell her Grayson had stopped by? That he knew about the affair?" Sabattini asked.

"No. To tell you the truth, I was angry at her. She'd lied about the state of her marriage and now I had to deal with the consequences. An irate husband in my office isn't good for my image. So I didn't feel the need to tell her. I didn't feel I owed her anything.

"Besides, she's the one who started the affair. And it had become increasingly clear she was pulling away. I could tell it was only a matter of time before our affair fizzled out and that was on her. Yes, I was pissed she was going to dump me. Not because I was going to be hurt, but because I'm the one who usually calls it quits. The fact her husband had found out and was angry really wasn't my concern. It was only fair she deal with the fallout."

"That's a bit of a cop out," Sabattini said.

The mayor shrugged as if it were of no consequence. "What can I say? I'm an asshole."

"Are you married, Mayor Matthews?" Sabattini asked.

"No."

"You mentioned Lydia's interest in the affair had appeared to wane. "Do you think there was someone else?" Sabattini asked.

"I don't know. Maybe." Matthews paused and then added, "Early the morning Lydia was murdered, I called her. Another woman answered the phone."

"Did she identify herself?" Sabattini asked.

"No." Matthews cleared his throat. "I asked her if I could speak to Lydia. She got awfully protective. Started asking me who I was and what I wanted and she wanted to know why I was calling at that hour. Kind of aggressive. I was a little taken aback. I asked again for Lydia. The woman told me Lydia was in the shower. I left a message asking for Lydia to call me back. I thought it a bit strange that this woman was in Lydia's home, answering her phone at seven in the morning."

"Was Grayson there?" Tony asked.

"I don't think so. He leaves early for work. I always made sure to call after I knew he'd left the house."

"Did you ask Lydia who this woman was?" Tony asked.

The mayor's expression crumbled. "No. Lydia didn't call me back. I eventually left for work. Got busy. Forgot to check in with her. To tell you the truth, I hadn't given her another thought that day until her husband showed up. Now she's gone." His voice hitched with emotion.

Sabattini remained unmoved. "Can anyone verify your movements?"

"Yes. Well, for most of the time. For the first little while I drove around aimlessly, trying to get my head sorted. Then I pulled into the Café on Kingsway in Caringbah and bought a coffee and a piece of lemon meringue pie. I'm sure if you check the surveillance cameras you'll find me there."

"What time was this?"

"I don't know. About one o'clock. I drank my coffee, ate my pie, made some phone calls. Tried to clear my head."

"What time did you leave?"

"I don't remember exactly, but I was there for a while. Maybe an hour?"

Charlotte made a mental note to request the CCTV footage from the coffee shop, along with Matthews' phone records.

"Where did you go afterwards?" Sabattini asked.

"I went back to my office. My secretary can verify that. I arrived there about half-past two and was there for the rest of the afternoon."

Thanking the mayor for his time, Charlotte and Tony walked back out to the reception area. Matthews' executive assistant was alone there. She eyed them curiously. Charlotte glanced at Tony, wordlessly seeking permission. Tony nodded. Charlotte walked up to the secretary's desk.

"Hi. You must be Sally."

"Yes." The woman's tone was cautious.

Charlotte gave her a friendly smile. "We're here about Lydia Thorpe. She was murdered nearly two weeks ago. Did you know her?"

Sally lowered her eyes and nodded. "Yes. She stopped by here sometimes to see Simon. I heard about what happened to her on the news. It was terrible."

"What can you tell us about that day?" Charlotte asked.

"Well, it started out just like any other day. Simon had a few meetings in the morning. Around lunchtime, a man came charging in demanding to see him. I asked him if he had an appointment, but he told me he didn't need one. That he was there to see Simon and if I didn't show him through he'd find him himself."

"What did this man look like?"

She smiled slightly. "To be honest, he looked a lot like Simon. For a moment, I thought they might be brothers. I asked him for his name. He told me he was Grayson Thorpe."

"Did that name mean anything to you?"

"Yes, of course. I guessed straight away he was Lydia's husband and I was almost certain I knew why he was there, all riled up and demanding to see my boss."

"What happened then?" Sabattini asked.

"I buzzed Simon and told him Mr Thorpe was there to see him. Simon told me to tell the man he was busy, so I did."

"How did Thorpe take that?" Charlotte asked, guessing the answer.

Sally grimaced. "Not well. He pushed past me and headed straight down the hallway toward Simon's office. I chased him down the hall, telling him he couldn't interrupt the mayor, but he just kept walking. Simon came out of his office and saw what was going on. He told me it was okay and he showed Mr Thorpe into his office. I went back to my desk."

"Did you hear them arguing?" Sabattini asked.

"Yes, of course. It got very heated and the faux wood paneling isn't thick. But it seemed it was Mr Thorpe doing all the shouting. After about ten minutes, he left. Simon came out not long after and told me he was going out."

"Did he return later that afternoon?"

"Yes. I'd just gotten back from my lunch break. It was about half-past two."

"How did your boss appear on his return?" Charlotte asked.

"He seemed more in control than before he'd left. I figured whatever it was the two men had argued about had been resolved."

"Did you ask him about it?" Charlotte asked.

"No. He's my boss. I... I understood the matter was personal."

"Did you know Lydia and your boss were having an affair?" Sabattini asked.

Sally looked away. "Yes. But it was none of my business."

"Do you think your boss is capable of murder?" Charlotte asked.

The woman looked aghast. "No! Absolutely not! Simon gets faint at the sight of a nose bleed. He could never have been responsible for what happened to Lydia."

"Thank you, Sally. You've been very helpful," Sabattini said. He fished in his pocket for a business card. "If you think of anything else, please call me."

Chapter Thirteen

Charlotte spent a restless night going over all they knew about the murder. She was relieved Grayson had been cleared and was no longer a suspect and when she had a chance, she'd unpack all the feelings she had for him, but she still felt a driving need to find justice for Lydia. The woman had fought hard for her life and had lost. The least she deserved was for the police to find her killer.

The next morning, she made sure she gave Raoul her undivided attention. She'd been so busy with the case, she'd hardly had time for anything else, including her beloved cat. As he settled himself on her lap, she stroked his soft fur. He purred with contentment. It seemed all had been forgiven.

Ten minutes later, she reluctantly pressed a kiss to his nose and set him back down on the floor. She glanced at her watch. If she didn't hurry, she'd be late for work. She was anxious to confer with Sabattini and go back over all that they knew, including the latest information from Simon Matthews.

Her gut told her the mayor's alibi would hold up. After all, what motive did he have for killing his former lover? By his own admission, the relationship had all but come to an end and though he admitted to being annoyed it had been Lydia who'd lost interest first, he didn't seem at all cut up about the fact the passion between them had died.

Of course, it could all be an act. A deliberate show of nonchalance to put them off the scent. He wouldn't be the first suspect to try that. With Sabattini's words ringing in her ears, she was determined to get irrefutable evidence before she dismissed Matthews as a suspect.

To her surprise, Tony was already seated behind his desk when she arrived, sipping from a mug of coffee. She dropped her handbag on her desk and peeled off her jacket. She glanced in his direction.

"Good morning."

Sabattini merely grunted.

Charlotte pulled out her chair and sat. "I'll get straight onto preparing a warrant for Simon Matthews' phone records." She paused and then added, "Maybe we should add Melissa Robinson and Lydia Thorpe to the request?"

Sabattini nodded. "I think we need to take a closer look at Robinson. Something about her seems off. We can corroborate what she said about the texts and phone calls she made to Lydia. While you're at it, put in a request for the CCTV footage at the Café on Kingsway."

"You got it."

Taking a seat, Charlotte drew the keyboard toward her. They already knew Melissa had been wrong about Grayson. He wasn't the man she'd seen outside the house. Both Charlotte and Sabattini thought it most likely a case of mistaken identity. Especially given Matthews and Grayson looked so much alike.

But if Matthews' alibi checked out that meant he couldn't have been the man Melissa Robinson had seen outside Lydia's house either. Tony had expressly put to Melissa that she might have been mistaken. Robinson had been adamant she was right.

Which means if Matthews is cleared, then Melissa's lying. At least about this...

The woman was quickly moving to the top of Charlotte's suspect list. Right now, Charlotte had no motive for Melissa to stab her best friend to death, but it was time to do some research into Melissa Robinson, starting with her social media pages. But first, Charlotte would do the paperwork necessary for the phone records and put in a call to the Café on Kingsway and request their CCTV footage.

After attending to both tasks, Charlotte clicked open a new search page on the web. Quickly and efficiently, she typed in the commands that would provide her with access to Melissa's Facebook page. There were hundreds of photos, along with an impressive number of friends. But there was very little interaction on any of Melissa's posts. Either her friends weren't interested in Melissa's material, or her "friends" were fake.

It wasn't hard to buy friends and followers. It could be done for any of the social media sites. Pay twenty dollars and get five thousand followers. It was as easy as that. Though some of the social media sites did their best to crack down on fake followers and friends, they weren't always successful.

Charlotte kept scrolling. Many of the photos were of other women. A few of them included Melissa. In one photo, she had her arms around another woman and was tongue-kissing her.

"I think Melissa Robinson's into women," Charlotte said.

Sabattini looked over at her. "What, as in she's a lesbian?"

"I don't know, but some of these photos are suggestive of that. Take a look."

She turned her screen toward Tony. He stood and moved closer for a better look. He reached for her mouse and clicked on several more photos.

Slowly he shook his head. "I think you're right. What else did you find?"

Charlotte turned the screen back to face her. "Well, it says here she's in a relationship." She pointed to the relevant box. "It also says she went to high school in Mount Druitt." She turned to Sabattini. "Didn't she say she and Lydia went to high school together?"

"Yeah."

The outer west suburb of Sydney was about twenty-five miles from the city. It was a low socio-economic area with a high crime rate and a growing number of gangs. It was hard to imagine Grayson's wife growing up there.

"Lydia must have worked hard to get where she was. It couldn't have been easy," Charlotte murmured.

Sabattini nodded. "We need to get Melissa in for another interview, but let's wait for the CCTV footage from The Café on Kingsway. That way we'll know if we can cross Matthews off the suspect list. Better still, we'll wait until we have the phone records. Then we can cross-check the other information she volunteered."

Charlotte agreed. "In the meantime, I'll call Mount Druitt High School and have someone verify Lydia Thorpe's enrolment. We don't know her maiden name, but we do know her age. According to Melissa, they were in the same class. It might not narrow down things completely, but it's a start. With a bit of luck, there might still be someone on staff who remembers one or both of them."

Sabattini nodded. "Good. Let me know how you get on."

Charlotte's mobile began to ring. Sabattini moved away. She glanced down at the screen, but there was no caller ID. She considered ignoring it, but at the last moment changed her mind.

"Charlotte. It's Grayson."

Her stomach somersaulted. Her pulse leaped. The sound of his deep voice did strange things to her insides. She had no business talking to him and he shouldn't be calling, but she couldn't bring herself to hang up on him. Especially now that he'd been cleared.

"Grayson. What is it?"

She heard him sigh softly. "I just wanted to talk to you."

Her heart skipped another beat. She told herself not to be stupid. She should have more self-control. His wife had been murdered and although he was no longer considered a suspect, the case was far from closed.

"You shouldn't be calling me," she said, silently cursing her husky tone.

"I know. But I can't help it." He sighed again. "I can't stop thinking about you. About us."

She ignored the tightening of her belly and frowned. "Have you been drinking?"

"No."

"Well, please don't call me again. At least, not while the investigation into your wife's death is still open. Okay?"

There was a long beat of silence. Finally he responded. "Okay."

Then Charlotte remembered about the call she intended to put in to Mount Druitt High School.

"Oh, by the way. What was Lydia's maiden name?"

"Her maiden name?"

She heard the confusion in Grayson's voice, but refused to explain. "Yes. Her maiden name."

"Why is that important?"

"It doesn't matter, but I'd be grateful if you could provide me with the information."

"It's Tucker," he said.

"Tucker?"

"Yes."

"Thank you."

"My pleasure. Anything else I can do to help?"

"No. Thank you."

"I miss you."

Her stomach flip-flopped. "Grayson..."

"I can't help it, Charlotte. That night we spent together... It was the most magical night of my life. I left that hotel feeling on top of the world. As sad as I was about the end of my marriage, I looked forward to being free to see you again. And then everything went to hell...

"But my feelings toward you haven't changed. You're all I think about. I can't concentrate; I can't sleep... I look like shit. People think it's because of what happened to Lydia, but the truth is, it's because of you..."

"Grayson... Please... Don't do this!"

"Please, Charlotte! Tell me you feel the same!"

"I don't know what I feel!" she cried. From the corner of her eye, she saw Sabattini glance in her direction. She lowered her voice to a whisper. "Things are complicated. You know that better than anyone."

"I need to see you."

The desperation in his voice touched her deep inside. These past few weeks must have been hell on him. She couldn't imagine the nightmare his life had surely become. But making any decision about the two of them filled her with panic. At the same time, she yearned to see him again.

"Please, Charlotte. Just meet me for coffee. Thirty minutes of your time. That's all I ask."

Charlotte sighed. Knowing she'd probably end up regretting it, but unable to refuse him, she heard herself say, "Okay. Thirty minutes. Coffee. Nothing more."

"Thank you, Charlotte. I'll meet you in the café right down the street from the police station."

"Give me fifteen minutes. First I need to make another call." She also needed to get the okay from Sabbatini, as the lead investigator, to let Grayson know he was no longer a suspect in his wife's murder.

Grayson checked his watch for the umpteenth time and tried to quell his disappointment.

She isn't coming...

She'd asked for fifteen minutes. He'd been there nearly twenty-five. Every minute she didn't appear drove another shaft of pain and doubt through his heart. It was too early to feel so strongly about her. He barely knew her. That might be so, but it didn't stop him from feeling she was his soul mate. They'd connected on a deeper level right from the start. The tumult of the past couple of weeks had only sharpened his awareness that life was too short not to take chances when opportunities for something special dropped in his lap. He was sure she felt the same way.

He was desperate to see her again. He understood her reluctance to get involved with him. It was true. Things were complicated. But nothing worth fighting for ever came easy and no matter the nightmare he was currently living, he wanted Charlotte Barrington in his life.

He was already on his second latté. He looked at his watch.

If she's not here in five minutes, I'm leaving...

After all, he still had his pride.

And then she was there, standing in front of him, looking beautiful and flushed and harried.

"I'm sorry. I got caught up on the phone. Thank you for waiting."

She set her handbag down on a chair and then went to the counter and put in an order. He watched her walk back toward him. She wore a charcoal-gray suit. The skirt ended at her knees. Her open-toed sandals had modest heels. She was dressed for work, all business, but to him, she couldn't have looked sexier.

The pale blue silk blouse fluttered open in the slight draft from the door, exposing a patch of creamy skin. He remembered the silky feel of it. The way it tasted beneath his lips. Blood rushed to his cock. He bit back a groan. As if aware of his erotic thoughts, she blushed and looked away. In silence, she took the seat opposite him.

Reflexively, he reached for her hands. She pulled them out of reach. Her reaction hurt, but he was determined to make the most of his time with her.

"Thank you for coming," he said. "I wasn't sure you'd show."

"Yes. Sorry about that. Like I said, I got caught up on the phone. It took longer than I expected."

"Was it to do with the investigation?"

"Yes."

"Anything you'd like to share?"

She pursed her lips and then nodded, as if coming to a decision. "What do you know about Melissa Robinson?"

"Who?"

"Your wife's best friend."

"Best friend? Oh, you mean Mel. I'm not sure I'd describe her as Lydia's best friend. I haven't even met her. I only know about her because Lydia mentioned her once or twice. I'm sure the woman's never been to our house."

"Oh, but you're wrong. Your neighbor, Cindy, told me Melissa often stopped by."

Grayson shook his head, perplexed. "Then it must have been while I was at work. Lydia owned her own business. She had more flexible hours than I did."

"Melissa told us she'd gone to high school with your wife. In Mount Druitt."

Grayson frowned. "Lydia didn't go to school in Mount Druitt. She was born on the lower north shore. She went to school in North Sydney."

Charlotte regarded him steadily. "Well that fits. I called Mount Druitt High School. That's who I was on the phone with before I got here. There was no record of Lydia ever being enrolled there, let alone at the same time as Melissa. I also spoke to some of the staff who worked there at that time. No one remembered Lydia Tucker."

Grayson pursed his lips. "I don't understand. Why would Melissa lie about something like that?"

Charlotte shrugged. "Perhaps she wanted us to think she was closer to your wife than she actually was."

"But why? What would she gain by that?"

It was a valid question and one Charlotte had already asked herself. She debated a moment about how much to tell Grayson and then decided he deserved to know the truth. Besides, she'd already received clearance from Sabattini to let Grayson know he was no longer a suspect.

"Melissa Robinson was the witness who was adamant she'd seen you outside your house the afternoon Lydia was murdered."

Grayson gasped. "But that's wrong! I didn't go back to my house. I already told you. I went straight back to the office."

"Yes. We got hold of the CCTV footage from the Shell Service Station on Botany Road. You were there fueling up at one-thirteen. There was no way you had time to get home from the council chambers, stab your wife to death and then be at that service station such a short time later."

Hope and relief flooded Grayson's face. "Does this mean I'm off the hook?"

She nodded reluctantly. "Yes. You're officially no longer a suspect."

The grin that split Grayson's face in two nearly took her breath away. It also took years off his face. She couldn't imagine how hard these past weeks had been for him. Sympathy welled up inside her, along with something powerful she refused to identify. He seemed to sense her softening attitude.

His eyes pleaded with hers. "This is all messed up, Charlotte. You. Me. Us. It's impossible. I know that. But that doesn't stop me from wishing things were different and wanting to be with you again."

Charlotte's heart skipped a beat and then her pulse took off at a gallop. She wanted so badly to remain unaffected, detached from his words and the emotion behind them. But how could she when she felt the same way?

Her coffee arrived, saving her from having to answer. She took a sip and carefully set her cup back down again. Grayson watched her expectantly.

"I don't know what you want me to say," she finally managed.

"I don't want you to say anything. All I want you to do is feel. I'm the same man you met that night at the Brass Monkey. Our attraction was instant, combustible. You remember how good it was between us. How good it could be again. And I want more from you than sex. I want to get to know you, to take you to dinner, to the movies, to concerts, to shows. I want to know what makes you tick, what makes you laugh, what upsets you. I want to wake up beside you and fall asleep with you in my arms."

He paused to drag in a breath. Charlotte sat there, stunned. Once again, he reached for her hands and this time she didn't pull away.

"You know I didn't kill my wife," he said in a low voice. "Her murder isn't something either of us can forget, but I beg you to put it aside for just a moment and think about us and where we might be if Lydia were still alive? I would have ended my marriage for good. I would have called you the very next day. I would have asked you out a hundred times already and you would have said yes every time."

Charlotte shook her head from side to side. Things were moving way too fast. "You don't know that," she managed.

Grayson's gaze built in its intensity. "Yes. I do. I know because you and I are destined to be together. I feel that in my heart. I've always felt it. Right from the first moment I saw you. And you felt it too."

A fresh wave of panic gripped her insides, "No, Grayson... It's too soon ... Dealing with the shock, the turmoil, the loss ... You need to give yourself time."

He picked up her hands and pressed a kiss against her knuckles. She felt the effects of it all the way down to her toes.

"Please, Charlotte. Don't deny it. I understand how scary this is for you. It's scary for me too. All I ask is that you give us a chance. Please. Meet me after work at the Brass Monkey. We'll go for a drink. Maybe even dinner."

Once again, Charlotte fought off her panic. She pulled her hands out of Grayson's and looked around for her handbag. Then she stood and prepared to leave.

His gaze burned into hers. "I'll be there from six."

"I'll think about it," was all she said and quickly made her escape.

Chapter Fourteen

Charlotte returned to work, her head full of Grayson. As much as she wanted to agree with him, something held her back. They barely knew each other. Apart from an amazing night of sex, what else did they have in common? He knew nothing about the person she was, the things she liked, the way she preferred to spend her leisure time. Hell, she didn't even know if he liked cats. And if not, that would be a deal breaker.

Even though she was now certain he was innocent of the murder of his wife, that didn't make things any less complicated. She wanted to be with him, but right now, while they were in the middle of an ongoing investigation that was impossible. She thought about his plea to meet him at the Brass Monkey after work. Once again, her heart lurched. The truth was, she really wanted to, but that probably wasn't a wise move. At the very least, she should wait until after the case was closed.

Then there was the speed with which things between them were moving. Was it possible to feel so deeply about someone she barely knew? And what about Grayson? Could she trust that his feelings were real? It was all so confusing.

She wished she had someone to talk to about it. None of her siblings were married. Only one of them was even in love. Christopher. Her oldest brother. Well, technically her half-brother. Christopher's falling in love had come as a surprise to everyone. As far as Charlotte was aware, until now he hadn't even had a serious girlfriend. He was forty-one years old. Charlotte was sure her parents had almost given up on the idea their eldest child would ever settle down. But it appeared he'd found the love of his life in the form of Lexi Greenaway.

Charlotte had met the beautiful widow at a recent charity fundraiser. It wasn't hard to see why Christopher was smitten. There was now talk of an engagement in the not too distant future.

Christopher hasn't known Lexi for long... A month or so at the most... He seems confident he's found the one... His soul mate.

Is it possible? After such a short period of time? She didn't know, but a big part of her really wanted to find out.

She jumped and squealed with surprise when Sabattini unexpectedly dropped a pile of papers on her desk.

"Tony!" she gasped, her heart thumping. "You startled me."

"Good work on following up with Mount Druitt High School. It appears that might be the second lie we've caught Robinson in."

Charlotte looked up at him. "So you're certain she lied about seeing Grayson outside his home? It wasn't just a mistake?"

"I'm not certain of anything at the moment, but things aren't adding up. While you were out, I received the CCTV footage from The Café on Kingsway. It shows our man the mayor seated at an outside table drinking coffee and eating cake."

"What time was this?"

Sabattini paused for effect. "Do you remember what time he said he arrived there?"

Charlotte thought back to the conversation. "He left right after Grayson and drove around for a while. I think he said he got to the café at one."

Sabattini compressed his lips and nodded. "Right. Only the CCTV footage of the carpark shows him pulling in thirty minutes later than that."

"He got there at half-past?"

"Yes."

"Do you think he got confused about the time he arrived there? He did say his head was all over the place."

"I don't know, but the CCTV footage doesn't lie. We know he left his office shortly after Grayson did. We estimate that to be about twelve forty-five. He shows up on the CCTV footage forty-five minutes later. Where was he during that time? He told us he was driving around, clearing his head, but his chambers are less than ten minutes away from the Thorpe residence. He could have gone straight there, confronted Lydia, stabbed her to death and then left again. The café is only a few minutes' drive from the Thorpe house."

Charlotte shot Tony a dubious look. "How does he appear in the footage?"

Tony compressed his lips. "Not covered in blood, if that's what you're getting at."

Charlotte nodded. "If our time estimates are correct, the mayor had about thirty minutes. I'm not saying it's impossible, but it's a very small window of opportunity to carry out the deadly deed. And where did he get the change of clothes?"

"Perhaps he took some of Grayson's? We both know how similar they are in shape and size."

Charlotte remained unconvinced. "I don't know, Tony."

He shot her a look filled with frustration. "Look let's just agree that at this stage we can't rule the mayor out. Robinson swears she saw Grayson or at least someone who looked like him outside the Thorpe house around one o'clock. We definitely know it wasn't Grayson, but it's entirely possible it was Matthews. The mayor isn't seen on the CCTV footage outside the café until half-past. I agree, the timeline is tight, but it's possible he's our man."

"Okay, so do you or don't you think Robinson was lying about seeing Grayson?" Charlotte asked.

Sabattini shrugged. "We've been here before. She's either mistaken about who she saw coming from the Thorpe house or she didn't see either of them and she's lying. It's not like she doesn't have form. She lied about being at high school with our vic."

Charlotte frowned. "Yes. But why? What does she have to gain? Unless she's trying to set Grayson up... Even though we know Grayson is in the clear, maybe she genuinely believes he had something to do with his wife's death? After all, she made it clear she knew all about their marriage problems and how unhappy Lydia was. She also appeared adamant about wanting justice for her friend. That was the reason she gave for coming forward in the first place."

"You're right. And who knows where the truth lies? Just something else we need to unravel." Sabattini pointed toward the pile of papers. "In the meantime, these are the phone records of Mayor Matthews, Robinson and Lydia Thorpe. Go through them with a fine-tooth comb."

Charlotte nodded. "Robinson told you she'd called and texted Lydia the day of the murder. Those, at least, should show up in these records."

"Yes. Though I'm not holding out too much hope she lied about them. After all, she volunteered that information. It doesn't make sense to volunteer something that can be so easily verified. Still, we need to be thorough. At the least, going through this pile of phone records might shed some more light on the relationship between Robinson and Lydia. It's obvious they didn't go to school together, but it's still bugging me that a woman who's purportedly such a close friend of our vic has never even met her husband."

Charlotte spent the next few hours poring over the phone records. She started with Simon Matthews. She recalled the mayor telling them he'd phoned Lydia around seven that morning and another woman had answered the phone. Charlotte flipped pages over and found the call. It had lasted one minute and forty-three seconds. Long enough for someone to have had a conversation.

Looks like the mayor was telling the truth... At least about that...

Though the CCTV footage had confirmed the mayor's alibi from half-past one until the time he returned to the office, there was still the time when he told them he'd been driving around that was unaccounted for...

Charlotte scanned the paperwork, working backwards. The phone records showed that several calls had been made during the time he was at the Café on Kingsway. The triangulation of his phone signal also showed his phone was pinging off a tower in the same area, nowhere near the murder scene. She went back further. There was only one call that had been made from the mayor's phone between half-past twelve and half-past one.

Charlotte's heart skipped a beat. The call had been made to Lydia Thorpe. The time was a little after one. Even more concerning was the fact the triangulation showed that at the time of the phone call, Matthews' phone had been pinging off a tower only a block away from Lydia's house.

He lied to us. He went to Lydia's house that afternoon before he stopped in at the café... Just like Tony suspected...

Charlotte's heart thumped. Then she studied the times again. Less than thirty minutes after he was in Lydia's neighborhood, Matthews had been drinking coffee and eating pie. She was dubious the first time Tony had suggested the mayor had had enough time to carry out the murder. She was just as dubious now.

Tapping on her keyboard, she accessed the CCTV footage they'd obtained from the Café on Kingsway. She found the frames which showed the mayor seated at an outdoor table. He was facing the security camera. Though she couldn't see below his waist, there was plenty of pristine white shirt visible on the screen. Unless he'd changed into Grayson's clothes, as Tony had suggested, there was no way Matthews had been involved in the bloodbath that had greeted them at the crime scene.

Charlotte gnawed on her fingernail. Despite what Sabattini had said, Matthews just didn't feel right as the killer. He didn't seem emotionally invested enough, to care too much either way about what had happened to Lydia. He certainly hadn't appeared to be heartbroken the affair was coming to an end. Of course, that could have been an act but Charlotte didn't think so. And then there was the time factor. As far as she was concerned, thirty minutes wasn't enough time to commit the murder, shower, change and get back on the road...and according to the phone records, Matthews had managed to place a call to Lydia somewhere along the line.

The phone call had been made just after one. Either Matthews hadn't yet committed the murder and was trying to ascertain Lydia's whereabouts, or he'd done the deed and was trying to cover his tracks by making out he had no idea she was dead. Either way, the timeline became impossible. No, the more Charlotte thought about it, the more she was convinced there was no way Simon Matthews had time to murder his lover, clean up and be seen on CCTV cameras all in the space of thirty minutes.

One thing about Matthews' presence at Lydia's house was that it could account for the person Melissa Robinson thought she saw outside the Thorpe residence. The mayor had told them he was just driving around, clearing his head. The phone records put a lie to that and though Charlotte was convinced Matthews didn't have enough time to murder Lydia, what was he doing there in her neighborhood?

Charlotte glanced across at Sabattini's desk, intending to bring him up to date with her findings, but his desk was empty. No doubt he'd gone out for lunch. She'd catch him up when he got back. She returned her attention to the phone records.

The pile of paper that contained Melissa Robinson's phone records for the same period was substantially thinner than the mayor's. No doubt her phone calls were limited for safety reasons because she was at work on a construction site. Charlotte stood and stretched, fetched a fresh cup of coffee from the tearoom and then returned to her task.

As she'd done with the mayor's records, she picked up a highlighter and systematically went through the data, underlining each phone call made and received during the relevant time. She compared that information with what Melissa had told Sabattini. There were a number of discrepancies.

Firstly, there was no call from Melissa Robinson's phone around one o'clock. Robinson had said she'd arrived at Lydia's house about one, knocked on the door and got no answer. She'd then apparently called her friend Lydia to ask where she was. Robinson had told them the call had gone through to voicemail and she'd left a message. The only thing was, she hadn't. In fact, the only call Melissa had made that day to Lydia Thorpe had been much earlier. At nine thirty-four, to be precise. The call to Lydia had lasted thirty seconds. Long enough to have spoken only briefly to someone on the other end.

Is that when they'd made arrangements to meet for lunch?

Charlotte consulted the triangulation data. Melissa's phone was pinging off a tower near the Thorpe house on the day of the murder, so that part at least was true, but when Charlotte looked closer, she realized Melissa's phone had also been in that vicinity since twelve twenty-seven, not one o'clock as she'd said, and she had remained there until around half-past two.

Why had Melissa arrived more than half an hour early? What was she doing there all that time? She'd told Sabattini that Lydia wasn't home and that she'd left shortly after. But if that were the case, why was Melissa's phone still pinging off a tower nearby more than two hours later?

Charlotte went back further. In the weeks before the murder, there were a large volume of both texts and calls going to and from Melissa Robinson's phone. Charlotte consulted Lydia's records. The same volume of calls and texts back and forth, showed up there.

Charlotte tamped down her growing excitement. She was onto something. She knew it. She felt it in her gut. Then she remembered something else Melissa had said. A text she'd received from Lydia at work, advising Melissa of her need to return home. That's the reason Melissa gave for being at the Thorpe house that day in the first place.

Charlotte scanned the texts received by Melissa on the day in question. There was a text from Lydia sent to Melissa at nine thirty-six. Melissa had told Sabattini her friend had texted her that she needed to return home to collect a patient file. That seemed true. Then Charlotte scanned the text.

I'm not doing this over the phone. Meet me @ home @ 12.30

Twelve-thirty? Charlotte frowned. The text didn't seem to reference an arrangement to meet for lunch or a missing file. What the text did explain was why Melissa had arrived at the

Thorpe house at twelve twenty-seven and not at one o'clock, like she'd said.

So why had Melissa been adamant she'd arrived on time for her meeting with Lydia at one? Why had Melissa lied? What was going on?

The questions continued to circle around in Charlotte's head. Taking out a pen and pad, she began to make notes. She went back to the older texts. This time, she read through all of the messages sent between the friends. Pages and pages of passionate writings had been exchanged. At last she looked up, dazed, as she came to the only possible conclusion.

The two women were in a relationship... They were in love...

Charlotte wondered if Grayson—or her lover, the mayor—knew.

With adrenaline coursing through her, she pulled her keyboard toward her and ran a background check on Melissa.

She had a criminal record. Charlotte scanned the entries. Petty theft. A couple of minor drug convictions. No crimes of violence. No jail time, which meant there would be no DNA on file. She made a mental note to ask Sabattini if he'd received the DNA results from the lab.

She looked at her screen again. There was nothing there to indicate Robinson could be capable of such a brutal murder. And yet, she'd lied to them about going to high school with the victim and again about seeing Grayson Thorpe at the murder scene. She'd also lied about her meeting time with Lydia.

What's Melissa hiding? Who's she protecting? Herself? Or someone else?

Once again, Charlotte looked across at Sabattini's desk. He still hadn't returned. She quelled a rush of impatience and prayed he hadn't decided to call it a day. She couldn't wait to share her findings and toss around her theories.

Lexi Greenaway brushed the hair out of her eyes and stared up at the man she loved. Christopher Barrington smiled down at her.

"So, what do you think?" he asked.

Lexi turned to stare at the old farmhouse. It was twice the size of the one she'd recently vacated and was surrounded by even more land. Six bedrooms, four bathrooms and the whole place was in excellent repair. There were horse stables, a riding arena, an established orchard, a flourishing vegetable patch. Several outbuildings that would be great for storage. A pool, a tennis court. Even a BMX track. Of course, it came with a price tag to match.

She turned back to Christopher. "It's beautiful. My dream house. But we can't afford it."

Christopher kissed her tenderly on the lips. "I think we can."

She laughed. "Have you taken leave of your senses? It's more than double our budget."

He reached out and tucked a stray strand of hair behind her ears. "That's what I wanted to talk to you about. I... I want to help you out. Remember that five hundred thousand dollar bonus my father gave me for sealing the Serenity deal?"

Lexi's smile faded. "Of course."

"I want to donate that to our cause. Put it toward the purchase of this house. And I'll make up any shortfall out of my own pocket."

Lexi had started shaking her head well before Christopher had even finished. "No. Stop. Christopher, I can't take your money."

He took her by the arms. "It's our money, Lexi. We're a team. Let me help you."

"But—"

He silenced her protest with another kiss. "I'm tired of living with my parents. As much as I love them, I want to have you all alone. In our own house. With the kids. All eight of them. I'd willingly have you all pile into my place in Waverton if it meant having you all to myself, but it would be one heck of a squeeze. Two bedrooms just isn't going to cut it." He looked back at the property they'd just inspected.

"This place is only down the road from Serenity. The kids can continue to go to their schools. The property has everything we want, with plenty of room to grow." He paused and gave her a winning smile. "Please, Lexi. Say yes. Let's do it for the kids. The eight you have and all the others who are yet to find safety and security under your roof."

He looked so earnest, tears pricked her eyes. She stared up at him, her heart flooding with love.

"How can I say no to that?" she choked.

Christopher's eyes widened. "So it's a yes? Are you kidding?"

Lexi laughed and cried at the same time. "It's a yes. Let's do it."

Christopher enveloped her in an enthusiastic hug and pressed another kiss against her lips. And then his expression changed, grew somber. If she didn't know any better, she'd think he looked nervous.

"Christopher? What is it? Don't tell me you've already changed your mind?"

He laughed, but it didn't reach his eyes.

Misgivings stirred in her stomach. "Christopher? This isn't carved in stone. What's wrong?"

He brushed away her concerns with a grin that looked forced. "Nothing's wrong. It's just that... I was hoping that while you're in the mood to say yes, you might say yes to this."

With that, he pulled a velvet ring box out of the pocket of his suit pants. Lexi stared at it in shock.

"Christopher...?"

Oblivious to the dirt and stones that lined the driveway, he went down on one knee. "Lexi Greenaway, will you do me the honor of becoming my wife?"

"Oh, my God! Christopher! Yes! Yes! Yes!"

He barely had time to slip the beautiful diamond-and-sapphire ring on her finger before she flung herself into his arms. Kissing his lips, his eyes, his cheeks she could barely contain her happiness.

Christopher looked just as pleased. "I can't wait to tell the kids."

Lexi laughed and took a moment to admire her ring. "They're going to be so excited."

"Patrice is going to scream."

Lexi nodded. "Oh, yeah. And probably Stella and Josie, too."

Christopher drew her in his arms and kissed her long and lovingly. "I love you Lexi."

"I love you too. Now and always."

Taking her hand, he led her back to the car. Lexi's heart overflowed with happiness. As Christopher climbed in behind the wheel, she turned to him and smiled.

"Let's call the kids right away. We can Facetime them so we can watch their reactions."

Christopher grinned. "Sounds good. But first, let's call the real estate agent and put in an offer. I don't want to lose this place."

Lexi looked back at the property she hoped to soon be able to call home. "It's perfect." She sighed.

Christopher squeezed her hand. "Just like you."

The minute Sabattini returned from lunch, Charlotte launched herself at him. Hardly able to contain her excitement, she perched herself on the edge of his desk and filled him in on what she'd discovered.

He nodded with approval when she'd finished. "Good work, Barrington. You've done well."

His praise filled her with warmth. "So, what do you want to do next?"

"First we bring in the mayor for questioning. It seems he wasn't wholly forthcoming the last time we spoke. I agree that the timeline is too tight for him to be our killer, but I don't like it when a witness withholds vital information. I want to let him know that, in case he's ever of a mind to do it again. Then we talk to Robinson."

"I'll get on it," Charlotte said automatically.

Tony cleared his throat. "Um, Barrington... In your enthusiasm to solve this case, I think you've forgotten you're not part of the formal investigation. While I hate to do this to you, I have no choice. I'll call Matthews and set up a meeting."

Charlotte's shoulders slumped with disappointment, but she put on a brave face. "Of course. I understand."

Sabattini gave her a reassuring smile. "Don't let this temporary setback affect you. You have the makings of a great investigator. Keep your head down, your nose clean and see what else you can find out."

She grinned, feeling better. "You got it."

Chapter Fifteen

Grayson found himself yet again seated by the bar in the Brass Monkey, but this time he was waiting for Charlotte to show. At least, he hoped she was going to show. There was no guarantee. She said she'd think about it. Whatever that meant. He hoped she didn't think too long and hard about it. He hoped she listened to her heart, not her head.

He was familiar with all the logical arguments about why the strength of his feelings for her was utter madness after knowing her for only a couple of weeks and primarily as a suspect in a homicide investigation! They'd only shared a handful of hours together and most of those had been spent horizontal. But he also realized logic didn't count when dealing with matters of the heart. His head was cool, calm and composed in the face of a crisis or when facing a judge in the courtroom. But his heart was awhirl with emotion whenever Charlotte was near and then his clear-headed thinking flew straight out the window.

It was sheer madness, but there was nothing he could do about it. His need for her was a physical ache that never went away or diminished. He'd never felt this way before, not even in his early days with Lydia. That's why he knew deep in his gut that this was more than passing lust.

With a weary sigh, he caught the bartender's attention and ordered a beer. He'd only taken the first mouthful when he caught sight of Charlotte's reflection in the mirrored wall behind the bar. His heart skipped a beat and then took off in full flight.

Charlotte spied Grayson the minute she walked into the Brass Monkey. He was seated close to where he'd been the first time they met. Being there right now was probably the stupidest thing she'd ever done, but she couldn't stay away from him. Like a moth to a flame...

Her head was still awhirl with the discoveries she'd made with the phone records and if she were truthful, she'd confess she was riding a serious high, but until Sabattini had spoken to Matthews again, there was nothing more she could do to advance her theory that it had been Matthews that Melissa Robinson had seen outside the Thorpe residence. Charlotte was convinced the woman who purported to be the victim's best friend was much more than that and might have had more to do with her death than anyone had realized.

Still, now wasn't the time to contemplate the intricacies of the investigation. The most important things right now were that Grayson Thorpe was innocent of anything to do with his wife's death and the way he was staring at her from the other side of the room made her feel like she was the most beautiful, most desirable woman in the world.

She closed the distance between them and took a seat beside him. "H-hello." Her voice sounded as nervous and breathless as the butterflies crowding her stomach made her feel.

"You came."

The simple words vibrated with emotion. The look in Grayson's eyes was every bit as intense up close. Dragging her gaze away from his, she drew in a breath and managed to order a glass of wine. When the bartender moved away, she spoke again.

"I went over all the reasons why this wasn't a good idea, and I'm fairly sure it isn't, but the fact is, I couldn't stay away."

His eyes darkened with emotion. He moved closer, reached out, cupped her cheek. Then his head moved even closer and his lips brushed over hers. The lightest of pressure, like the wings of a butterfly, and yet her body burned with fire.

This is so crazy... How can I feel like this...?

From the look on Grayson's face when he pulled away, he felt just as off kilter as she did. Charlotte took refuge in her wine. Grayson took a swallow of his beer. Charlotte's body trembled with need. Her heart pounded. No matter how crazy this whole thing was, she wanted him. Badly.

Taking another large gulp of wine, she swallowed and focused on the warmth of the alcohol sliding down her throat. She glanced at him. His gaze was back on her. "So, what do we do now?"

"Let's talk. There's so much we don't know about each other."

She nodded agreement. "Were you born in Sydney? Tell me about your parents."

"To answer your first question, yes. I was born in Sydney. In the Royal Hospital for Women, actually."

"In Paddington?"

"Yes."

"Didn't they close that hospital awhile back?"

He nodded. "Yes. I must admit, I wasn't surprised. I think it was nearing its use-by date even before I was born."

They both grinned. "Your turn," Grayson said. "Where were you born?"

"Have you ever heard of a town called Broken?"

"No."

She laughed. "Don't worry. Not many people have. It's a small country town in the southern highlands. About ninety minutes' drive south of the city."

"That's a nice part of the world. I have a cousin who has a farm near Bowral."

"Wow. Bowral's only a bit further down the road."

"So you were born in Broken. Do your parents still live there?"

"Yes. At least, they have some acreage on the edge of town." She left out the bit about the fact her father was the owner of a billion-dollar mining company. It wasn't relevant. Besides, she wanted Grayson to like her for who she was and not be influenced by the fact she came from serious money.

"Nice."

She shot him an impish smile. "If you had to choose between ice cream and chocolate, what would it be?"

Grayson smiled. "Why do I need to choose?"

"Because I said so." She grinned.

"That's not an answer."

"Chocolate or ice cream?" she persisted.

"Neither. Crackers and chips. I'm more of a savory man."

She stared at him in mock horror. "You don't like sweets?"

He shrugged. "Meh."

Charlotte shook her head. "I'm afraid that's a deal breaker. If we're going to get serious, you need to commit to at least one of them."

He quirked an eyebrow. "Do I now? You're awfully bossy all of a sudden."

She poked out her tongue. He laughed.

"So, tell me about your parents," she said.

Grayson took another sip from his beer and then set his glass back down. "John and Barbara Thorpe. They moved to the central coast a few years ago. Retired to the beach. Dad spends most of his time playing golf. At least, he did before his surgery. He's just had a knee replacement."

"Oh. I hope everything went well."

"Yes. I spoke to him the other night. It's slowed him down a bit, but he's doing okay."

"What about your mother?"

Grayson smiled fondly. "Mom's a member of so many different volunteer organizations, I'm surprised she has time for anything else."

"She sounds kind."

"She is. She's a nurturer. Always wanting to help out the less fortunate."

Charlotte's mood sobered. "How are they taking Lydia's death?"

Grayson sighed and reached for his glass again. He took another sip before replying. "I'm sure you can imagine. It's been difficult for all of us."

Charlotte's heart clenched. "Of course."

Sadness filled his eyes. Charlotte hated to see him upset. Even worse, in this instance she'd been the one to remind him of all that had happened. She drew in a breath and gathered her courage around her. She took a fortifying mouthful of her wine and then reached for his hand. "Come home with me."

His eyes widened at her suggestion. The sadness in his gaze was slowly replaced with a look so heated it scorched her. Without a word, he finished his beer and set the glass down on the counter. Then he took her by the hand and led her to the exit.

With her butterflies now beating a tattoo against her stomach, nervous laughter bubbled up inside her.

I can't believe I'm doing this... Again.

And yet she was and she couldn't wait to get him naked. This time they wouldn't be strangers, but two people with all the time in the world to explore and re-learn the shape, the taste, the feel of each other. It was way too early to be thinking about the "L" word, but there was no denying she lusted after Grayson in a way she'd never experienced.

"I'll hail a cab," he murmured after giving her a quick kiss.

As they arrived outside her unit, nerves once again fluttered in her stomach. The moment she turned the key in the lock and opened the door, Grayson started kissing her. In a frenzy of passion, they tore at each other's clothes until they were naked and then came together again, kissing and tasting and touching like there was no tomorrow.

At one point, Raoul came out of one of the bedrooms to see what all the fuss was about. He rubbed against Charlotte's bare legs. She laughed and pulled away from Grayson long enough to put the cat outside on the patio.

"You don't have to do that," Grayson said. "I love cats."

Her heart melted. "Really?"

"Yes. I wanted to get one, but Lydia was allergic."

Charlotte took him by the hand and led him across the living room.

"Nice digs," he said, looking about.

"Thank you," she murmured and continued down the corridor toward her bedroom. She pushed the door all the way open with her shoulder and they stepped inside. Once again, Grayson took her in his arms. His lips were firm and supple. He kissed his way across her mouth, her jaw and then nuzzled her ears. Desire rippled through her, pebbling her nipples.

She shivered and tightened her hold on him. He continued his sensual exploration. At the same time he walked her backwards until she felt the mattress behind her legs. Together, they fell on the bed and kept kissing.

She ran her hands over the smooth planes of his back. Muscles rippled beneath her fingers. For someone who spent most of their time behind a desk, he was impressively built. She guessed he spent a fair amount of time at the gym and absently wondered where he found the time.

Then his mouth closed over one of her nipples and all thoughts of the gym and workouts fled her mind. Her back arched as pleasure ripped through her. She buried her fingers in his hair and held his head in place. He licked and suckled and teased until she couldn't stand it another minute. Gasping, she lifted his head away from her breast and fused her lips with his.

They kissed until they were breathless. Then they rolled so she straddled him. His cock lay thick and hard against his stomach. She reached for it and encircled it with her hand. She squeezed.

"Oh God," Grayson groaned.

Sliding lower, Charlotte opened her mouth and guided his cock between her lips. The silky smooth skin, hot and hard, filled her mouth. She licked and sucked and stroked the firm flesh. At the same time, she tightened her hand around his shaft. She dipped her tongue into his slit and tasted salty liquid.

Taking him even deeper, she continued to pleasure him with her mouth. Her hand stole down between his thighs and cupped his balls. They were full and heavy and tight, desperate for release. She massaged them gently with her fingers, all the while keeping up the sucking motion of her mouth.

He groaned again. "Oh God, Charlotte. If you keep that up, I'm gonna come."

She smiled with satisfaction. "I want to drive you crazy." She renewed her efforts and was rewarded with another moan of desire. A moment later, Grayson reached for her and rolled her onto her back. The next moment he was straddling her, a triumphant look in his green eyes.

"Now we'll see who's going to drive who crazy."

With that, he kissed his way down her body. Her breasts received another round of lavish attention from his tongue before he moved lower. His lips skimmed over her ribcage and across her flat stomach. His tongue paused to dip into her belly button before continuing his descent. When he reached his goal and pressed a soft kiss against her womanly flesh, her stomach quivered with pent-up need.

Moving lower, his tongue stroked her silky folds with confidence, laving her over and over again. She clenched her hands into fists, doing her best to withstand the sensual onslaught. Desire built to a fever pitch and still he continued to stroke her with his magical tongue.

She stirred restlessly against him, needing more. As if reading her fevered thoughts, he slipped a finger inside her. First one, then two and though it felt so good, it wasn't enough."Please. Grayson. Fuck me."

The intensity in his green eyes flared hotly. His expression was glazed with passion.

"Condom," she gasped. "Bedside drawer."

She indicated which side with her head. He reached over and found what he was looking for. Quickly and efficiently, he sheathed himself and then positioned himself between her thighs. She wrapped her arms around his shoulders and clung to him, silently urging him on.

He nudged her entrance. Unlike the last time, when he'd eased himself into her, this time he plunged, filling her with one hard thrust. The force of his entry stole her breath. Gasping, she tightened her hold on his shoulders, lifted her thighs around his hips and buried her face against his neck.

Together, they pressed their bodies hard against each other, desperately seeking to obliterate the last weeks of trauma in a maelstrom of pleasure. Palming her butt,

Grayson lifted her higher against him and drove harder into her, giving them both what they needed. With a simultaneous cry of triumph and relief, they peaked together and found oblivion.

It was a long time later that Charlotte recovered enough to speak. She turned on her side to look at him.

"That was amazing," she said and gave him a soft smile.

He smiled with satisfaction. "Right back at you."

She reached for his hand and entwined her fingers with his. "This is so crazy."

He regarded her solemnly and then nodded. "Yes. It is."

"Who would have thought a one night stand might lead to this?"

He smiled again and tightened his hold on her hand. "Not me. I had a few hot and heavy romances at university, before I met Lydia, but you were my first one night stand."

She looked at him in surprise and laughed. "Me too! I remember waking up that first morning. You'd already left, but I remember thinking how wonderful our night together had been and how much I wanted to repeat it."

"I felt the same. But then I felt guilty and sad and confused. I knew my marriage was over, but I didn't celebrate that fact. I arrived home and... You know what happened after that."

Charlotte compressed her lips and then reached over and kissed him. "Neither of us saw that coming. Let's not think about it. The good news is you've been cleared as a suspect and I'm quietly confident we're closing in on Lydia's killer."

Grayson started in surprise. "You are?"

"Yes. But I can't talk about it. Let's just say, with a bit of luck you can soon put this nightmare behind you and we'll be free to start exploring whatever this is."

He was silent for so long, Charlotte began to feel concerned.

Don't tell me he doesn't feel the same way? Don't tell me he can't see me in his future...

She went to move away, but Grayson was having none of it. He put his arm around her shoulders and pulled her in close against him.

"I never imagined my life turning out like this," he said quietly. "When I started law school, I thought I had my life all planned out. Finish university, get a job in a great law firm, marry the woman of my dreams, make partner, have a couple of kids... But everything started to unravel. Lydia and I wanted different things. We began to argue, grow apart. She didn't want to be part of my dream and I..."

He looked chagrinned. "To tell you the truth, I hadn't even thought about what Lydia wanted. I was focused on the future I had mapped out for myself. Somewhere along the line, I failed to convince Lydia to come along for the ride."

He made a sound of disgust in the back of his throat. "Then again, maybe that was a deliberate, subconscious decision. Maybe I didn't want to think about what Lydia wanted. Maybe deep inside I already knew we weren't on the same path."

"That doesn't mean your marriage was destined to fail," Charlotte murmured.

Grayson sighed. "You're right. But it certainly didn't help matters. Now she's gone." He shook his head. "I still can't believe it."

"How many times have you been back to the house since it happened?"

He compressed his lips and grimaced. "Not many. Only to get some clothes and personal effects. That's what I was doing there the day I saw you and your partner next door. It's hard for me to be there, knowing what went on. Every time I close my eyes, I see her there, on the floor, lying in a pool of blood. So much blood..."

"I understand. That's something no one should have to see."

He looked at her. "How do you do it? How do you attend murder scenes?"

She compressed her lips. "It's never easy to confront death, whether it's murder or an accident. You have to find ways to cope. Talking to other cops always helps. I'm lucky two of my brothers are cops. They're my go-to people when things get tough." She paused and then added, "This was my first homicide."

Grayson looked distressed. "Oh, Charlotte! Oh, no!"

"Hey," she said. "Don't worry about it. I love my job. This might sound weird, but being in homicide is all I've ever wanted to do. I burn for justice. More so when a killer's on the loose."

Grayson sighed. "I hope for everyone's sake you find him. Nothing's going to bring Lydia back, but knowing her killer is behind bars will help ease some of the guilt and pain."

Charlotte looked at him. Nerves swirled in her stomach. "Do you still miss her?"

Grayson held her gaze. "The house seems empty. I felt so alone in there when I went back. I wish I could say I actually missed her. Am I a bad person for saying that?" He drew in a ragged breath.

"Our marriage had been in trouble long before the night you and I met. I was telling you the truth when I told you I was separated. Okay, so I hadn't had the conversation with Lydia at that point, but earlier that day, after discovering she was having an affair with the mayor no less, I knew it was over. We were done. I thought about calling her after I confronted him, but that didn't seem right. I didn't want to do it over the phone. I was going to tell her that night and by then I'm sure the mayor would have let her know about me coming to his office..."

Charlotte remembered what Melissa Robinson had said about Lydia. That the woman was supposed to tell Grayson that night that she was leaving. She wondered if he knew she'd been planning to walk out.

She briefly considered asking him, but then decided against it. Lydia was dead. There was no point. And then Grayson was pressing a tender kiss on her lips and there was nothing to focus on but him.

When he pulled away, he looked at her, his eyes filled with tenderness. "As to the future..."

Charlotte held her breath. Her heart pounded. She stared at Grayson, willing him to speak. And then he did.

"The truth is... I want to explore this... I want to see where it takes us. I want us to take a chance, together."

Joy exploded in her heart. She threw herself against him, laughing and kissing him with abandon and as the passion built between them, they made sweet, hot love all over again.

Tony arrived at work early, the first time he'd done so in over twelve months. It wasn't the only first. Last night had been the first night since his wife's death that he hadn't drunk himself into a stupor. The first morning he hadn't woken up with a dry mouth, a thick tongue, a sore head that felt like every thought was being filtered through a mountain of nail-ridden cotton wool. In fact, he felt better than he had for a long time and he had his new partner to thank for it.

He'd thought having someone young enough to be his daughter working beside him would bring back memories that were unbearably painful and he'd been right. But gradually, Charlotte Barrington had grown on him and the pain had dulled a little. She was nothing like his quiet and shy daughter who'd preferred to spend her time buried in books and playing the piano rather than spending time with other people.

Brielle.

Just thinking of her brought back a rush of painful memories. She'd been shy to the point that it had been difficult to watch her on the rare occasions that she was forced to interact with society. Even asking for the time or for directions or for anything really, took an agonizing amount of effort. Neither he nor his wife knew how she'd come to be like that.

It wasn't as if they didn't socialize. Tony often had mates around for a barbeque or friends over for drinks. But Brielle had never felt comfortable in a crowd, or among anyone other than with her parents. She and Charlotte were polar opposites in that way. And it was because they were so different that he'd been able to look at Charlotte and talk to her and not see his daughter every single time.

There were also other differences. Charlotte was slim and petite with a cloud of dark hair. Brielle had been short and stocky and her short locks were the color of straw. Charlotte was excitable. Brielle had rarely gotten excited over anything. Charlotte was bossy, opinionated, even when she tried so hard not to be. Brielle always agreed with everyone.

Tony had begun to realize his partner had something to offer and could very well be an important asset to his investigation. She'd proved she was just as tenacious as he was about finding out the truth. It was a good quality for a detective to possess.

Tony had gone against his better judgment, had ignored an order from his superior by including her, even on the periphery of his investigation. He wasn't sorry that he'd done it. In fact, he was quietly hopeful of the possibility they might make a good team in the future. It was something to feel positive about, something to look forward to and God knew, positivity had been absent from his life these past twelve months.

Chapter Sixteen

The next morning, Charlotte was embarrassed to arrive at work nearly half an hour late. She'd overslept despite her alarm and by the time she'd showered and dressed, fed Raoul and sent a text to Grayson thanking him for a wonderful night, the time had gotten away from her. She'd half-expected Grayson to stay the night, but he'd explained he had a court appearance and needed to get into the office and do some final preparation.

She hung up her jacket in her locker and had just stepped into the tearoom for coffee when Wendell strode in.

"Barrington. In my office. Now." His face looked like a thundercloud.

Charlotte's heart dropped at his terse order. She didn't even bother to wait for her coffee. She hurried toward Wendell's office. Sabattini was already there.

She flashed him a look filled with questions. He merely shrugged. Drawing in a breath, she tried to control her panic.

Wendell's expression turned even more severe. His brow furrowed. His heavy brows drew together until they almost formed a straight line. Charlotte's panic ratcheted up a notch.

"I just had a call from Simon Matthews." Wendell growled.

Dread formed an icy block in Charlotte's stomach. She glanced at Sabattini again. He was staring straight ahead.

"The Mayor of Sutherland Shire's very unhappy," Wendell continued in the same angry tone. "He demanded I get my detectives to stop harassing him. Apparently, he's already told them everything he knows."

Wendell glared at Charlotte and then turned his glare on Tony. "The mayor mentioned two detectives—a middle-aged man and a young woman," Wendell said. He gave Charlotte a pointed look. "Please tell me it wasn't you."

Charlotte's cheeks heated with shame. She stared down at the floor. "I'm sorry, sir. I... I just—"

"I specifically removed you from this investigation, Barrington. Did you forget that?"

"No, sir, I... I only—"

Sabattini interrupted. "It's my fault, Wendell. I asked her to tag along. She has excellent observational skills. I wanted a second set of eyes on the mayor."

Wendell's gaze remained fixed on Charlotte. "You were given an order, Barrington. If you think you can go off half-cocked and do whatever you want, you're in the wrong place. I have no room for that kind of cop in my team."

Once again, Charlotte's cheeks heated with shame. "Yes, sir. I'm sorry, sir," she mumbled.

Wendell's gaze switched to Sabattini. "I'm disappointed in you, Tony. You knew what my decision was in this regard and yet you encouraged Barrington's participation."

"Yes, sir."

"What do you have to say for yourself?" Wendell asked.

Sabattini cleared his throat. "We've ruled out Grayson's Thorpe's involvement in his wife's death. He has iron-clad proof in the form of eye witnesses and CCTV footage that he couldn't have been at the crime scene at the time his wife was murdered. Barrington's potential conflict of interest had involved only a fleeting contact with the victim's husband and like I said, he's now been cleared beyond doubt."

He glanced toward Charlotte and then looked back at their boss. "In my defense, Barrington rode along only as an extra set of eyes. She didn't actively participate in the questioning of a potential suspect. As far as the mayor goes, Barrington only observed my interview with him. She asked no questions and otherwise didn't try and insert herself into the investigation."

He flicked his gaze toward Charlotte and then continued. "I asked Barrington to do some legwork, going through the phone records of some of the people involved. As a result, she's come up with some credible information that might break this case wide open. Some of the new information involved the mayor. No matter what Matthews told you, he wasn't completely forthcoming. I spoke to him again this morning and clarified a few things."

Wendell pursed his lips. "Perhaps that's what prompted his call to me."

Tony nodded. "Most likely. I didn't play nice. I'm like that when someone tries to pull one over me. Anyway, the bottom line is the mayor didn't have the opportunity to carry out this crime. He's no longer a suspect."

He paused and then added in a more conciliatory tone. "Wendell, I'm sorry for involving Barrington on any level in this investigation, but I don't believe it's jeopardized the case. In fact, it could help us lead to an arrest."

"Do you have any other credible suspects?" Wendell asked in a mollified tone.

Sabattini nodded. "Yes. Melissa Robinson. She approached us early on with information and told us she was the victim's best friend. We have reason to believe she's lied to us about a number of things and recently, we discovered she was having a sexual relationship with the deceased."

Wendell's eyes widened with surprise. "Wow. That's interesting."

"Very interesting," Sabattini agreed. "It also gives her motive," Sabattini said.

"How so?" Wendell asked.

"I have a theory," Charlotte offered and then held her breath. She glanced at her boss.

He nodded. "Go ahead."

Charlotte drew in a breath and spoke quickly. "From their text messages, it appears Lydia Thorpe and Melissa Robinson were involved in a romantic relationship in the four months prior to Lydia's murder. For the past six months, Lydia had also been having an affair with Simon Matthews, the mayor."

"And then there was the husband," Sabattini added dryly. "Talk about a love triangle. Or is that a love quadrangle?"

"Grayson told us he and his wife hadn't been intimate for months," Charlotte said.

"Perhaps that's why," Wendell said wryly.

"Anyway," Charlotte continued. "I think Melissa somehow discovered Lydia's affair with Matthews. I think she made the discovery on the same morning Lydia was murdered. Grayson had already left for work. Though it was early, Melissa was there at the Thorpe house. Matthews called Lydia early that morning. His phone records support this. He said Lydia's phone was answered by a woman who got quite defensive when he asked her if he could speak with Lydia."

Charlotte paused and drew in another breath. "I think Melissa put two and two together and if she didn't immediately realize Matthews was yet another significant other in Lydia's life, she certainly was suspicious. She didn't confront Lydia right away. We know this because the time of death isn't until much later, closer to midday—at the earliest. I'm guessing Lydia left for work as usual and Melissa continued to dwell on the phone call from Matthews. At some point, she decided to confront Lydia about it.

"Hence the phone call Melissa made to Lydia around half-past nine that morning. It only lasted for thirty seconds. Long enough for the two of them to make arrangements to meet. Melissa told us she was meeting Lydia for lunch, but I think the meeting was to be a conversation about Matthews. Lydia sent a text to Melissa right after the phone call saying words to the effect that she wouldn't deal with the conversation over the phone. That she would meet Melissa at twelve-thirty at her home."

Sabattini took up the recital. "Lydia leaves work around lunchtime and goes home. Melissa is already there. The phone data supports this. Once again, Melissa confronts Lydia about Matthews. The two get into an argument. Melissa stabs Lydia to death. Melissa has plenty of time to clean up the crime scene. She knows Grayson never comes home for lunch. She also knows he works late most days. Lydia had complained to her before about Grayson's long hours. Melissa had no reason to suspect he'd come home early that day. We know from the triangulation of the telephone data Melissa was there until about half-past two."

Charlotte spoke again. "At some point, around one that afternoon, the mayor also arrived at the house to talk to Lydia. By then, he'd been visited by Grayson and was aware that Grayson knew about the affair. The triangulation data showed his phone pinging off the same tower as Melissa's.

"He was seen by Melissa outside the Thorpe home. Though she told us she saw Grayson and she'd been sitting in her car, we believe she was still in the house and she saw Matthews, instead. We're not sure if she knew it wasn't Grayson and she decided to set him up, or if it was a genuine case of mistaken identity, but Melissa was adamant it was Grayson she'd seen."

Sabattini once again took over. "When I confronted Matthews this morning with the evidence that put him at Lydia's house that day, after some blustering he reluctantly confirmed that he was there. He told me that after his confrontation with Grayson, he took off and went straight over to Lydia's office to speak with her. He happened to pass by Lydia's house on his way. He saw her car parked in the driveway. He couldn't find a parking spot close to the house, so he pulled up a few houses down and walked back. He knocked on the door and called out to her, but there was no answer. About this time he put in a call to Lydia. It wasn't answered. Eventually, he gave up and left."

A lightbulb went off in Charlotte's head. "I'll bet that's why Melissa said she saw Grayson's BMW in the driveway. She must have known what kind of car he drove. She didn't see Matthews' car because he wasn't parked where she could see from inside the house."

Sabattini nodded. "That sounds plausible. It'll be interesting to hear what Robinson says when we put that to her."

"Have you found the murder weapon?" Wendell asked.

Sabattini shook his head. "No. It's my guess Robinson brought the knife to the murder scene and then took it with her."

"If so, that shows pre-mediation." Wendell looked grim. "So where do you go from here?"

"I'm going to interview Melissa Robinson again," Sabattini replied. "I'm going to hit her with some hard evidence and see how she reacts. You never know, I might just secure a confession," he half-joked.

Wendell nodded. "Very well. Make it happen." His gaze moved to Charlotte. "I'm going to allow you to sit in on the interview, but don't go making a nuisance of yourself, all right? This is Tony's case."

Charlotte could hardly contain her excitement. "Yes, sir. Thank you, sir."

Wendell shot her a look of warning. "Keep yourself on a tight leash, Detective. Don't make me sorry for this."

"I won't sir. I promise."

If anyone had cared to ask, Charlotte would have freely admitted she was nervous about the upcoming interview with Melissa Robinson, but she was also excited. As Sabattini brought the woman into the interview room, Charlotte drew in a calming breath to get her adrenaline under control.

"This is Detective Barrington," Sabattini said, making the introductions.

Robinson merely offered a grunt in Charlotte's direction. After dealing with a few preliminaries, Sabattini got straight to the point.

"Where were you on the day of Lydia Thorpe's murder?"

Robinson appeared calm and relaxed. She leaned back against her chair. "I was at work for most of it. The only time I wasn't on site was when I took my lunch break."

"And where is your worksite?"

"I'm working on a construction site in Hornsby."

Charlotte didn't bother hiding her surprise. "Meeting your girlfriend at her home in Cronulla's a fair way to go for lunch. It must have taken you at least an hour to get there."

Robinson shrugged and looked away. "What can I say? I have an understanding boss."

"Did Lydia know you were gay?" Sabattini asked.

Charlotte caught a flash of surprise before Melissa quickly averted her gaze. "Of course. We were best friends. She knew everything about me."

"Were you ever involved romantically?" Charlotte asked.

Melissa scoffed. "With Lydia? Hardly. She was married."

Charlotte sensed an undertone of anger. She pushed a little harder. "I mean before. Back in high school."

Melissa shook her head. "No."

"Not even mucking around?"

"No."

"Did you want to?"

Anger now flooded Melissa's face. "What's your point, Detective?"

"Tell me about your partner," Charlotte said, swiftly changing the subject. "Did she know about your close relationship with Lydia?"

"What are you talking about? I don't have a partner."

Charlotte feigned surprise. "Oh? And yet your social media profile states you're in a relationship. Was it a recent break-up?"

An ugly red stain began to spread across the woman's cheeks. The look she gave Charlotte was deadly.

Interesting... I've hit a nerve...

Charlotte was keen to exploit that. She needed to probe even deeper and ascertain which of her questions had elicited that reaction.

"What's the name of your partner?" she demanded in a no-nonsense tone.

"You're not listening, Detective. I don't have a partner." Melissa emphasized her curt response with a pointed finger.

"Oh, so you were being deceitful when you wrote on your profile that you were in a relationship, or were you referring to your relationship with Lydia?"

Anger once again blazed in Melissa's eyes. She leaned toward Charlotte in a threatening manner. Charlotte held her ground. They were in a police station and she wasn't alone. She was confident the woman wouldn't attempt anything.

"Are we done Detective? Because I'd like to get back to work."

"Oh, yes. Your construction job. Do you enjoy that kind of work?" Charlotte asked.

Melissa looked slightly taken aback at the change of direction in the questioning. She offered another shrug. "I guess. The hours are good and it pays well enough."

"The hours. Of course. So flexible you're able to meet a girlfriend for lunch more than an hours' drive away. Very understanding, your boss."

Melissa's jaw tightened. Her fists clenched. She stared at the table between them. It was obvious she was fighting hard not to react.

"What's the name of the construction company you work for, Melissa?" Sabattini asked.

Melissa turned her attention to Tony. "Boston Earthmoving. It's a small operation subcontracted to a larger contractor."

"How long have you worked for them?" Sabattini asked.

"A couple of years."

Tony nodded. "You drive a machine or are you behind a desk?"

"Mostly I'm on a dozer."

"And what's your boss's name?" Charlotte asked.

Melissa shook her head. "What does he have to do with anything?"

Charlotte gave her an insincere smile. "Just leave the questions to us. Now, his name?"

Melissa glared at her. "Joe Boston."

"His contact number?" Charlotte asked.

Melissa reluctantly provided the information. Charlotte duly made a note of the name and number on the paper in front of her. She handed the paper to Tony who nodded. He pushed away from the table and tapped against the glass that faced out into the corridor. A few moments later, another detective appeared and opened the door.

"You need something?" the detective asked.

"Yeah," Sabattini replied. "I need you to make a phone call." He handed over the piece of paper.

Melissa frowned. "What's happening?"

Charlotte gave her a bland smile. "We're going to call your boss, check that the information you just gave us is good."

A look of alarm crossed Melissa's face. "Of course it's good. Why would I lie about where I work?"

"We're just being thorough, Melissa. You want us to find Lydia's killer, don't you?"

"Of course," Melissa said tightly.

The detective left the room. Tony resumed his seat. Charlotte's smile disappeared. She eyeballed Melissa. "Why did you lie about going to high school with Lydia?"

The woman glared. "I didn't lie."

"Of course you did. Lydia Thorpe went to school on the lower north shore. Nowhere near Mount Druitt."

Charlotte caught the confused look that briefly filled Melissa's face and explained: "You have the information about your high school on your social media pages."

The woman's cheeks turned crimson. She looked like she was about to combust. Charlotte lightened her tone and took another tack.

"How long were you at the Thorpe house that day?"

"Only a few minutes, ten at the most."

"What time was this again?" Sabattini asked.

"I've already told you. We'd agreed to meet at one o'clock. When Lydia didn't show, I left."

"And before you left, you saw Grayson Thorpe leaving the house, right?"

"Yes."

"I'm curious. Did you speak with Grayson?" Charlotte asked.

"No."

Once again, Charlotte feigned surprise. "Really? You didn't ask him about his wife? Why she wasn't home? You didn't tell him you were supposed to be meeting her? You were on your lunch break after all. Time was ticking."

Melissa's expression remained tense. "No. I didn't talk to Lydia's husband about any of those things."

Charlotte pretended to be confused. "Why not? Didn't you want to know if he knew why she hadn't showed?"

"I just didn't, okay? He and I weren't exactly on friendly terms."

"In fact, you and Grayson Thorpe had never met, had you?" Sabattini asked.

"That's right."

Charlotte regarded her steadily. "Strange, don't you think? Given that you and Lydia had been best friends for so many years."

The woman stared down at the table in stony silence. Charlotte lightened her tone.

"Where did you go after leaving the Thorpe house?"

"I went back to work."

"Straight away? You didn't hang around in the hope that Lydia might arrive? I mean, she could have just been running late."

"No."

"Are you sure?"

"Yes."

"You had your phone with you that day, didn't you? You told Detective Sabattini you tried to call Lydia when she didn't answer your knock on the door."

"Yes."

With deliberate casualness, Charlotte slowly sat back in her chair and stared at the woman she was convinced had murdered Lydia Thorpe.

"See, Melissa. The thing is, we checked your phone records. The only call you made to Lydia that day was about nine-thirty in the morning. She replied with a text, telling you she'd meet you at her house at half-past twelve. There was no mention of her having to go home to collect a forgotten file."

While Melissa was digesting that morsel, Charlotte dropped another bomb. "We've also done a triangulation on your phone. Do you know what that means?"

Melissa regarded her with a surly expression. "No, but I'm sure you're going to tell me."

"Triangulation tells us what tower your phone was pinging off at any given time." Charlotte leaned toward the woman. "Do you know what we found out about yours?"

Melissa went for a nonchalant shrug, but didn't quite pull it off.

"Your phone was pinging off a tower about a block away from Lydia's house."

"So what? I already told you I was there."

Charlotte smiled. "So you did. At one o'clock, right?"

"Right."

Charlotte narrowed her eyes at the woman. "Wrong. The data shows you were in that neighborhood from twelve twenty-seven until half-past two. How do you explain that, Melissa?"

The woman's expression remained belligerent, but uncertainty flashed in her eyes. She shifted in her seat and compressed her lips. It was obvious she had no answer. Just as she hadn't been able to explain any of the other anomalies Charlotte had already exposed.

"Why did you lie about seeing Grayson Thorpe that day?" Charlotte asked.

Melissa recovered some of her composure and glared at her. "I didn't lie, Detective. He was there. At his house."

Sabattini gave her a pointed look. "Except he wasn't, Melissa. He provided an alibi. It checks out. We have him on CCTV footage at a service station more than half an hour away from his home right around the time you said you saw him."

The door opened and the detective re-entered. Tony stood. The two men moved away. Charlotte heard the detective speaking quietly into Tony's ear. Charlotte glanced up at him.

Tony's expression was grim.

A few moments later, the detective left and Tony regained his seat. He gave Melissa a hard look.

"My colleague has just had an interesting conversation with your boss, Joe Boston," he said. "Or should I say, former boss. Boston told him you were fired several months ago. Apparently you had a little difficulty turning up."

Charlotte managed to refrain from punching her fist in the air. Their case was coming together. They had the murderer in their sights.

Melissa turned red and spluttered. Her earlier cockiness seemed to have disappeared. For the first time, Charlotte saw fear in the woman's eyes.

"Were you in love with Lydia Thorpe?" Charlotte asked.

Shock was visible on the woman's face moments before she brought her reaction under control and offered Charlotte a bland look. "That's ridiculous."

"Is it? The two of you were having a sexual relationship, weren't you?" Charlotte continued.

Melissa opened and closed her mouth several times, but nothing came out.

Sabattini shook his head in disgust. "Don't bother denying it, Melissa. It's obvious from your texts. How long had it been going on?"

Melissa eyeballed Tony for a long moment and then her shoulders slumped on a sigh. Once again, Charlotte had to stop herself from punching the air in triumph.

Sabattini's done it! She's going to confess!

"You're right. Lydia and I were lovers," Melissa admitted. "It had been going on about four months. But I swear I didn't kill her. I... I loved her."

Melissa's voice cracked with emotion. Sabattini appeared unmoved. "Keep talking," he prompted. "How did you meet?"

Melissa drew in a deep breath. "We met online. We chatted for a while. Lydia confessed she'd been bisexual in college and had begun to crave something more than what sex with a man could offer. We agreed to meet. It went from there."

"Did you know she was married?" Charlotte asked.

"Not at first. Later, when she brought me back to her house, I saw the wedding photos."

"That must have come as a surprise," Charlotte murmured.

The woman grimaced. "Yes."

"What did you say to her?" Sabattini asked.

"Nothing. I didn't care. I knew she'd been with men in the past."

"So you didn't care she was still sleeping with her husband?" Sabattini asked.

"She told me they hadn't had sex for months."

"Did you believe her?" Charlotte asked.

"Yes." A slight smile turned up her lips. "Our relationship got hot and heavy fast. She was a generous and passionate lover. She made me feel like I was the most important person in the world." She looked up and eyeballed Charlotte. "There was no way she was still sleeping with her husband."

Charlotte held her gaze. "But you never met him, did you?"

"No. We made sure we only met while he was at work."

"Where did you meet?" Charlotte asked.

"At her house, mainly. She'd meet me after her husband left for work, or leave her office and meet me during her lunch hour."

"And you were meant to meet her for lunch the day she was murdered, right?" Sabattini asked.

"Right."

"Except you were there much earlier than what you told us, weren't you?" Charlotte stated.

Melissa stared down at her hands that were now clenched in her lap. Finally, she looked up and nodded. "You're right. I didn't get there at one. I arrived there half an hour earlier."

"More like several hours earlier. You were at her house at seven that morning. You answered her phone when Simon Matthews tried to call her, didn't you?"

Once again, Melissa debated over her answer, but it appeared she realized the game was up. She looked at Charlotte and nodded. "I didn't know it was him, but yes, I answered her phone."

"Why were you at the Thorpe house so early?"

"I'd come over to talk to Lyds about leaving. I was there to have another go at convincing her to run away to Queensland with me. To start a new life together."

"Lydia was resistant to the idea?" Charlotte asked.

Melissa grimaced. "Not exactly resistant, but she wasn't sure she wanted to leave her life behind. She told me it had nothing to do with her husband. She didn't care about her marriage. It was over. But there were other considerations. Her counseling practice, for one."

"You left her place and called her at half-past nine that morning," Charlotte said. "You'd put two and two together and realized there was someone else in her life. Simon Matthews."

"No! I didn't know anything about him."

Charlotte stared at her. "I don't believe you. I think you worked out pretty quickly while you were talking to Matthews that he was someone important in Lydia's life. Someone you hadn't known about. You didn't confront her right away. After all, you needed time to think about it, to plan how you were going to react. You headed home and Lydia left for work. You eventually called her at half-past nine to confront her about your suspicions."

"No! You're wrong."

Charlotte regarded her coldly. "I don't think so. Lydia texted you shortly after that phone call. Words to the effect that she wouldn't deal with "it" over the phone. That's when she agreed to meet you at her house during her lunch break, at twelve-thirty, like she'd done many times before."

Melissa narrowed her eyes at Charlotte. "We were having lunch. Nothing more."

Charlotte glared at her. "Don't take us for fools, Melissa. Lydia's text message makes it clear something was going on. You weren't meeting for lunch. You were meeting to talk about the fact you'd just found out she was having an affair with someone else. The mayor of Sutherland Shire."

"No!"

"See, here's what I think happened," Charlotte continued on, unperturbed. "You found out she was cheating on you— not with her husband, but with another man. You were furious. How dare she? You were in love with her! How could she hurt you like that? You'd even talked about going away together, moving to Queensland. Now you'd discovered that was all a lie. Your relationship was all a lie. You meant nothing to her!"

Melissa brought her hands up over her ears and began shaking her head from side to side with increasing ferocity. A howling sound came out of her mouth. It sounded like a wounded animal. A shiver ran down Charlotte's spine, but she forged on.

"Sometime between Lydia's text and when she arrived at the appointed time, you made plans to kill her. You got your hands on a knife and lay in wait. She came home and you confronted her. Maybe you got into a fight. Maybe you didn't even give her a chance to explain. That's not important. What is important is that you took to Lydia in a frenzy of anger and hurt and stabbed her thirty-seven times."

"No! No! No!" Melissa howled.

Charlotte spoke above the noise. "Then you had to clean up. Shower. Change. I'm guessing you kept spare clothes at Lydia's house. All of that took time. That's the reason your phone was still pinging off a nearby tower until half-past two. At around one o'clock, Simon Matthews arrived, looking for Lydia. By now she was already dead, but of course, he didn't know that. You saw him arrive, heard him calling out for Lydia, and you stayed silent. Eventually he left.

"Only you thought Matthews was Lydia's husband. There's no dispute they look alike. A simple mistake to make. You saw an opportunity to frame Grayson. After all, when a wife is so brutally murdered, the first person the cops look at is the husband, right?

"That's why you told us you saw Grayson's car parked in the driveway. A navy-blue BMW. Only it wasn't Grayson and his car wasn't there. You just made that bit up because you knew it would steer the police investigation away from you and toward Lydia's husband. In fact, the car that was parked in the driveway belonged to Lydia."

Melissa had stopped howling and now remained ominously quiet. She glared at Charlotte. "Say whatever you like. You can't force me to admit to anything."

"Oh, we're not forcing you to do anything." Charlotte looked at Sabattini. He inclined his head and then nodded. It was all the confirmation she needed. She glared at Melissa.

"Melissa Robinson, you're going to be charged with the murder of Lydia Thorpe."Charlotte and Tony stood. Charlotte pulled out a set of handcuffs and secured them around Melissa's wrists. The woman twisted her head and spat in Charlotte's face.

"You think you're so smart!" she screamed. "You know nothing! I won't forget this, bitch."

Tony took Melissa by the elbow and jerked her toward the door. "That's enough out of you. Be careful, or we'll slap an assault charge on you too." With that, Tony pulled open the door and marched the woman toward the charge room.

Charlotte pulled a pouch from the shelf, opened it and calmly wiped her face with the towelette, threw it in the trashcan then leaned against the wall, breathing hard. It took a few moments to recover her equilibrium. She was exhausted, but she was also elated. Slowly, realization set in.

I did it! I've just helped to put my first killer away!

She couldn't wipe the smile off her face. Her very next thought was that she couldn't wait to tell Grayson.

Chapter Seventeen

G rayson finished dictating a letter for his EA and then set the dictaphone aside. Though his concentration was still shot to hell, he couldn't take any more time off work. Besides, sitting around in a hotel room was driving him insane. The truth was, it was better for his mental health to keep busy and the best way to do that was to be at work.

Burying himself in the minutiae of probate disputes, juggling court dates, difficult clients, preparing statements and everything else that went into the running of a busy law practice had given him some reprieve from the endless cycle of questions about Lydia and her murder that had taken up residence in his brain. Then there was Charlotte.

The speed with which he was falling for her made him feel unsettled. He wanted to take a step back, slow things down, catch his breath. At the same time, he wanted to be with her all the time. He wanted to call her, hear her voice. He wanted to sleep with her, hold her close. His conflicting emotions, grief, needs and desires were exhausting and another reason why he'd barely slept since the murder.

The ringing of his phone interrupted his thoughts. He glanced at the screen. No caller ID. He let it go through to voicemail. A few moments later, his phone beeped, indicating a new message. Tapping his phone, he listened. At the sound of Charlotte's voice, his heart skipped a beat. Warmth spread through him.

God... I'm hopeless... A goner for sure...

She asked him to call her as soon as he could. She sounded...excited. He wondered if there had been a breakthrough in the case. Quickly, he dialed her number. She answered on the second ring.

"Grayson! You're not going to believe it!"

She went on to tell him her news but also some information about Melissa and Lydia's relationship that shocked him all over again. How could he not know all this? He tried not to show how much the news affected him. He listened patiently as Charlotte told him how she and Sabattini had pieced the evidence together. How Melissa Robinson had been charged with Lydia's murder.

"Thank God!" he cried, unable to keep the relief out of his voice. Finally a resolution to this nightmare and a chance of justice for Lydia. Perhaps now he'd be able to get some sleep...

"We should go out to celebrate," Charlotte suggested.

Grayson sighed. "I'd love to, but not tonight. Do you mind if I beg off? This is tremendous news, but I think I need time to process."

"I understand."

Grayson heard the disappointment in her voice and winced. The last thing he wanted to do was hurt her.

"Would you like some company?"

The hope that laced her question filled him with remorse. He wanted so much to accept her offer, but he knew some time alone to sort through his thoughts was for the best. Dragging in a deep breath, he declined and told her he'd call her in the morning. He ended the call and breathed out a heartfelt sigh of relief and thought about all that had happened over the past few weeks.

It was mind blowing. Simply unbelievable. No wonder his head was in a spin. And though he was terribly sad about what had happened to Lydia and stunned that she'd been seeing not only the mayor, but a woman on the side, he didn't feel guilty about meeting Charlotte.

She was the only breath of fresh air in all the darkness that had overwhelmed him since coming home and finding Lydia dead. It might not be the right time to be thinking about another woman, or of inviting her into his life, but he couldn't help it. What he felt for Charlotte was a once in a lifetime thing. And though the timing wasn't great, he didn't want to throw away the chance of finding something wonderful with her simply because it might seem like it was way too fast for him to be moving on.

What the people around him didn't know was that his marriage had been over long before he'd met Charlotte and before his wife had been killed. Recent events had cemented for him the belief that life was too short to allow other peoples' judgment to get in the way. Grayson hadn't said anything to his work colleagues or friends about Charlotte, but he wanted to. Fortunately, his bosses had stood by him throughout the investigation into Lydia's death and his closest friends had remained supportive. He only hoped they continued to feel that way when he eventually told them about the new woman in his life.

The sound of his phone ringing interrupted his thoughts. He checked the screen. Once again, there was no Caller ID. Thinking it might be Charlotte again, he answered the call.

"This is Grayson."

"Grayson Thorpe?"

The gravelly voice definitely didn't belong to Charlotte. "Yes?"

"This is Roger White from the Lidcombe Morgue. I'm just calling to let you know your wife's body has been released for burial. Or whatever it is you wish to do with her remains."

Grayson swallowed. In all the turmoil, he'd barely given a thought to making funeral arrangements. Of course, he'd known nothing could be done until the police had given the morgue the all clear to release her body. Now it seemed that time had come. Lydia's parents were both dead and she'd been an only child. He was the last person in her family, left to mourn her.

Dragging in a deep breath, he thanked the morgue technician and told him he'd make the arrangements right away. There was a funeral home he passed by every time he drove into the city. He'd give them a call.

The next hour was spent on the phone answering what seemed to be a lot of pointless questions from the attendant at the funeral home. Finally the questions came to an end. A private cremation was what Lydia would have wanted. He'd spread her ashes over Cronulla Beach. She'd always loved swimming there. It had been one of their favorite spots. He'd lay her to rest where they both had good memories. He hoped she was finally at peace.

The day dragged on. Grayson battled his way through affidavits, applications, emails and phone calls. He also forced himself to dig out Lydia's will. He spoke to a colleague about taking on the administration of Lydia's estate and was grateful when his colleague acquiesced to Grayson's request without hesitation.

Exhausted from the day's events and the weeks of trauma, pain and stress, he decided to leave work early and head for home. He owed it to himself to spend an evening alone processing everything that had happened and finding his feet again before reconnecting with Charlotte.

Bidding farewell to Anne, he wished his EA a good weekend and with a slight spring in his step, headed for the lifts. It felt like a weight had been lifted from his chest. It was the best he'd felt for a long time and he had Charlotte and her news about the case to thank for that.

Saturday evening rolled around quickly. Charlotte was filled with nervous anticipation at the thought of spending time with Grayson again. He'd called her as promised and they'd talked through all that had happened. He told her he'd spent his first stress-free day in weeks savoring the little freedoms, talking with his parents, reconnecting with this friends and thinking of her. The last admission lifted any doubts she'd had and filled her with warmth. She couldn't wait to see him again.

Opening the door to the Brass Monkey, she spied Grayson at the bar. Once again, he'd arrived ahead of her. While she'd been disappointed not to have celebrated with him the evening before, she understood and if truth be told she'd also needed the time to process developments and consider possibilities.

Looking at him now, she couldn't deny he looked even sexier than memory served in his Levis, brown leather loafers and a form fitting white T-shirt that clung to his impressive biceps and well-defined pectorals. His hair was wet and looked like it had been finger brushed, probably straight from the shower. As if sensing her scrutiny, he swiveled on the barstool and snagged her gaze. His face lit up. His sensual lips turned upward in a slow and sexy smile.

Her heart skipped a beat and then started pounding so hard she felt breathless. Butterflies had her giddy with excitement.

He stood as she approached. "Congratulations on closing the case. I'm sorry I couldn't do last night," he murmured, drawing her close and kissing her on the lips.

He smelled of pine forest and clean skin. His shampoo was sweet and fruity. His mouth was a combination of heat and cold and yeast, no doubt as a result of the half-full glass of beer that stood on the bar in front of him. She moved slightly away and took the empty seat beside him.

The bar was filling up and the crowd was loud and boisterous. People letting their hair down on a Saturday night. A band had set up in one corner, but as yet there was no sign of the musicians.

"What would you like to drink?" Grayson asked.

"A red wine please," she replied.

He caught the attention of the bartender and put in her order. A few moments later, the bartender returned with her drink. Grayson handed over a twenty.

"Keep the change," he said.

The bartender murmured his thanks and moved away. Grayson turned back to her. "Let's go somewhere a little quieter, where we can talk."

Charlotte nodded. They picked up their drinks and wended their way through pockets of people until they came to the seating area in the back. Sliding into a vacant booth, they took seats opposite each other. The noise level had dropped considerably from the main area.

"That's better," Grayson said. "Now I can hear myself."

Charlotte chuckled. He was right. The booths were much more conducive to conversation.

"So, can you tell me how you managed to find the killer, or is that classified information?"

She laughed and took a sip of wine. "It's not really classified. It will all come out at the trial, but for now, let's just say it was my exceptional detective skills that cracked the case." Her smile widened.

He winked. "I have no doubt you have exceptional detective skills, even if you don't look like any cop I know."

His gaze moved meaningfully over her body. She'd taken the time to dress in a form-fitting, hot pink mini dress. It wasn't quite as provocative as the black leather number she'd worn the first night they'd met, but the strapless, low-cut bodice displayed enough of her cleavage to entice any hot-blooded male. Topped with a generous amount of exposed tanned thigh and stilettos high enough to drive a man crazy, she was pretty confident her outfit had what it took to drive Grayson wild. And from the way his green eyes darkened to emerald as his gaze scanned her from head to toe, she knew she'd been right.

She blushed and cleared her throat. "More importantly, how are you feeling? How was last night and today? I can't even begin to imagine how horrible it's all been."

He shrugged. "It was hard, especially talking with my parents. I told them everything. They were shocked and upset and finally resigned. They asked me to pass on their gratitude to you for catching the killer."

Charlotte ducked her head, embarrassed. "It wasn't just me. Detective Sabattini did his part. Both of us were only doing our job."

She saw that he was about to protest and cut him off with another request. "Tell me more about your family. You told me a little bit about your parents, but I'm sure there's plenty more to know about your family."

He smiled. "Sure. What would you like to know?"

"I don't know." She sipped from her wine. "Do you have any siblings?"

"No."

She raised her eyebrows in surprise. "No? Are you kidding? Not a single one?"

"Not a single one."

"But, how can that be? I have eight."

This time it was his turn to smile in surprise. "Eight? Heck, what were your parents thinking?"

Charlotte chuckled. "We always used to joke they'd been trying for their own soccer team."

"It must have been noisy at meal times."

"Oh, yeah. Everyone talking over the top of each other, all wanting to have their say. It's still like that when we all get together. We were lucky. Mom and Dad rarely dissuaded us from sharing our opinion. It was okay to disagree."

Grayson nodded. "That must be why you're so bossy now," he teased.

"Hey! I'm not bossy!" Charlotte protested.

"No? What about when you demanded I come on board with ice cream and chocolate? That wasn't up for negotiation."

"That was different! I was nervous and I couldn't stop talking and I didn't demand you come on board with both..." She stopped. "Why are you laughing?"

"Because you look so sexy when you get all mad."

"I'm not mad! I'm just...explaining my position."

He leaned over and kissed her briefly on the lips. "So where do you fit in this impressive lineup of Barringtons?"

"Actually, I'm a triplet."

"What? Are you kidding?"

She giggled at the surprise on his face. "No, I'm not. I have a brother, Trace. He's also a cop. And I have a sister, Molly. She's a paramedic. They form the rest of the trio. We come in at numbers four, five and six."

Grayson's answering smile was filled with yearning. Charlotte thought about all of her siblings and wondered what it had been like for him as an only child. She couldn't imagine growing up without her noisy bunch of brothers and sisters. Sometimes they drove her insane with their opinions, but they probably felt the same way about her. At the end of the day, she loved them all to bits and wouldn't want to face life without them.

"Tell me about the other five," Grayson said quietly.

"Well, let's see. My oldest brother is Christopher. He turned forty-one about a month ago. He's actually my half-brother. My mom had him years before she met my Dad. When Dad and Mom got married, Dad legally adopted Christopher."

"That's so nice," Grayson said.

"Yes. They're nice people. My second oldest brother is Vaughan. He's forty. He was also adopted."

"Is he another half-brother?"

"No. He'd been in and out of foster homes for the first eleven years of his life. Mom and Dad took him out of foster care and adopted him."

Grayson looked at her with eyes wide with wonder. "Wow. That's amazing."

"Yes. The thing is, they didn't think they could have kids of their own. They tried for a year or two after they married, with no success. They wanted a sibling for Christopher and so they adopted Vaughan. A couple of years later, Mom discovered she was pregnant with Lincoln."

"So Lincoln comes in at number three."

"Yes. He's twenty-seven."

"Is he a cop, too?"

"No. He's ex-army." Charlotte's mood sobered as she thought about Lincoln.

Seeing the change in her expression, Grayson leaned closer. "What is it?" he asked softly.

"Lincoln served three tours in Afghanistan. It...changed him."

"Three tours?" Grayson slowly shook his head. "Wow. That must have been tough."

"Yes. He's been different since he came back. We're all trying to give him some space, but it's been six months... No one quite knows what to do."

"I get that. It must be difficult."

"Yes. Especially when we're so used to sticking our noses into each other's business. We all have an opinion on what's right or wrong for each of us. It's hard because none of us know what to say to Lincoln. Everyone wants to help him, but none of us know how to go about it."

"Maybe he just needs time," Grayson suggested. "Not everything can be fixed overnight. As long as he knows he has your love and support, I'm sure he'll be fine."

Tears burned behind Charlotte's eyes. She gave Grayson a grateful look. "I hope so."

They both took refuge in their drinks for a moment. Then Grayson spoke again. "So, who comes after the triplets?"

Charlotte chuckled. "That would be Wade. He's a park ranger in a teeny tiny town called Watervale. It's literally in the middle of nowhere. I spent a year as a probationary constable there. Let's just say it was an experience." She grinned. "I can't imagine living anywhere but Sydney, but Wade loves it out there."

"How old is he?"

"Only a year younger than me. Twenty-five."

"A baby," Grayson teased.

Charlotte did her best to look outraged. "Oh, like you're so ancient! You haven't even told me your age."

Grayson's eyes sparkled with humor. "Guess."

Charlotte rolled her eyes. "Really?"

"Yes. Guess."

Charlotte grinned mischievously. "Okay." She pretended to think. "Um... Thirty-nine."

"Thirty-nine!" Grayson shouted.

Charlotte giggled. "What? Not old enough?"

He shook his head ruefully. "Minx."

She held up her hands in a sign of surrender. "Okay, okay. I'll take another guess." Once again, she pretended to think. "Um... Thirty-two."

"At least that's a bit closer. I'm twenty-eight."

Charlotte smiled. "Twenty-eight. Nice."

Grayson took a sip from his beer. "So you haven't finished telling me about your siblings."

"Who was I up to?"

"Wade."

"Right. Wade. Well, after Wade comes Zac. He's twenty-four. And before you ask, yes, he's a cop."

"Does he live in Sydney?"

"No. He's another brother who enjoys living in the country. In fact, he works in the same small town where I grew up."

Grayson looked surprise. "Broken?"

Charlotte nodded, pleased he'd remembered. "Yes. Zac's never ventured far from home. He's a momma's boy."

"Really?"

She laughed. "No, not really. In fact, until recently he was stationed on the Central Coast. Now he's back in Broken. It's a running joke in the family because he goes home for dinner at least two or three times a week."

"He's not married?"

"No. None of us are. Although Christopher recently met someone. We're all quietly confident she might be the love of his life."

"That's nice," Grayson said.

Charlotte looked at his wistful expression. "Are you thinking about Lydia?" she asked softly.

He stared down at his lap and then slowly shook his head. "No. I was just thinking how wonderful your family sounds. What Lydia and I had together... We started out all right, but something changed. Maybe we both changed. I don't know. Don't get me wrong, I'm sad about what happened to her. She didn't deserve that. But our marriage had been over for a long time before the murder. And we didn't have children... I miss what we used to be, but I'd already come to the conclusion before she was killed that our life together had come to an end."

"I'm just glad we were able to put away her killer," Charlotte murmured.

Grayson grimaced. "Yeah. Me too. I got a call from the morgue. They've released Lydia's body. I made the funeral arrangements this afternoon. A private cremation."

"Oh, Grayson! Are you okay?"

He nodded. "Yes. I'm fine. But thanks for asking."

"Hey, there's one more Barrington I haven't told you about," she said in an effort to lighten the mood.

"Oh, yeah? Who is it?"

"I've saved the best for last. My little sister, Hannah. At the ripe old age of twenty-three, she's the youngest mine manager I know."

Grayson's eyebrows lifted in surprise. "She works in the mines?"

"Yes. She manages Dad's coal mine up in the Hunter Valley."

"Wow. That's...interesting."

Charlotte laughed. "The truth is, she doesn't know what she wants to do with her life. She was sitting around home doing nothing, getting on everyone's nerves. Dad needed a supervisor. He suggested she take on the job there while she thought about what she wanted to do."

"Fair enough."

Charlotte grinned. "By all accounts, she's loving it. Who'd have thought?"

Grayson looked at her. "So your father's involved in mining?"

Too late Charlotte remembered she'd intended to keep her family's wealth a secret. She sighed inwardly. Grayson was bound to find out sooner or later. She just hoped they knew each other well enough and that he already had strong feelings for her, regardless of who her family was or their financial status.

She nodded. "Yes. He has several mining interests. A coal mine in the Hunter Valley. A couple of iron ore mines in the Pilbara in Western Australia."

It took Grayson a few beats, but she knew the exact moment when he made the connection. His expression turned incredulous.

"Oh my God! You're not one of those Barringtons, are you?"

Her lips tightened, along with her stomach. "If you mean is my father Frank Barrington, CEO of Barrington Mining, then yes. I'm one of those Barringtons."

As if sensing something in her tone, Grayson looked immediately contrite. "Charlotte, I didn't mean anything by that. You just took me by surprise. I... I had no idea you were related to one of the wealthiest families in Australia."

She narrowed her eyes at him. "So? Is that a problem?"

He shook his head, looking slightly bewildered. "A problem? Of course not. I couldn't give a damn who you're related to. I like you." He paused and then added in a husky tone, "I like you a lot."

The raw emotion in his eyes caused Charlotte's heart to skip a beat. At the same time, she was filled with warmth and a yearning so overwhelming it snatched her breath. Hastily, she reached for her wine and realized her glass was empty.

"Can I get you another?" Grayson asked.

She nodded. "Yes, thank you." She handed Grayson the empty glass. Sliding out of the booth, he headed for the bar. She watched his broad shoulders and trim body disappear into the crowd and took the time to regain her equilibrium. She also wondered how she'd gotten so lucky.

He was everything she could ask for in a life partner. Smart, sexy, hardworking, sensitive and kind. He even loved cats. He was the complete package and now that he knew about her family and it didn't seem to change his attitude toward her... She couldn't keep the smile of anticipation off her face.

Chapter Eighteen

Grayson shouldered his way through the crowd that filled the Brass Monkey and wondered at his luck. He couldn't believe a woman as beautiful, as smart, as self-possessed as Charlotte had chosen him. Or maybe they'd chosen each other. Whatever. He kept wanting to pinch himself to make sure this wasn't a dream.

And then he remembered everything that had happened with Lydia and his smile faded. There was no way this was a dream. He was just glad Lydia's murderer had been found. After the cremation, he'd do his best to try and put all of this behind him.

With that thought top of mind, he ordered a fresh round of drinks and brought them back to the booth. Charlotte smiled her thanks and took a sip of wine. The band had started to play and she tapped out the rhythm on the table with her fingers.

"Would you like to dance?" Grayson asked.

Charlotte smiled. "Yes."

Leaving their drinks on the table, they slid out from the booth. Grayson reached for her hand. It was small and soft in his. At the same time, there was a quiet strength in her fingers that belied her petite frame. He knew from experience she was tough, inside and out. Nobody could work in homicide without those qualities.

The music had an upbeat tempo. Grayson prided himself on being a better than average dancer. It was nice that Charlotte could hold her own. She moved to the beat with natural rhythm, matching his steps without the least hint of self-consciousness.

"You're a good dancer," he commented.

She winked. "So are you. That's one of the first things I noticed about you."

He grinned. "My mother sent me to ballroom dancing lessons when I was a kid."

She looked at him in mock horror. "Oh, you poor boy!"

He chuckled. "Actually, I enjoyed it. She did me a favor. I still love to dance."

Charlotte's eye sparkled. "So do I."

With that, Grayson took her by the hand and spun her around and then twirled her under his arm and back again. She followed the intricate steps and did not falter. The music changed, slowed tempo. He drew her into his arms and held her close.

Bending his head, he breathed in the soft sweetness of her hair. She'd left it loose and flowing around her shoulders. So different from the tidy bun he'd seen her wear at work. He preferred this softer, more sensual Charlotte. The woman who could laugh and joke and dance. She made him feel good when he was around her.

He hoped that whatever it was between them would continue to blossom and grow into something substantial. Though it was early days yet, and no doubt his friends would caution him about going slowly, deep inside he knew there was something very special about what they'd found together. He hoped she felt the same.

As if sensing the direction of his thoughts, her arms tightened around him. He pulled her even closer and kissed her softly on the lips. It was meant to be a quick kiss, a touch because he couldn't go this long without doing it, but passion ignited between them and all of a sudden Charlotte was kissing him back. With her arms clinging tightly around his neck, she pulled his head down to hers and held it in place. She kissed him with everything she had.

Her tongue stole into his mouth and danced with his. Her breasts were crushed against his chest. His body throbbed, his cock ached. If he didn't have her, he might combust...

Once again, she seemed to sense his thoughts. Slowly, reluctantly she lifted her head and smiled.

"Do you want to come back to my place?"

Nothing on earth could keep him away.

Charlotte dropped her handbag on her desk and hung up her jacket. It had been six days since they'd put Melissa Robinson behind bars. It had also been six nights that Charlotte had spent in Grayson's arms. She could hardly wipe the smile from her face.

In the days following charges being laid against Melissa Robinson, Wendell had urged both Charlotte and Tony to take a few well-deserved days off. Charlotte had been only too happy to do so. It had been a difficult few weeks. She was glad for some time to rest and recharge. Even better, she convinced Grayson to take a few days off with her. Fortunately, his boss had readily agreed.

She and Grayson had spent most of their time off together. It had been wonderful getting to know the real Grayson, not just the guy she'd encountered that night in the Brass Monkey and then later, as the husband of a murder victim.

Right from the start, they'd been compatible in bed, but as the days went by and they got to know each other on a deeper level, it was clear they had a lot in common in other ways. He liked cats, for one. Every time he came over, he took the time to sit with Raoul and talk to him and pet him. And Raoul seemed just as taken with him. It was sweet to see them together and even more reassuring that Grayson had really meant it when he'd told her he loved cats.

He also liked to cook. Though Charlotte knew her way around a kitchen, she was often too tired after a twelve-hour shift to do much more than a basic meal. Having Grayson around inspired her. He loved to try out new things, experiment. He admitted that he hadn't spent a lot of time cooking over the past few years. Lydia preferred to eat out and he'd worked long hours. Neither were conducive to him standing over a hot stove and whipping up gourmet meals. But things were different now and it was good. He was changing and he thought that was good too.

The ringing of her phone interrupted her musings. Reaching for her mobile, she automatically checked the screen and smiled.

Trace.

During the time she'd immersed herself with Grayson, calling her brother, or anyone else for that matter, had completely slipped her mind. Now she was pleased to speak with him again.

"Trace. How are things?"

"Not bad, little sis. I hear congratulations are in order. Sorry it's taken me so long to call. I've been out of town working on a case. I only got back in last night. Heard the news this morning."

Charlotte's thoughts immediately went to Grayson. She flushed with embarrassment and wondered how Trace, or anyone else, could possibly know about her blossoming relationship.

"Um... Gee, thanks. How did you...?"

"Hear that you'd solved your first homicide? It's the talk of the department. We're all impressed with what you've managed to achieve. And Tony, of course. I thought you said he was a has-been?" Trace teased.

Charlotte flushed again, but this time it was for an entirely different reason. Though she was relieved news about her and Grayson hadn't yet hit the family rumor mill, she was equally embarrassed about the way she'd carried on with Trace about her partner. Her comments had been ill-advised and completely without basis. She told Trace as much.

"Oh, so you're a fan of Sabattini now, are you? Glad to hear that. He's had a rough time of it this past year or so, but he's still a damn fine cop."

"You're right," she agreed. "He is."

"So, what's next for Sydney's up-and-coming crime fighter?"

Charlotte waved away Trace's question with a laugh. "Onward and upward, brother. You know how it is. There's always another criminal to bring down."

Trace's tone sobered. "You've got that right. It does my head in some days."

While Trace preferred the quieter life in Broken to working in a busy city station, he faced his fair share of crime. Particularly with the rise of methamphetamines creeping out to small country towns. It was a headache for everyone, especially law enforcement.

"Have you heard from Vaughan?" Charlotte asked, changing the subject.

"No. Have you?"

"Nope. Last I heard he'd emailed Dad to say he was okay and that he needed to take some time off."

"Yeah. Same with me. I called his phone a couple of times, left messages, but he hasn't called me back. I spoke to Christopher the other day. He said he thinks Vaughan has taken off somewhere. He drove by Vaughan's unit and no one was home. The mailbox was full of junk mail. It looked like Vaughan hadn't been there for a while."

Charlotte sighed. "I guess we just have to trust he knows what he's doing. It's obvious he wants some space. I wonder if it has anything to do with him turning forty last month…"

"Who knows? He didn't seem hung up about his age at the party, but maybe he was putting on a good front?"

"Yeah. Well, let me know if you hear from him. It would be nice to know where he is."

"Right back at you."

Charlotte chuckled. "Of course. You know we have no secrets from each other, brother."

As she said it, Charlotte flushed with guilt. She hadn't told anyone in her family about Grayson. It was way too early. Right now, she looked forward to the times they spent together and so far things had been more perfect than she could have imagined—but what if things fizzled out? She wanted to be more certain about the way they felt about each other before she involved her family. If they got even a hint she was seeing someone, they'd be all over her with questions. Especially Molly and Trace.

From the corner of her eye, she spied Sabattini walk into the squad room. He came to a halt beside her. She looked at him, wondering what was going on. He motioned for her to wind up her phone call.

"Um, Trace? I have to go. I'll call you back later."

She ended the call and turned to her partner. "What is it?"

"Did you hear?"

"About what?"

"Robinson made bail."

Charlotte felt like she'd been sucker-punched. "She what?"

Sabattini's expression turned grim. "Yeah. Managed to get some hotshot lawyer to plead her case before the Supreme Court. Pretty strict conditions, but still…"

Charlotte shook her head from side to side. "I don't believe it! Why would a judge release her on bail? There's a presumption against bail for murder charges. Our case is strong! We're almost certain to get a conviction. I just don't get it."

Sabattini compressed his lips. "Apparently this is her first serious offense. The judge agreed with her lawyer she wasn't a flight risk. He also agreed she wasn't likely a danger to the community." Sabattini shrugged. "He let her out."

"Damn. After all that hard work," Charlotte complained.

Sabattini offered her a half-hearted smile. "Hey, cheer up. She's out on bail. It's not like the case has been dismissed. You'll get your day in court."

Charlotte grumbled under her breath. Sabattini's expression filled with understanding. "You did good on this case, Barrington. We might have gotten off to a rocky start, but... You'll do okay."

Charlotte looked up at him, her heart flooding with warmth and gratitude. "Thank you, Tony. Coming from you, that means a lot."

Now it was Tony's turn to grunt under his breath. He looked away, as if uncomfortable, but she saw the flush of pleasure on his cheeks. And then he went and ruined it by saying, "Just don't go disobeying direct orders ever again, or I'll personally see to it that you kiss your career in policing goodbye forever. Got it?"

"Yep. Got it."

Vaughan Barrington's breath came fast. His feet pounded the wet sand that stretched for miles into the distance along the Nusa Dua coastline. It was early. A little past five. The only time during the daylight hours that the humidity in Bali was bearable this time of year. It meant he could get in his daily run without having his T-shirt already sticking to him before he'd left his house.

He'd been in Bali a little over a month. Apart from his initial email to his father, he hadn't been in contact with his family. The truth was, he didn't know what to say to them. As close as he was to them, this was something no one had seen coming. It definitely wasn't something he could drop in a casual email.

Oh, by the way... You know how we all thought I was an orphan? Well, it turns out that's not true. In fact, my biological mother's alive and well and living just down the road from my family home... Who would have thought? And not only that. Turns out the woman who gave birth to me is none other than Elizabeth Craigdon. Yes, that's right. Christopher's step-mother...

It sounded crazy even to him and he had the letter to prove it. That's if it was true. It was so easy to put a hoax together these days. People fell for them online every day. Calls and emails purporting to be from the tax office or some other equally important, authoritative body.

Is that what this is? A cruel hoax?

He had no proof the letter had come from Elizabeth Craigdon. Okay, so the correspondence had been written on her personal embossed letterhead, but so what? These days anyone with half a brain and a computer and a printer could create a fake letterhead that could pass as an original.

But what would they have to gain, except to throw his life into disarray? Perhaps this had something to do with Barrington Mining? After all, his father was always walking a tightrope between government regulations, unions and other private players with competing interests and motivations. As one of the high level executives in Barrington Mining, Vaughan's absence in the office would have been noticed. It would have given his father a headache to have to step in and fill the void, even temporarily.

Of course, there was nothing Frank Barrington didn't know about his company. After all, he'd started it from the ground up. But over the years, Vaughan had taken on more and more responsibility. Was that what this letter was about? A fabricated and shocking disclosure to send him running for the hills, dropping everything in his father's lap? Were their competitors even now circling like piranhas, just waiting for Frank to make a mistake and give them a chance to move in?

He couldn't deny the possibility the letter purporting to be from Elizabeth Craigdon was nothing more than a hoax. In fact, that made more sense than not. Either that, or the woman claiming to be his mother was lying. He couldn't figure out her motivation for deceiving him, but he'd been told by so many people all his life that his biological mother was dead. Had all of them lied? Or had they just assumed?

He shook his head to rid himself of the endless questions that circled through his mind. So many questions and no answers and yet, he wasn't ready to face anyone yet. He was also still so angry at Elizabeth Craigdon. Why had she waited this long? Was she telling the truth? Was she his biological mother, or was this all part of a grand scheme to bring Barrington Mining to its knees?

He didn't know and right now, he didn't want to know. Keeping well clear of the drama by hiding out in Bali was his best plan of action for now. He needed more time to think, to clear his head, to come to terms with the possibility this wasn't a lie and that the mother he'd believed dead all these years was in fact alive and well...and wanting to meet him.

Melissa Robinson was seething. She'd been forced to use all of her savings to secure her release. A total of fifty thousand dollars had been put up as surety. Fifty thousand dollars! It was a joke. As if she was a threat to society. As if she had the potential to kill again. This had been all about Lydia. If the woman hadn't betrayed her like that... With a man, no less.

It had been bad enough when Lydia resisted her attempts to persuade her to walk away from her boring life in the suburbs and start afresh with Melissa interstate. Melissa had made enquires. The construction industry was booming in Brisbane. She'd have no difficulty picking up work.

As far as Lydia went, her work was just as mobile. Counseling services were in high demand everywhere. It seemed the whole human race was battling some form of mental illness or other. Bullying, low self-esteem, depression, irrational fear. The list was endless. Melissa was confident Lydia would have no trouble finding clients.

No, the problem hadn't been their ability to find work. The problem had been Lydia. She'd kept giving Melissa excuses.

"I can't just walk out on my marriage... Okay, so my marriage might be over, but what about my work? I can't desert my clients. They need me," Lydia had said.

"But I need you too," Melissa had argued. "I love you, Lydia. I want us to be together. We can't do that while you continue to stay in this dead end marriage. You already told me you and Grayson are over. You said it again just now. What's keeping you here? What are you afraid of?"

"I'm not afraid of anything," Lydia had said. "I want to be with you too. It's just that..."

"Just what?" Melissa demanded.

Lydia had merely shrugged and averted her gaze. "Things are complicated."

"How? You pack your bags and leave your sorry sap of a husband a note. Tell him whatever you want. Just make it clear you've moved on and that's that. How hard can it be?"

Lydia had given her a pained look. "You don't understand. It isn't as easy as that."

Melissa's anger had stirred at Lydia's continued resistance. "You're right," she cried. "I don't understand. I love you and you love me. That's the only thing that matters."

"You're right," Lydia said with little conviction.

Melissa hadn't given up hope of convincing Lydia to run away with her. Of course, that was before Melissa had found out about the mayor.

Simon Matthews.

So, it had been the mayor who'd come calling on Lydia that day. Figures. After all, he'd phoned Lydia early that morning. It was too bad she hadn't realized how much Matthews looked like Grayson Thorpe. It would have been just as easy to point the finger at the mayor. But she'd honestly thought it was Grayson outside his house. She should have realized her mistake when he didn't bother to come inside. Instead, he'd merely called out to Lydia and after a few moments had left.

Melissa had been inside, frozen with panic. Lydia's body still lay in full view on the living room floor. Melissa had been canvassing her options, including using the knife on the man she'd believed was Grayson, when he'd turned and left. In her relief, she hadn't stopped to ponder why.

But it had been Matthews. That's why he didn't use a key. Now that she knew, she wasn't surprised the mayor had turned up outside Lydia's house. When he'd called earlier that morning, he'd wanted to speak with Lydia. Melissa had put him off by assuring him she'd pass on his message to Lydia, but of course she hadn't. She'd begun to suspect there was more to the mayor's early morning call and so she'd started doing some digging.

She'd lied when she'd told that cop she knew nothing about Simon Matthews or the fact he was sleeping with her girlfriend. The truth was, she'd started nosing around in Lydia's text messages the moment the mayor was off the phone. It had been pathetically easy. The two of them hadn't even tried to disguise their relationship. Their text messages were numerous and explicit. It angered Melissa to discover the affair had been going on even longer than the relationship between Lydia and herself.

All this time I thought I was her one and only... She'd told me over and over her marriage was over... I had no idea she was playing me right along with her stupid husband... The joke was on me...

Except, Melissa had made sure Lydia paid for her deception. No one played Melissa Robinson like that and got away with it. Hell no. Lydia Thorpe chose the wrong woman to cross. And she'd found that out the hard way.

It was a shame. Melissa missed her. They might have only known each other four months, but they'd clicked right away. Slept with each other within hours of finishing their first lunch. It had been amazing, magical, like nothing Melissa had ever experienced. She'd been with women before, but no one as beautiful and sophisticated as Lydia Thorpe.

The detectives had put together more of the story than Melissa would have guessed, but they didn't know everything. They didn't know how much Melissa had loved Lydia and how killing her was the only option open to her after Lydia betrayed her. Lydia didn't love her the same way Melissa loved Lydia. She couldn't have or she wouldn't have been able to carry on an affair with the mayor at the same time she was snuggling up to Melissa.

Someone that deceitful couldn't be allowed to keep breathing. It was as simple as that. Just like her parents. Like Lydia, they'd found out the hard way Melissa didn't tolerate dishonesty. No one had suspected the fifteen-year-old daughter of setting the fire that took her parents' lives. It had been a simple enough matter to research on the Internet. An electrical fire, that's what the police had determined. The house and everything in it was destroyed, including the computer she'd used to research how to start an electrical fire.

Everyone talked about how lucky she was to have escaped with only minor burns. Child services had momentarily stepped in and made motions to have her put into foster care, but she soon put paid to that idea. She moved in with the family of her teenage girlfriend. Unlike her close-minded and bigoted parents who'd pretended to respect her choices. Behind her back her parents had turned around and arranged for psychiatric appointments meant to denigrate and humiliate and rid her of her aberration...

Jacqui's parents were much more understanding. She would have continued to live with them indefinitely if Jacqui hadn't moved on with someone else. She didn't blame Jacqui. Shit happened. At least the girl had the decency to be upfront with her when her feelings waned.

Not like Lydia. Cheating on her husband times two. What a joke.

The cops just didn't understand: Melissa had only one choice and that was to end Lydia's life. They were determined to paint Melissa as a cold-blooded killer, but they didn't know how it really was. Especially the bitch cop.

Charlotte Barrington.

Who the hell did she think she was? She thought she was so clever, putting all the pieces together. The phone records were what had done Melissa in. If it weren't for them, the police would be no wiser about what had gone on.

Charlotte Barrington.

Young, beautiful, confident, smart. All the things Melissa yearned to be, but never would be. Sometimes life dealt out a shitty hand. When it did, you did everything in your power to change that. To balance things. Even the score. That was something the Charlotte Barringtons of the world didn't understand. But the bitch cop would soon understand only too well. Hell, yeah. She would.

Chapter Nineteen

G rayson hummed along to the song playing on his speaker and tapped his foot to the beat. It had been a month since his wife's murder. He still woke up some nights breathing hard after a nightmare wherein he arrived home to find her gasping her last breath, but those times were becoming less frequent and he had Charlotte to thank for that.

She was a ray of light in his otherwise sad and sorry life. She helped him remember he was very much still alive, with a lot to offer and a life to live. Over the past week, they'd grown closer, shared confidences, discovered common ground. It felt nice to be in a relationship where the other person actually looked forward to his company. Who took his phone calls. Who teased him, who made him laugh.

It was the light-hearted moments he'd missed the most when his marriage had begun to fail. He worked in a somber, serious job. One where he was often surrounded by angry, vindictive people, all wanting their day in court. No doubt it was the same for lawyers who specialized in family law. He made a mental note to call his colleague and friend, Flynn Craigdon. Maybe invite him out for a drink. Chew the fat. Share some laughs. Relieve some stress. They could all do with more of that.

In the early days of his marriage, Lydia had often made him laugh. Her stories of things that had happened in the course of her day or even something she'd read online or seen on TV had amused them both.

He couldn't pinpoint the time when they'd stopped sharing those moments. It had occurred so gradually he didn't realize it had happened until it was too late to get them back. By then they were arguing over almost everything and she'd shut herself off from him, both emotionally and physically. No wonder they'd never had the discussion about children. That had been the furthest thing from both of their minds.

It was the reason he hadn't come out and told Charlotte too much about the way he felt. The truth was, the strength of his feelings for her overwhelmed him. He'd never felt this way. He was also wary of jumping into another relationship so soon. Not because his wife had died in such terrible circumstances, but because he needed time to properly assimilate all that had happened and how it had changed him.

One thing he was determined to do was cut back on his work hours. It had been the biggest thing he and Lydia had argued over. He could see now that there were more important things than climbing to the top of the career ladder and though he hadn't lost his desire to make partner one day, he no longer felt the urgency to achieve that dream in the shortest amount of time possible.

He'd rather have time to draw breath, appreciate the sunset, spend time with the woman he was falling for fast. It wasn't as easy as he'd anticipated, dragging himself away from his clients, his files, his paperwork, but he was determined to make the change, no matter what it took.

Like now. He'd taken the afternoon off work so he could cook Charlotte dinner. It was their one-month anniversary. A whole month since they'd first met. He wanted to celebrate by cooking her something wildly extravagant. Something that would blow her mind. He'd bought all the ingredients from a nearby farmers' market and had already begun preparations.

The plan was for him to cook all the dishes at his house and then surprise her with them at her unit. Over the weeks, he'd been slowly forcing himself to spend more time in his house. It had been difficult at first and no doubt his visits back home had contributed to some of his nightmares, but this was his home, with all his belongings. He needed to come to terms with what had happened and find the courage to accept it and move on. He was also getting tired of living out of hotel rooms.

At some stage, he'd put the place on the market, sell it and move on. There was no way he would live there for longer than necessary. Too many memories. He'd probably lose money on his investment. After all, the law required that potential buyers be informed if a property had been the scene of a homicide. That tended to have a negative effect on the asking price. But he'd take what he could get and start over. The alternative, staying there indefinitely, simply wasn't an option for his peace of mind.

With a sigh, Grayson tossed a handful of baby potatoes into the sink and gave them a good wash. Along with the small steamed potatoes garnished with garlic butter and herbs, he'd chosen Oysters Kilpatrick for starters, made from scratch. Charlotte had once told him how much she loved seafood and he wanted to let her know he'd listened.

He'd sourced the fresh Sydney Rock Oysters from the fish markets. Right now, they were in the fridge. He'd prepare the bacon topping here and cook them under Charlotte's grill so they could eat them straight afterwards. Nothing beat hot, fresh Oysters Kilpatrick. He salivated at the thought.

Next on the menu were lobster tails with lemon-and-chive-infused butter. It was a simple dish that looked and tasted fabulous and another nod to Charlotte's love of seafood. As a side, he'd add the baby potatoes and crisp green broccolini. Finally, for dessert there was bombe Alaska. It was an ambitious dish where the timing was all important, but he looked forward to the challenge. He hadn't actually cooked it before, but he was confident he could pull it off. He just hoped she enjoyed it.

He barely heard the sound of his phone ringing over the music. Picking up the remote, he silenced the song and answered the call. When Charlotte spoke, he smiled.

"Hi, you. I was just thinking about you," he said.

"Really? I'm always thinking about you too."

Charlotte's response sent warmth rushing through him to center in his groin. Images of her naked limbs wrapped around him and the feel of her wet heat pulsing around his cock flooded his mind. He cursed under his breath.

"What are you doing?" Charlotte asked.

"Not much. Just tidying up a few things."

"Do you have court this afternoon?"

"No. I'm actually out of the office."

"Oh?"

He could hear the curiosity in her voice and smiled. No doubt she was dying to ask him where he was, but she wouldn't. They hadn't quite reached that stage in their relationship where they felt comfortable asking for that kind of accountability. Right now that played in his favor. If she asked too many questions there was a chance he might inadvertently give something away. He didn't want her to guess what he was up to.

"Yeah, but listen, I'm in the middle of something at the moment, so I'm going to have to go."

"Oh. Okay. Well, will I see you later?"

Her tone was filled with hope, but it was also tinged with uncertainty. He was flooded with guilt.

"I don't think so. It's my poker night, remember?"

"Oh. Yes, that's right. Poker night."

She sounded so disappointed. He bit down on another surge of guilt.

"Well, I get off work at six. Should be home by six-twenty if the traffic's good. I'll be home all night alone, if you change your mind about poker."

He smiled at her teasing tone. "Sure. Thanks for the offer, but don't wait up for me. I've already told the boys I'll be there. Still, hold off on an early dinner in case they cancel. Then I'll take you out. But it's not likely they will."

Once again, she sounded disheartened. "Okay. Well, have a good night. Bye."

Eager to get off the phone, he ended the call and went back to his preparations. He felt guilty about lying to her, but he wanted to surprise her. It was their anniversary. Besides, she'd been working so hard. Even with Robinson's trial now in the hands of the prosecutor's office there was always work to be done.

He wanted to do something special for her. To let her know how much he cared. To let her know he remembered the night they met. It had been a night that had changed his life. He couldn't wait to see the look on her face when he arrived with their dinner.

Charlotte dropped her phone back on her desk and stared blindly at her computer screen. She was bummed Grayson hadn't remembered their one-month anniversary. Okay, so it was silly to place so much importance on a stupid date, but she felt disappointed anyway. She never begrudged him the nights he spent away from her. After all, he had a life of his own; things that he liked doing and had been part of long before she'd come into his life. Poker night was one of them.

She was glad he had friends to spend time with and unwind. He worked long hours, even now. Though he'd started talking about reorganizing his priorities and perhaps cutting back time he spent at work, so far she hadn't seen any evidence of that. Still, there was nothing she could do about that and it was silly getting all worked up about an anniversary that really wasn't an anniversary at all. The best thing to do was to forget about it and look forward to the next time they got to be alone.

Yes, that's what she'd do. She'd put the whole thing out of her mind. Just because Grayson hadn't remembered didn't mean he didn't care. It was a guy thing. Girls got so much more hooked up on special dates and little signs. Most of the time men passed through oblivious. It would do her good to remember that.

In fact, the more she thought about it, the more she was grateful for a night alone. She'd wait a bit in case his card night was cancelled, then heat up a frozen dinner and eat it on the couch while watching the Netflix series she hadn't had a chance to watch for weeks. After that she'd take a nice long bath, light some candles, drink some champagne. It was the perfect way to end another busy working day.

Melissa looked at the time. It was going on for five. Still plenty of time. She was only minutes away from her destination. She'd been parked down the road from the bitch cop's complex for more than an hour, scoping out the neighborhood, familiarizing herself with her escape route, running through the plan in her head.

It had been easy enough to discover where the Barrington bitch lived. All Melissa had to do was follow the stupid cop home one night. She'd kept back far enough not to cause suspicion and had driven right on by when the bitch had pulled into the driveway of an older style unit block. The beach was spitting distance away.

"Trust that bitch to live right near the beach."

Melissa hadn't given much thought to a detective's salary, but obviously it was much more generous than she'd guessed. Beachside living in Cronulla didn't come cheap. Either that, or the woman had a rich husband who paid the bills.

Melissa had staked out the place over several days, taking care to remain out of sight. So far, she'd seen no sign of a husband. In fact, the only additional person she'd spied was Grayson Thorpe. At first, she guessed he was there on police business, tying up loose ends. But when it was obvious he was spending the night there, his presence took on a whole different light.

She's fucking him... Lydia's husband... The selfish bitch... Has she no sense of decency?

Though Melissa didn't care about the husband, she did care about her late girlfriend. Lydia had only been dead a month and already her husband had moved on. It seemed disrespectful somehow.

Then again, what did she care about that? It was obvious Lydia had been right. Her marriage had been over a long time before Melissa had come into her life. She wondered how many others had been before her. The mayor, for one. But could there have been others...?

It just went to show she'd done the right thing when she'd plunged that knife into Lydia's chest. The woman was a conniving, deceitful cheat. She deserved everything that had been done to her.

The good news was, Grayson Thorpe wasn't at the bitch cop's place every night. Melissa had studied the house long enough to establish a kind of pattern. Two nights together, the third one apart. The next night together and then the next one apart. They spent the weekends together unless the bitch cop had to work. Then Grayson went back to his house.

Tonight was a night they usually spent apart. Melissa was counting on it. She didn't need any witnesses for what she had in mind for the bitch cop. A sneer curled up her top lip. Anticipation flooded her veins. She fingered the handle of the six-inch knife that rested in her lap. It was the same knife she'd used on Lydia, taken from Melissa's house and returned to its scabbard after the murder. Lucky she'd had the foresight to hide it before the cops came with their search warrant. Now it was going to be used again on the very woman who thought she had Melissa bested.

Like hell.

There was a kind of poetic justice in that.

Chapter Twenty

The day dragged on forever. Charlotte knew it was because she kept hoping to get a call from Grayson, apologizing for forgetting their anniversary and agreeing to cancel poker night with the boys so he could spend the night celebrating with her. But when five o'clock rolled round and she hadn't heard from him again, she resigned herself to spending the night alone.

Though Charlotte had taken pains to keep things casual between them, it seemed their libidos had other ideas. And it wasn't just hers. Grayson was every bit as eager to spend time with her as she was with him. But that didn't change the fact he'd been through tumultuous times. Death was so final. To have it happen to someone he'd been close with and in such a shocking manner would take some adjusting to, whether he realized that or not.

No, it was best she didn't make a big deal of their one-month anniversary. It seemed trifling compared to everything he'd been through. She'd go home and when she was hungry, pull out a frozen meal, zap it in the microwave and catch up on some of her favorite shows with Raoul. And then she'd have that soaking bath. It sounded like a perfect night in. And in another hour, she could sign off and set her plans for the night in motion.

Great.

Sensing a presence beside her, she looked up and found Wendell a few feet from her desk. Nerves immediately swarmed in her belly. He hadn't spoken to her about wrapping up the Thorpe investigation. She wondered if that was what he intended to speak about now.

"Sir? Is there something you need?"

He perched his tall frame on the edge of her desk and cleared his throat. "I wanted to say congratulations for your work on the Thorpe case. Tony filled me in on the part you played in bringing together the evidence which resulted in murder charges being laid."

She blushed under his warm regard. "Thank you, sir. I was only involved in the periphery. Really, it was Tony who did all the work."

"I'm sure Tony did what Tony does best. He has an enviable success rate. But I wanted to let you know I'm pleased my instincts weren't wrong about you. You're going to make a fine investigator and a valuable member of this team."

Charlotte's embarrassment deepened. "Thank you, sir. I really appreciate that." Inside, she was jumping for joy.

Wendell held up his hand. "Just one thing before you go getting a swelled head. If you ever disobey a direct order again, you'll be out on your ass so quick you won't know what happened. Understand?"

Her mood sobered. Though it nearly killed her, she looked him straight in the eye. "Yes, sir. It won't happen again."

Wendell nodded, satisfied. "Good. Now, get back to work."

She gave him a cheeky salute. They both grinned. Charlotte's disappointment faded. It didn't matter that Grayson hadn't remembered their anniversary. Today was a great day.

Melissa took a sip from her hip flask and let the warmth of the rum slide down her throat. Dusk was fast approaching. The street lights had come on, illuminating the encroaching darkness. She rubbed at the goosebumps on her bare arms. The nights were getting cooler. It was mid-May. Winter was closing in.

She'd dressed with care. A black T-shirt and black jeans. All the better for concealing herself in the shadows. She hadn't quite decided how she was going to get access to Charlotte's unit, but she was sure she'd work something out. She was nothing if not resourceful.

The bitch cop lived on the ground floor of a red brick three-story walk-up. What it lacked in style, it made up for in beach views. The front yard was covered in neatly mowed grass. Best of all, it was unfenced. There were two windows in the bitch cop's apartment that faced out on the street. Right now they were open, but Melissa had noticed that the woman routinely closed the curtains on her return home.

All the better for concealing what was going on inside...

That suited Melissa perfectly. Now all she had to do was wait for her quarry to arrive. She slid her finger along the wicked knife blade and smiled.

Charlotte swung into her driveway and activated the remote for her lock-up garage. She drove in and parked. The roller door closed behind her.

Gathering her handbag and a bottle of wine she'd splurged on at the last minute, she climbed out of the car and went inside. Raoul met her halfway across the kitchen. He meowed his welcome. She set her things on the counter and crouched down to scratch behind his ears.

"Hey, there mister. How was your day? Did you miss me?"

Raoul wrapped himself around her legs and meowed again.

"I'm sorry, Raoul. Grayson's not here. It's his poker night tonight, remember? I'm afraid it's just you and me puss."

She stood and brushed her hands on her pants. Then she crossed the room and closed the curtains against the night. Walking back into the kitchen, she opened a cupboard and brought out Raoul's bag of cat food. After filling his bowl, she uncorked the bottle of wine and poured herself a glass.

She took a sip of the rich dark liquid, savoring the woody taste of it with a soft sigh. This wasn't exactly the way she'd imagined spending the night, but what the heck. There would be other milestones, other anniversaries to celebrate. The way she and Grayson felt about each other, she was sure of it.

Clinging to that thought, she pulled open the freezer door and dug through the contents. She hadn't heard from Grayson again, so she assumed his poker night was still on. She settled on a chicken dish. The picture on the outside of the box looked much more enticing than she knew it would actually look and taste, but what did she expect? Though a TV dinner was a far cry from a fresh home-cooked meal, tonight it would suffice.

Slipping it out of the box, she put the packet into the microwave. Now home, she was hungry. Raoul brushed up against her legs, meowing again.

"Okay, puss. I get it. You want to go outside."

She picked him up and walked down the corridor that led to the front door. Undoing the deadbolt and releasing the security chain, she set him down on the concrete path.

"There you go. Go and do your business and have a look around. Let me know when you're ready to come back inside."

With that, she closed the door, not bothering with the chain or deadbolt. She knew from experience that in ten minutes or so, Raoul would be back at the door, meowing for her to let him in.

The ding of the microwave announced that dinner was ready. She opened the door and withdrew her meal and tipped it out onto a plate. Grabbing her wineglass and some utensils, she switched on the TV and settled down on the couch.

Melissa watched the bitch cop drive into her garage. The roller door lowered behind her. A few minutes later, lights came on in the unit and true to form, the bitch closed the front curtains.

So far, so good...

Melissa waited a few more moments and after checking her surroundings for people and oncoming cars, she carefully slipped the knife into the waistband of her pants and climbed quickly out of her car. Jogging up the paved driveway that led to the bitch cop's unit, Melissa stayed close to the shadows. She waited in silence, concealed from the street by an overgrown bush.

Adrenaline filled her veins. Her heart hammered. She took a moment to breathe deeply, centering herself in the moment. And then she sensed someone looking at her. She froze, trying to work out from which direction it was coming.

Her gaze scanned the quiet dark street. Not a car in sight. Ditto for people. Then she looked down near her feet. A chocolate point Siamese sat a few yards away, watching her with a curious expression on his face. She almost cried out in fright.

With her pulse racing, she made an effort to get herself back under control.

Just a stupid cat... Nothing to be afraid of...

And then she recognized him as the same cat the bitch cop had let out about ten minutes before. A thought came to her. She started to chuckle quietly.

This is too good an opportunity to pass up...

The cat tilted his head to one side as he looked at her, as if trying to work her out. And then he meowed. Acting fast, Melissa lunged at the animal. She caught him around the shoulder. His cry of alarm was silenced when in one quick, smooth motion, she sliced the knife across his throat.

Grayson packed the last of his thermal bags—containing the gourmet meal he'd prepared—into the back of his car. He was thrilled with the results. The oysters Kilpatrick were marinating in their special sauce. A few minutes on Charlotte's grill and they'd be done. The lobster tails looked as good as they had in the recipe book. Even the bombe Alaska had turned out great but he'd have to get it into Charlotte's freezer quickly.

It was half-past six. Even with traffic heavier than usual, Charlotte should be home by now. He thought about phoning her to check, but didn't want to face more questions about his supposed poker night. No, better to leave it. Just surprise her at the door. He couldn't wait.

His heart hammered with anticipation and excitement. She was going to be overwhelmed. He hadn't given her so much as the tiniest hint he'd remembered their anniversary. He just hoped she forgave him the deceit.

He'd already started the ignition when he remembered the two bottles of expensive French champagne he'd left chilling in the fridge. With a sigh, he climbed out of the car and walked back inside to fetch them.

Charlotte finished her TV dinner and set the plate down on the coffee table. She glanced at her watch. She wondered where Raoul was. It had been nearly twenty minutes since she'd let him out. Plenty of time to do his business. Pushing off the couch, she stood and walked down the corridor to the front door. She pulled it open just wide enough for the cat to slip inside.

"Raoul? Puss, puss? Where are you, puss?"

She listened for his meow. He always came when she called. Over the noise of the TV, she heard what sounded like the fluttering of a bird. It sounded like it had flown away fast. Like it had been disturbed. She wondered if Raoul was to blame.

"Here puss. Here puss, puss. Raoul? It's time to come inside. Puss?"

Leaving the door ajar, she returned to her spot on the couch. She was sure he'd return when he was ready.

Melissa watched the bitch cop from the shadows. She carried the dead cat by his tail. Blood dripping everywhere, on the pavement, on her shoes. Not that she cared. Soon she'd be covered in a whole lot more blood than this. That was the problem with using knives. They were so messy.

But they were also so satisfying. The slippery, slurpy sound as the knife sunk deep into flesh and then when it was pulled out again. Every now and then, she'd encounter bone. Her wrist would be jarred from the impact. It had been like that with Lydia.

She'd taken her lover by surprise. A knife attack was the last thing Lydia had expected. She'd come home, thinking she'd sort everything out by talking. Huh. When did talking get anyone anywhere? Talk, talk, talk. That's all Lydia believed in.

Not Melissa. She was more into action.

Lydia had tried to talk her way out of the accusations Melissa had leveled at her: that she was sleeping with the mayor. Lydia should have known Melissa was way beyond listening to anything she might have had to say. She'd had hours to plan her ambush. She'd lain in wait inside Lydia's house, waiting for her to arrive home. She was right on time. Lydia prided herself on being punctual and Melissa had been counting on that.

Melissa had hidden the knife inside her jacket. She'd decided to at least give Lydia a chance to explain. But Lydia wasn't interested in explaining anything. All she wanted to do was deny. To make out it was Melissa with the problem.

"You're over-reacting, seeing things that aren't there... I love you, remember? What you're talking about is nonsense! Me? Having another affair? And with a man? Ha! That's nonsense! I think you've been working too hard, Mel. All that heat and dust has addled your brain..."

It went on and on. Eventually Melissa knew she had no choice. Lydia had to die. Just like the bitch cop.

Of course, Melissa wasn't half as angry with the detective, but she had to die, nevertheless. Without her nosy interference, Melissa might very well have gotten away with murder. After all, it wouldn't be the first time...

Remembering back to the fire everyone thought had claimed her parents' lives, Melissa smiled. Of course, the cops never knew she'd already stabbed them beforehand. She'd taken care to ensure they were wounded only enough that they lost enough blood to lose consciousness. Otherwise there would be no smoke in their lungs.

She'd watched enough crime shows to know that. No smoke in the lungs meant they weren't breathing when the fire started and that wouldn't be good for anyone, most of all their loving daughter who'd narrowly escaped the same tragic death.

But that was a long time ago. No need to dwell on it now. Right now she had another kill in her sights. She heard Charlotte calling out to her stupid cat. The front door opened. Melissa flattened herself back in the shadows. The bitch cop merely called out to the cat again and then walked away, leaving the door ajar.

Melissa looked down at the cat that swung lifelessly from her hand.

What do I do with it?

She wanted the bitch cop to see what she'd done. Feel the pain of loss right before she died... With that thought in mind, Melissa tossed the dead cat toward the bitch cop's front door. The body made a soft thudding sound as it connected with the wooden panel. Melissa smiled with satisfaction and once again flattened herself against the wall so the cop wouldn't see her when she returned to her front door. Now all Melissa had to do was sit back and wait.

Charlotte heard a soft thud against her front door and frowned. She got up off the couch again and went to investigate. The corridor was empty, but the door now stood wide open. Her gaze was drawn to the floor. She screamed at the sight that confronted her.

"No! No! No!" she howled.

Racing forward, she crouched low and collected Raoul's limp body in her arms. Blood dripped onto the tiles from the wound on his neck and stained her clothes. She stared down at her beloved pet in shock.

Before she could comprehend what had happened and who had done such a terrible thing, the open doorway filled with a shadow. Charlotte stared in horror into the cold eyes of Melissa Robinson. The woman stood there, her eyes wild and unfocused. She held an evil-looking knife in her hand.

"Move!" Melissa shouted, gesturing with the knife.

Frozen with fear, it took a few moments for Charlotte to respond. Cradling the body of her cat to her chest, she started walking backwards, her gaze fixed on the madwoman who kicked the door closed behind her and followed Charlotte down the corridor and into the open plan kitchen and living room.

Whimpering with fear and trying desperately to get ahold on the shock and heartbreak that threatened to overwhelm her each time she looked down at the soft bundle of fur in her arms, Charlotte tried to think.

Melissa stood before her, brandishing the knife. She swung it slowly from side to side. She cackled like a crazy woman, her eyes filled with insanity.

"Not so brave now, are you bitch?"

She waved the knife before Charlotte's face. It was all Charlotte could do not to flinch. Blood still dripped from the knife. Charlotte was certain it was Raoul's. She stifled a sob and tried to think past her terror to come up with a plan of escape before the woman in front of her took another life. Hers.

Grayson placed the bottles of champagne on the back seat and once again climbed into his car. Charlotte's beachside unit was only a few miles away. Right now she was probably contemplating what she might have for dinner. Little did she know he was enroute with a feast. He smiled. He couldn't wait to see the surprise on her face.

He pulled up at a set of lights. While waiting for them to change, he looked across at his local mall.

Some flowers would be nice...

Flicking on his indicator, he switched lanes. As soon as the light changed, he joined the traffic turning into the entry for the mall. Five minutes. Ten at the most. That's all it would take to duck inside and select a nice bouquet of flowers. Roses. Or maybe a bunch of fragrant oriental lilies. He'd see what they had.

Chapter Twenty One

Charlotte's chest was tight with a fear so paralyzing it was all she could do to speak. She was alone with a vicious killer. No one knew what was happening. Grayson was at his poker night. Her brothers and sisters had no reason to stop by, especially on a week night. She had no one but herself to rely on to get her out of there with her life intact.

I need to get to my phone... I need to call 000...

But her phone was all the way over on the coffee table. A lifetime away from where she stood, facing off with Melissa in the kitchen.

I need to get her talking, distract her. If I can't reach my phone, can I make a run for it? She closed the door behind her, but it's not locked. If I can move fast enough, I might make it outside before she has a chance to react... But first, a distraction...

"Why are you here, Melissa? You must know you won't get away with this."

The woman merely smirked. "Says who? I have in the past."

Charlotte frowned. "What are you talking about?"

The woman went on to tell Charlotte about the death of her parents in a fire.

"It was ruled an accident. Electrical fault. Of course, only I knew the truth."

Charlotte stared at her. "Why? Why would you kill your parents?"

Melissa's expression hardened. "They refused to accept me for who I was. They took me to doctors, to shrinks, even to our local pastor. They were convinced there was something wrong with me and that they could fix whatever it was."

"You mean, the fact you're a lesbian?"

"Yes! They couldn't even say the word! They refused to allow me to spend time with my girlfriend. They wouldn't even let her come to our house! It was like she had a disease, something contagious. They blamed her for making me believe I liked girls instead of boys. It was sick."

"They were reacting out of fear. They were at a loss as to what to do. It's not uncommon," Charlotte replied.

"Bullshit. They did it to destroy my life! They couldn't bear to see me happy! They had to destroy what little contentment I had! They hated my girlfriend and they hated me!"

Melissa's breaths were coming fast; her eyes were wild. She twisted the knife back and forth. Light glinted off its sharp edge. Charlotte pulled Raoul's body in closer and tried to hold back a whimper. She knew she had to stop thinking about Raoul and focus on making her escape. That was her only hope. There would be plenty of time to mourn the loss of her beautiful baby later, after the woman who'd so cruelly murdered him was once again behind bars.

"Why me, Melissa? What did I ever do to you? And why my cat?"

The woman smiled and gave a half-shrug. "Because I could, that's why. I'm sick and tired of people making my decisions, telling me what I can and can't do. From now on, I'm in charge. I'll do whatever I feel like. Tonight I felt like killing your cat." She gave Charlotte a smile that was almost angelic. "But don't worry. You won't have long to feel bad about it. You're next. You must know that."

Melissa started advancing toward her, evil in her eyes. Charlotte guessed this was exactly how Lydia had felt right before she'd been stabbed thirty-seven times. Despite the promise of death Melissa had just delivered, Charlotte sent up a silent, frantic prayer that she'd be spared. She started to move slowly backward, toward the living room, inching toward her phone. She visualized it on the coffee table where she'd left it.

She risked a glance over her shoulder. Sure enough, the phone was there. Only a few yards away, but well out of reaching distance.

So close, yet so far away...

She took a few more steps in that direction, all the while keeping her gaze fixed on Melissa. Finally she was close enough that it was possible for her to stretch out her arm and reach it. Coming to a decision, she made a lunge for it...

Her fingers skimmed over the glass screen. She clenched them closed, but only succeeded in pushing the phone further away. It fell to the floor and landed on the rug.

Melissa's eyes gleamed with malice as she continued to advance. She waved the knife back and forth, licking her lips. Charlotte stared in terror, praying it would be over quickly as she waited to die.

Grayson arrived at Charlotte's unit and pulled up to the curb outside. He couldn't see her car in the street. Then again, she usually parked in her garage. He switched off the ignition and climbed out. For a moment, he contemplated bringing all the food bags in together, but then decided to savor the moment of her surprise when she first caught sight of him.

Instead, he took out the flowers and champagne. He'd come back for the rest afterwards.

Walking up the paved driveway, he noted the lights inside her unit. His heart skipped a beat.

Great. She's home...

As he approached the front door, he saw what looked like blood spatter all over the wooden panel. He frowned with confusion.

Strange.

He paused and looked around him. The neighborhood was still and quiet. Not even the sound of a passing car disturbed the silence. He looked down at the weird stains again and then bent down to wipe at them with his finger. It came away wet. He brought his finger up to his nose.

Definitely blood... Very strange...

His body went on alert. With his heart in his throat, he put his ear to the door to listen. He could hear voices. Female. More than one.

Is it the TV? Is that what I hear?

Then he heard Charlotte cry out a name that made his blood run cold. Melissa. With shaking hands, he fumbled for his phone and dialed 000. In a low voice, he put in an urgent request for the police.

"A home invasion. Escaped criminal... Dangerous... Please, hurry..."

He gave the operator Charlotte's address and then ended the call with another plea for them to get there as fast as they could. Setting the wine and flowers down on the ground, his feverish mind set about formulating a plan to save the woman he loved.

Charlotte stared at Melissa, not daring to look away from the madwoman. The knife continued to wave threateningly toward her face. There was no point in making another attempt to grab her phone. Melissa had picked it up and thrown it as hard and far as she could. It had smashed all over the marble tiles in the corridor that led to the front door.

Charlotte needed to stay calm so she could think. She needed to come up with an escape plan. Something that didn't involve her phone. She wished Grayson was there. She didn't want to die, let alone die alone.

On the other hand she was glad his poker night had meant he wasn't with her. Imagine the two of them at the mercy of this crazy woman. She didn't wish the utter fear and terror that consumed her on anyone, most especially the man she'd fallen in love with.

Think, Charlotte! Stop feeling scared and think! Don't let her do this! At the very least, put up a fight! Like Lydia.

Poor Lydia... She'd put up a fight all right. The numerous defensive wounds on her fingers and hands had been proof of that. In the end, it hadn't mattered. She'd still ended up dead.

No! I'm not going to die like Lydia... I'm going to find a way...

She thought longingly of her service revolver that was locked up in the safe at work. Police protocol demanded that be done for firearms for any off-duty cop. It was for the safety of everyone, including the cops. But she sure could have done with it now. At the very least, it would have acted as a deterrent.

Once again, Melissa advanced upon her and once again Charlotte took a few steps back. She kept her gaze fixed on the wicked blade. At the same time, she instinctively tightened her hold on Raoul.

I need to have both hands free... I need to set him down...

Putting the thought into action, she eased herself over to the couch and gently lay Raoul down. Melissa merely chuckled.

"Oh, the poor kitty! Even now, with his throat slashed, you still care... How touching..."

Charlotte decided to try and appeal to Melissa's softer side, if she had one. "Please, Melissa. It doesn't have to be this way. You've only been charged with murder. That doesn't mean the prosecutor will secure a conviction. There's every chance you'll walk free," she lied.

"You got bail, didn't you?" she continued. "The court wouldn't have done that if they were confident in the strength of the police case. But if you kill me, it's all over. You might have gotten away with the murder of your parents, but there's no way you'll get away with four. Besides, I'm a cop. Cops look after their own. There isn't a cop in all of Sydney who won't be hunting you down."

She paused to gauge Melissa's reaction. The woman appeared to be listening. Charlotte continued. "Do you really want to live like that? Always looking over your shoulder? Knowing that at any time someone's going to find you and when they do, they're going to do everything in their power to see you go down? You'll get life. Imagine that. Never roaming free in the world again?"

"You're lying," Melissa spat. "I'm not stupid. Even if I let you go, there's no way I won't do time."

"No! I'm not lying! I promise, you let me go, I won't say a word to anyone. There's only you and me here. Nobody else has to know."

Melissa's face turned puce with anger. "Shut the hell up! I know you're lying bitch! As if I'm going to fall for stinking promises from a dirty cop. I'm done with talking. Time to finish this."

Grayson heard the faint sound of sirens in the distance and nearly collapsed with relief. Even so, he was beyond anxious about what was going on behind the closed door. He couldn't just stand there and do nothing, not while Charlotte's life was at risk.

He stepped forward and tried the doorknob. It turned easily under his hand. His belly somersaulted with both relief and terror. The only time Charlotte left the door unlocked was when she was waiting for Raoul to come back in. So far, Grayson had seen no sign of the cat.

With his heart in his throat, he crept forward on silent footsteps. There were more drops of blood on the tiles, along with pieces of a smashed phone. The voices got louder. He eased his way down the corridor, flattening himself against one wall. Then he spied Melissa and Charlotte and his gut nosedived with fear.

They were in the living room, not far from the couch. Melissa had her back to him and was slowly advancing toward Charlotte, who kept moving backwards, step by step. Charlotte looked terrified. Grayson understood why when he noticed the vicious-looking knife in Melissa's hand.

He knew the instant Charlotte became aware of him. The slightest widening of her eyes. The most infinitesimal movement, but he was watching her so closely, he noticed. He breathed a silent sigh of relief that she was too well trained to give anything away, including the fact he was there.

The sirens grew louder. Melissa's agitation increased. "Fuck you! You called the police!" the woman screamed.

Charlotte shook her head. "No! I swear. How could I? You've been with me the whole time. Besides, you broke my phone, remember?"

The woman seemed to consider Charlotte's explanation and then dismissed it with another ugly curse. "You fucking bitch! You're lying!"

Charlotte looked desperate. "No! Please!"

Melissa lunged toward her, slicing and slashing with the knife. Charlotte screamed and reached for her face. At the sight of the blood pouring out between her fingers, Grayson was frozen with terror. Seconds later, he reacted.

A primal growl of fury erupted from his chest. He rushed toward Melissa and threw the full force of his weight against her. Taken by surprise, she barely had time to twist away before they crashed to the floor. Grayson landed hard on top of her. The madwoman struggled in earnest. The knife slashed the air around his face. If he didn't get hold of it, he was as good as dead.

On a burst of adrenaline, he seized her wrist. It took all of his strength to force the deadly blade away from him. Slowly, he forced her hand toward the floor. He kept squeezing. She howled in pain and glared at him from eyes that had lost their grip on the world.

Slowly, slowly he forced her arm backwards, all the time increasing the pressure on her wrist. When her hand was mere inches from the floor, Grayson called on an extra surge of strength and smashed her hand against the tiles. Melissa screamed again along with the sound of breaking bones and it was an awful sound, but she finally released her hold on the knife.

Charlotte was quick to kick it out of the way, well clear of Melissa's reach. Grayson was still on top of her, breathing hard, holding her down, when the police arrived.

As realization set in that the nightmare was over, Charlotte's legs buckled. She sank inelegantly to the floor with hardly a murmur. Grayson called out her name, scrambling over to her side.

"Charlotte? Are you all right?"

Blood still seeped out of the wound on her face, but she knew enough about knife injuries to know hers wasn't fatal. Still, she'd lost a lot of blood and the wound would need to be stitched. She was just so relieved it was over and that Grayson had arrived in time.

"Thank you, Grayson. You saved me," she breathed.

"Yes. No. We saved each other," he said. Bending over her, he pushed the hair matted with blood back off her forehead. "I can't believe how close I came to losing you. Oh God. I was so scared."

Charlotte managed a weak smile. "Me too."

A paramedic came over to see to her injuries. It wasn't until she was almost beside her that Charlotte realized it was her sister. Molly was as white as a sheet, but after a few deep breaths, she appeared to call on her inner professionalism and got on with her job.

"Charlotte! Oh my God! I can't believe you were involved in a home invasion," her triplet said.

Charlotte grimaced. "I'm sorry you were on call, Molly. I wish you'd been spared this."

"Nonsense. This is all part of my job. I'm just a little taken aback to discover the patient is my sister."

Grayson looked back and forth between the two women, interest clear on his face. "Wait a minute. You're sisters?"

Charlotte grimaced. She wished she had a bit more time before introducing Grayson to her family, but it seemed that had been taken out of her hands.

"Grayson, this is my sister, Molly. Molly, this is Grayson. My..."

"Boyfriend," Grayson quickly supplied.

Molly's face was immediately suffused with surprise, quickly followed by speculation.

"Boyfriend, huh?" Her gaze cut back to Charlotte. "Seems we have some catching up to do."

Charlotte blushed at Molly's faintly accusatory tone. Her sister had every right to be peeved. If their situation were reversed, Charlotte would feel the same way. Opting to leave further discussion about Grayson for another time, Molly quietly and efficiently set about checking Charlotte over, paying particular attention to the knife wound. Molly came to the same conclusion as Charlotte.

"That's a nasty cut. You going to need stitches. And a tetanus shot. God knows where that knife's been. We're taking you to the hospital."

Out of habit, Charlotte opened her mouth to protest. She hated being bossed around, even by her little sister. Okay, so Charlotte was only a couple of minutes older, but still...

"Uh, uh. No arguments," Molly said in a no-nonsense tone.

In short order, Charlotte was placed on a stretcher. She barely had time to say goodbye to Grayson before Molly and her partner were wheeling her outside.

"I'll meet you at the hospital," Grayson shouted as she disappeared from view.

Slumping against the pillows, Charlotte breathed a sigh of relief that the nightmare was over.

Chapter Twenty Two

Grayson watched the doors of the ambulance close on the woman he loved and wished he could go with her. Unfortunately, the police hadn't finished questioning him. Detective Sabattini had been one of the first officers on the scene. They'd handcuffed Melissa and had taken her away in the back of an ambulance, followed closely by a police vehicle. Sabattini and another cop had remained behind.

"Are you okay?" Sabattini asked. There seemed genuine concern in his eyes.

Grayson nodded. He had a few minor cuts on his hands from where he'd struggled with the knife, but was otherwise unharmed.

"Yeah, I'm fine."

"I'd like to ask you some questions."

Grayson nodded. "Of course."

Sabattini pulled out a notebook and pen. "Start from the beginning."

With a sigh, Grayson recounted what he knew. The first moment when he realized Lydia's killer was inside with Charlotte came back to him with a vengeance, making him weak with delayed reaction.

Something in his face must have alerted Sabattini. The detective's gaze filled with concern. "Are you sure you're okay?"

Grayson grimaced and then drew in a deep breath. "Yeah. It's just that... It's hard, you know. I... I thought I was going to lose her."

His voice cracked on a surge of emotion. He saw the surprise in the detective's eyes. Obviously Charlotte hadn't said anything to her partner about their relationship. Grayson understood her need to be discrete. He'd felt the same way. But now, after they'd both had such a close brush with death, he didn't care who knew. Life was short. Way too short to worry about the rights and wrongs of things, or to care about what others thought.

The detective continued to regard him with surprise. "You and Barrington... You have something going?"

Grayson held the man's gaze. "Yes. I'm in love with her."

Sabattini's thick eyebrows rose a notch. He shook his head. His expression was filled with amusement and tinged with disbelief.

"Well, I never..."

"We did nothing untoward," Grayson said hurriedly. "It didn't start until after you'd cleared me of any suspicion."

Sabattini shot him a dry look. "Except if you count the time you spent together the night your wife died."

Grayson flushed. "Can we get back to your questions about what happened here? I really want to get to the hospital."

"Yes, of course," Sabattini replied, all business.

Sabattini asked more questions and Grayson did his best to answer them. All the time he was conscious that Charlotte had been taken to the hospital. He wanted to be with her, to hold her hand, offer her comfort, reassure himself once again that she was all right. Finally the detective indicated they were done.

Grayson sighed with relief and turned away, eager to leave. His gaze drifted to the couch where a police photographer was busy taking pictures. Raoul's lifeless body still lay there. Grayson's heart clenched with pain. He could only imagine the devastation Charlotte felt.

Waiting until the officer had finished and moved away, Grayson wrapped Raoul gently in a towel and carried him into the laundry. He didn't want Charlotte to see the poor cat lying there the moment she returned from the hospital. Grayson would talk to her and see what she wanted to do with him. There were places where people could take their pets to be cremated. He'd heard good things about them. Ultimately, it would be Charlotte's decision.

It was more than an hour later that Grayson pulled into the hospital carpark. He walked into the emergency department and asked about Charlotte at the triage station. He was directed to a room down the hall. Opening the door, he stepped quietly inside. She turned and saw him and smiled.

The tenderness in her eyes choked him up inside. All of a sudden, he was reminded again of how close he'd come to losing her.

"Hey," he whispered, "how are you feeling?"

She grimaced and touched the white bandage on the side of her face. "Like I've been carved up with a knife."

"Where's Molly?" he asked.

"She had to leave. She's still at work." Charlotte grimaced. "Don't worry. By now every Barrington will have been notified I'm here. We're going to be bombarded any moment." She paused and then added, "But I'm so glad you're here."

Grayson walked closer, suddenly shy. The strength of his feelings overwhelmed him and he wasn't sure how she felt. Neither of them had spoken the "L" word.

What if it's too soon? What if she doesn't feel the same way?

His chest went tight with panic and he silently castigated himself. It didn't matter if she didn't feel the same way. He was sure she'd get there one day and he was prepared to wait for however long it took.

He stopped beside her bed and reached out to cup her good cheek. "You can't imagine how glad I am to see you," he whispered. "When I saw that woman holding that knife... Oh God. I thought I was going to lose you."

Charlotte placed her hand over his. "You're not going to get rid of me that easily."

Though she chuckled, he noticed the humor didn't reach her eyes. "It's okay, Charlotte. You don't have to be brave anymore. It's over."

It was as if his words had released the dam that had been holding back her emotions. Her eyes flooded with tears. She turned toward him muttering about Raoul and how afraid she'd been. At the same time, he stepped close and pulled her into his arms.

She cried for so long, his shirt was soaked through by the time she'd finished. All the time, he stroked his hand up and down her back and whispered mindless words of comfort. At last, her sobs lessened. She slowly pulled away and looked up at him with eyes that were swollen and red.

"I'm sorry. I didn't mean to do that. It's just that... Oh God, Grayson... She killed Raoul! And she wanted to kill me! I've never been so scared in my life."

"Me neither," he choked. Reaching up, he placed his hands on either side of her face, taking extra care with her injured side. Slowly, he brought his mouth down to hers. His kiss was soft and gentle and filled with all the love he felt inside. And then he decided to throw caution to the wind and tell her.

"I love you."

Her eyes went wide with surprise and delight. "Really? You love me? Are you sure?"

He laughed. "Yes, I'm sure! I know it's too soon, but I can't help the way I feel. I'm just hoping you feel the same."

Her smile widened. "Of course I do."

Now it was Grayson's turn to be flooded with surprise and delight. "You do?"

She nodded. "Yes, I do. And you're right. Everything's happened so fast. It's way too soon to feel like this. But I do. I love you and I'm not going to apologize for that."

He kissed her again, this time lingering on her lips. "There's nothing to apologize for," he whispered. "Nothing at all."

Their lips met in another tender kiss. Mouths opened, tongues entwined. The sound of someone loudly clearing their throat was the only thing that forced them apart.

Grayson looked across and saw the room filling with people. They all bore enough resemblance to Charlotte that he could tell they were related. An older woman with stylish dark hair and twinkling green eyes stood at the front of the pack.

"So, you must be Grayson. Molly's told us all about you. I'm Evelyn. Charlotte's mother. It's so very nice to meet you."

THE END

Get a free book when you sign up for Chris Taylor's newsletter at: http://www.christaylorauthor.com.au

If you enjoyed Charlotte and Grayson's story, don't forget to leave a review at your favorite digital retailer. Every review is greatly appreciated and really helps with visibility so that other readers can find and enjoy my books.

Broken Bonds is the next book in the Barrington Family Series. Keep reading below for a sneak peek at **Broken Bonds**:

CHAPTER ONE

Cassie Webster's stomach churned with dread. Tension kept her shoulders taut. She climbed out of her car and headed up the paved path that led inside the Broken Police Station. In all of her twenty-four years living and growing up in Broken, she'd never had cause to visit the police station and she was eternally grateful for that. But now her run of luck had come to an end.

The squat, red brick building circa 1970s, with its chocolate brown tiled roof and wooden framed windows perched on a generous block of land it. A decent sized police station for a town with less than ten thousand people. She glimpsed a couple of patrol cars parked alongside the building. A uniformed officer climbed out of one of them and scratched idly at his hair.

A fresh wave of nerves and dread washed over her. There was something intimidating about being this close to a police station. She was an upright and law abiding citizen, but that didn't lessen the abject fear that threatened to overwhelm her.

Walk inside... That's all I have to do... One foot in front of the other...

The closer she drew to the front door, the more unreasonable her fear grew. If it weren't so imperative she speak to an officer, she'd turn tail and run. Her belly somersaulted on a rush of nausea. She gulped and glued her lips closed, praying she'd hold onto the contents of her stomach

I can do this... For Oscar I can do this...

Thinking of her brother spurred her on. She opened the glass door and went quickly up to the front desk. A young uniformed constable greeted her with a friendly smile.

"Hi. What can I do for you?"

"I-I need to speak to someone about a missing person. My brother."

"I see. Can I have your name?"

"It's Cassie. Cassandra Webster."

The constable jotted the name down on a notepad in front of her and then looked back up at Cassie. "Take a seat and I'll have one of the officers attend you."

"Thank you," Cassie managed, her voice a hoarse whisper.

Turning away, she took a seat on one of the hard plastic chairs that were lined up in a row on the back wall. Posters decrying drink and drug driving, domestic violence and an upbeat poster for a youth club run by the police filled a noticeboard that hung on the wall beside the counter. The place smelled of antiseptic, like it had been recently cleaned. The astringent odor burned Cassie's nostrils.

With her hands clutched tightly around her handbag, she dragged in a ragged breath and did her best to get her pulse rate back under control.

I did it... I'm here... Inside the police station... Now for the next challenge...

A side door she hadn't previously noticed came open and the space was filled with the tall and imposing figure of a man. He wore a suit and tie. This early in the morning, it was still crisply knotted. His shirt was a blinding white. He looked about her age, maybe a little older, with short dark hair, blue eyes and olive skin that

spoke to Mediterranean heritage. He walked toward her and smiled.

"Cassandra Webster? I'm Detective Trace Barrington."

She stood on trembling legs. He extended his arm in her direction. Her hand was swallowed up by his. His handshake was firm, his skin warm. She sensed a strength in him that gave her confidence. She blew out a shaky breath and squared her shoulders.

"Please, call me Cassie."

He acknowledged her comment with a slight inclination of his head and then chuckled. "Relax. You look like you're facing your executioner. I won't bite. I promise."

She made a strangled sound in the back of her throat in response. It was all she could manage. He shot her another curious glance and then turned and headed back the way he'd come. He held the door open for her.

"After you."

She murmured her thanks, pleased that her inward terror hadn't displaced her manners. She found herself standing in a carpeted corridor with closed doors on either side running the length of it.

"Just in here," the detective said.

He moved to open the door nearest to them and once again indicated for her to precede him. The room was small and claustrophobic. Not a single window in sight. A pale gray Formica table and two plastic chairs were the only furniture. A camera stood perched high on a bracket fixed to one wall.

"Take a seat," the detective offered.

Holding onto her courage, Cassie reached for the one nearest. The large detective took the seat opposite. He dropped a notepad and pen on the table and then folded his hands in front of him. He had long fingers. His nails were clean and cut short.

"So. You're here to file a missing person's report. Is that correct?"

She blinked and forced herself to concentrate on her reason for being there. "Yes." Her voice was barely above a whisper. She cleared her throat and tried again. "Yes. My brother. Oscar. Oscar Webster."

The detective wrote the name on the blank page and then looked back up at Cassie. "How old is he?"

"F-fourteen, but he looks younger. He's small for his age and... He has autism."

"Non-verbal?"

Cassie instinctively gave a brisk shake of her head. "No. He communicates well and he's exceptionally bright, but he... He has a rather simplistic view of the world. He sees the best in people. He's very trusting."

The detective made some more notes. "Has he disappeared like this before?"

Cassie bit her lip. "Yes, but he's never been gone this long."

"How long is he usually gone for?"

"I don't know. A few hours. Never all night."

"How often does he disappear?"

"Every now and then. When things get too much for him. When he needs to get away to think and clear the noise from his head. Maybe once every few months. Lately it's been more often than that."

"So what changed?"

"I don't know," she said honestly. "He and my stepfather haven't been getting along so well lately. They've always butted heads, but it seems the older Oscar gets the more he irritates Malcolm. I don't really blame Malcolm. Oscar can be a handful. But it annoys me that Malcolm loses his temper. I mean, he's the adult. And Oscar isn't exactly a normal teenager. He deserves to be cut some slack."

"What's Malcolm's last name?"

"Russell. Malcolm Russell."

"How long has he been with your mom?"

"They've been married five years."

"Do you think your stepfather might have something to do with Oscar's disappearance?"

Cassie stared down at the worn table. She hated having to air their dirty laundry in front of anyone, but if she wanted them to look for Oscar, she had no choice.

"Oscar and my stepfather got into an argument last night. Something about Oscar not doing his chores. I only caught the tail end of the dispute, but Malcolm was furious."

"Do you think that's why your brother ran away?"

Cassie pulsed with irritation. "I didn't say he'd run away. I told you he was missing. We don't know whether he ran away or... If something terrible happened to him."

The detective eyed her steadily. "Is that what you think? That something terrible might have happened to him?"

Her frustration boiled over. "I don't know!" she cried. "That's why I'm here! I need you to find him!"

The detective continued to regard her calmly. He made a few more notes and then glanced up at her again. "Tell me about your father. Is he still in your lives?"

Cassie stared stoically at her hands which were knotted in her lap. "We haven't seen our father for years. Not since Oscar was a baby. He... He went to jail a long time ago. We never saw him again."

"Do you know where he is?"

"No."

The detective scrawled on the paper. "What about your mother? Why isn't she here with you?"

Cassie tried not to squirm, but deep-seated embarrassment about Marie Russell made it difficult. She dragged in a deep breath and stared at the detective defiantly.

"My mother was too upset to come with me. She was happy for me to be the one to report Oscar missing."

The detective frowned but remained silent. Cassie saw the curiosity in his eyes, but refused to elaborate.

"Have you called your brother's friends? People he hangs out with?"

"Of course I have. I've called everyone I can think of. The thing is, he only has one close friend. He told me he hasn't seen Oscar since they were at school on Friday afternoon."

"They didn't see each other over the weekend?"

Cassie shook her head. "Apparently not."

"What's this friend's name?"

"Joe. Joseph Lahood."

"Any relation to the Lahood's who own the café on Main Street?"

"Yes. He's their son."

"What about a girlfriend?"

"Oscar doesn't have a girlfriend."

Once again, the detective made notes. Cassie clung to her patience.

This is taking so long! My brother is out there somewhere, cold, hungry, scared... He might even be hurt...

"Please. Are we nearly done? My brother's out there. We need to find him."

"Does your brother have a phone?"

"Yes. And before you ask, I've called him over and over through the night. It goes straight to voicemail."

"Tell me more about your stepfather? What does he do for a living?"

"Malcolm's a park ranger. Works for National Parks." She paused and then added, "I haven't seen him since last night, either."

At the detective's raised eyebrow, she hurried to explain. "That's not unusual. He tends to take off for a few days after one of his outbursts."

"So you're not reporting him missing?"

She flushed with embarrassment. "No. He...um... Like I said, this isn't out of character for him. I'm sure he's just gone somewhere to cool off."

"When did you last see him?"

Cassie closed her eyes and willed away another wave of embarrassment. God, she hated having to do this... But she had no choice. If she wanted the police to help find Oscar, she had to answer their questions.

"I last saw Malcolm dragging Oscar by the ear up to the back shed. I'd just returned home. I'd stayed back late at work to catch up on some paperwork and prepare for this week's lessons. As I said, I only caught the tail end of the argument."

"What did you hear?"

"I heard Malcolm yelling at Oscar for not doing his chores and threatening to teach him a lesson."

"What do you think Malcolm meant by that?" the detective asked.

Cassie drew in a ragged breath and let it out on a weary sigh. "I thought he was going to discipline him," she said quietly.

"In a physical way?"

She shrugged. "Sometimes."

The detective's gaze remained on hers. "Has he ever hit Oscar before?"

"Occasionally. When he's had too much to drink. Or when he's stressed or had a bad day at work. He's not like that most of the time and like I said, Oscar can test the patience of a saint." She tried for a smile, but it fell flat.

"Did you follow them up to the shed?"

She hung her head as shame overwhelmed her. "No."

"How long were they up there?"

"I don't know. Maybe ten minutes. I heard Malcolm take off in his truck a little while later and that's when I went up to the shed. I wanted to comfort Oscar and make sure he was all right. He's usually upset after a run-in with Malcolm."

She drew in another ragged breath. "But he wasn't there. I looked around for a bit and called out to him, but he didn't answer. I thought maybe he'd gone off somewhere to be alone. But that was twelve hours ago. He's never stayed away so long and never on his own. I've called everyone I can think of. No one's seen him. Where can he be?"

Her voice cracked with emotion. To her horror, her eyes welled up with tears. She swiped at them impatiently with the back of her hand.

The detective regarded her compassionately. "Is there a special place your brother might go when he wants to be alone?"

"Not really. He likes the bush. The National Park backs onto our house. But he's afraid of the dark. I don't think he'd go there at night."

"What time was the altercation with your stepfather?"

"About eight last night."

"What was your brother wearing last night?"

Cassie frowned in thought. "A pair of blue jeans and a long-sleeved black T-shirt. Nike cross trainers. Oh, and a red jacket."

The detective wrote the information down. "Do you have a recent picture of him?"

"Yes." Cassie opened her handbag and reached for her phone. She scrolled through her photos until she found one of Oscar. "This was taken a couple of weeks ago, at my birthday. I can airdrop it to you, if you like."

The detective reached into his pocket and pulled out his phone. A few moments later, the photo appeared on his screen.

Trace Barrington gazed at the picture of the kid who filled his screen. Oscar Webster looked a lot like his older sister. Dark auburn hair, pale skin, green eyes, freckles. A wide smile filled the boy's innocent face as he clowned it up for the camera.

Trace set his phone aside and focused again on the woman who sat across from him. She appeared genuine in her distress for her missing brother, but something didn't seem quite right. What was with the mother? Too upset to report her son missing? Too upset to turn to the people who might be able to help find him? His cop instincts told him something was awry.

He thought of Oscar. Several possibilities ran through this head: The kid had run away. It happened all the time. Maybe not so often in Broken where the total population was less than ten thousand people, but still... It happened. Second possibility: The prince of a stepfather might have taken him with him. After all, he hadn't been seen by the family since last night either.

"Have you spoken to your stepfather? Asked him about Oscar?"

Cassie grimaced. "No. I tried to but his phone's either switched off or flat. The calls go straight to voicemail. I've left messages, but I haven't heard from him."

"Have you called any of Malcolm's friends? His work colleagues?"

"I don't have any numbers for his work colleagues. I called his office. They haven't heard from him."

Trace noted Cassie's responses on the paper in front of him. There was a third possibility and one he didn't particularly want to consider, but had no choice. It was possible the boy could have been kidnapped. Not from the back shed, but from wherever he'd gone after the argument with his stepfather. The boy was small for his age, sweet, innocent-looking. The sister had mentioned how trusting he was.

Despite the quaintness of Broken, it wasn't without its vices. There were two registered sex offenders living inside a five mile radius of the town. Not as many as some, but more than Trace was comfortable with. There was always the possibility one of them had come across Oscar and taken him. The thought weighed heavy in his gut.

Still, there was no point in getting ahead of himself, or worrying the family unnecessarily. He looked at Cassie. "Thank you for coming in. You did the right thing. I'll speak to my superior and get onto this right away. What's the best way to contact you?"

She provided him with an email address and a phone number. "I'm a teacher at the local high school, so it's a bit tricky to get hold of me during the hours of nine and three. I'm on my way there now." She glanced at her watch and frowned. "In fact, if I don't hurry, I'm going to be late."

Her eyes met his. They were filled with storm clouds. "I'm just so worried about him. I mean, please God he walks into our living room any moment, but what if he doesn't?" Her gaze became haunted, her tone beseeching. "What if he doesn't?"

CHAPTER TWO

Cassie climbed into her car and started the ignition. Though dread still formed a hard, cold lump in the pit of her stomach, she was relieved she'd gone to the police. There was something about the tall detective that instilled confidence. She could tell he'd taken her concerns seriously. She just hoped he'd find her brother.

Please, God. Bring him home...

Looking over her shoulder, she checked for oncoming traffic and then pulled out onto the street. She headed toward the high school. She made the journey by memory. Her mind was full of Oscar and what more she could do to find him. The detective had quizzed her about Oscar's favorite haunts and it shamed her to admit she really didn't know. He'd always been partial to spending time roaming the trails in the National Park that bordered the rear of their property, but that was only during daylight hours. She had no idea where he went after dark.

On those occasions when he'd taken off after a disagreement with their stepfather, he hadn't ventured far. Mostly they found him at his best friend's house. Joe Lahood only lived down the road. But she'd already checked with Joe. He hadn't seen Oscar at all last night. In fact, he hadn't seen him since school.

As she turned into the staff carpark, she realized she was going to be late for roll call. There was nothing to be done about that now. As she made her way into the school building, she made a plan to find Joe in the first break and ask him again if he'd heard from Oscar. Perhaps her brother had texted his friend and Joe hadn't yet informed her. Or maybe Joe had come up with a better idea than she did about where Oscar might be. It was worth asking the question again.

She could also talk to his teachers. Maybe one of them might have some insights into where Oscar might have gone. As embarrassing as it would be for her to admit to them she'd been out of touch with her younger brother for the last little while, she'd set her pride aside for Oscar's sake. She just hoped someone could help her find him.

After seeing Cassie Webster out, Trace picked up his coffee mug and headed for the tearoom. He'd just finished filling it with black coffee when his brother, Zac, walked in.

"Morning. How's it going?" Zac asked and reached for a mug.

"Not bad. You?"

Zac shrugged. "You know. The usual."

Two years younger than Trace, Zac was a junior detective who'd recently relocated from a position with the DEA on the central coast to Broken. The sleepy rural town was far removed from the stress and adrenaline of working in a busy metropolitan station. While Zac claimed to love small-town policing and Trace well understood that, he suspected Zac's return to their hometown had more to do with a certain woman who'd broken his heart then any real desire to spend his life dealing largely with DUIs and break and enters in Broken.

Zac and Emily Wilson had been high school sweethearts. As so many young romances did, theirs had ended in tears. Trace didn't know all the details, but ever since the breakup, Zac had been withdrawn and circumspect. Not at all like the cheeky, fun-loving brother Trace had grown up with. He hoped Zac moved on from Emily and found someone else to keep him warm at night. Or go back and make things work with Emily. Either way, Trace didn't care. He just wanted to see his brother happy again.

Of course, it was also possible it was their mother's cooking that had Zac moving back close to home. It was a running joke in the family how Zac still ate dinner at home at least two or three times a week. Not that Trace could blame him for that. His mother was a superb cook.

Still, Zac and his tumultuous love life wasn't Trace's concern right now. A child was missing. Though he didn't want to jump to conclusions, the fact was there were two registered sex offenders living in Broken: Charles Morley and Kevin Turner. Morley had been released from jail only a couple of months earlier. They were supposed to be monitored, but there were ways and means around that if the guy was smart and knew his way around the system.

From what Trace knew about Charles Morley, the man had the brains to do exactly that. Released from Long Bay Correctional Centre in March, the convicted sex offender had once been a high flying human rights lawyer living it up in Sydney's wealthy eastern suburbs before his spectacular fall from grace. As far as Trace was concerned, the man was a germ. Anyone who preyed on vulnerable children deserved to be put down. Some might find his attitude harsh, but that was the way Trace felt and he wouldn't apologize for it. Morley was the first person Trace intended to pay a visit.

He regarded his brother over the rim of his coffee mug. "You busy?"

"Not really. I have to file some paperwork with the court on that Croft case. I've got a few statements I need to finish up. Why? Do you need some help?"

Trace filled him in on Oscar Webster.

Zac nodded thoughtfully. "Fourteen, you say? Not exactly a child. Are they sure he didn't just spend the night with friends?"

"Yes. The sister says she's called everyone she can think of. No one's seen or heard from him. The thing is, he's autistic. That puts this into a slightly more serious category than the average fourteen-year-old."

"So what's the plan?" Zac asked.

"We go out and start asking questions. Charles Morley and Kevin Turner are at the top of my list."

Zac nodded. "Sounds fair. You want me to ride along?"

Trace tossed him a set of car keys that belonged to a police cruiser. "I thought you'd never ask."

Charles Morley lived in an average part of town that was popular with a mix of blue collar workers, retirees and young families. Though his rented house wasn't situated in the immediate vicinity of children, it was close enough to make Trace uncomfortable. Not for the first time, he wished the law allowed him to warn the families who lived nearby.

Zac pulled up outside the small weatherboard house. Though the paint was fresh and the corrugated iron roof was new, the place was surrounded by an air of neglect. Trace and his brother climbed out of the cruiser. The front gate squeaked in protest when Trace pushed it open. Junk mail overflowed the mail box. The lawn was overgrown. However Morley now spent his time, it wasn't spent in his front garden.

They walked up the cracked concrete path and climbed the steps that led to the front door. Trace rapped his knuckles against the wooden panel and then stood back to wait. Half a minute passed. Then another. Trace knocked again.

"Mr Morley? It's the police. We'd like to speak with you."

Once again, they were met with silence. Trace knocked a third time.

"Charles Morley? Is anyone home?"

"Yeah."

"We should take a look around." Zac murmured.

They'd only just cleared the steps when their attention was captured by a man who'd sidled up to the dividing fence. He wore nothing but a singlet and loose jeans that hung from his hips. His white hair was mussed, his cheeks grizzled.

"You lookin' for Charlie?"

Trace walked closer. "Yes. Who are you?"

"I'm his neighbor. Mark Ratcliffe."

"Do you know where he is?" Trace asked.

"He's gone."

Trace frowned. A registered sex offender was obligated to notify the police of their movements. As far as Trace was aware, no one at the station had been contacted by Morley.

"Gone?" he asked.

"Yeah. Up north. His mother's sick. Dyin', I think."

"Whereabouts up north?" Trace asked.

"Queensland. Gympie, I think he said."

"When did he leave?" Zac asked.

"'Bout a month ago. Asked me to keep an eye on the place."

"Did he say when he'd be back?" Trace asked.

"Nope. I guess that depends on how long his old lady lasts." The man began to cough and wheeze. Trace waited him out. At last the man hawked up a globule of phlegm and lobbed it not far from Trace's feet.

Trace grimaced and ignored the man's unspoken insult. "And you haven't seen him in all that time?"

"Nope."

Trace thanked the man for his time and then headed back to the car. Zac followed.

"So, I guess that rules Morley out," Zac murmured.

"That's if Ratcliffe's telling the truth. He didn't seem to be a fan of cops. Let's see if we have better luck with Kevin Turner."

Zac put the cruiser into gear and headed in the opposite direction. According to Turner's file, he'd been employed as a technician by one of the electricity companies prior to his conviction for having sex with a minor. Trace wasn't sure what the man did now, but being on a register for sex offenders would have narrowed his options somewhat. Still, Trace was surprised when they pulled up outside Turner's house.

In stark contrast to the neglect evident at Morley's place, Turner's front yard was neat and tidy. This late in autumn, the trees had changed color and provided a background of rosy reds and orange against the clear blue sky. Flower beds were filled with neatly pruned plants and shrubs in preparation for the oncoming winter. The grass was freshly mown.

As Trace and Zac made their way up the front path, Trace noticed the three-seater loveseat on the front verandah. The area was cool and shaded and provided a clear view of the street. Turner lived only two blocks from Oscar Webster. It hadn't escaped Trace's notice that the boy would have to pass by Turner's house every day on his way to and from school. Unless he caught a ride with his sister, which was always possible. After all, Cassie Webster was a teacher at the high school.

Turner answered Trace's knock after only the first attempt. He was dressed in T-shirt and jeans. Though faded and worn, his clothes were clean. His feet were bare. Through the screen door, he eyed them warily.

"What can I do for you?"

"Are you Kevin Turner?"

"Yes."

"I'm Detective Trace Barrington. This is my off-sider. We want to talk to you about Oscar Webster."

The man frowned. "Who?"

"Oscar Webster. A young teenager. He lives not far from here. He's gone missing."

"Never heard of him."

Trace fished in his pocket and pulled out his phone. He found the photo Cassie had given to him.

"Here," he said, offering the phone to Turner. "See if this refreshes your memory."

Turner squinted at the photo. Slowly, he nodded. "Yeah. I've seen him. Didn't know his name was Oscar."

"How do you know him?" Zac asked.

"I don't know him. I've seen him pass by here every now and then on his way home from school. That's all."

Trace held his gaze steady on the man's face. Turner was clean-shaven. His hair was neatly trimmed. Though he had a slight belly protruding over the waistband of his jeans, he looked reasonably fit for a man in his late forties. No one looking at him would guess he was a sex offender.

That was the problem. These men—and the vast majority of them were men—went about in society with nobody the wiser about what went on in their sick minds. It was one of the reasons they went undetected for so long. There were two registered sex offenders in Broken, but Trace was under no illusion there were no doubt others who were yet to be caught. Sometimes that knowledge kept him up at night.

"When was the last time you saw this boy?" Trace asked.

The man shrugged. "I don't know. I don't keep records."

Trace bit down on his impatience. "Give us a ballpark. Did you see him come by here this morning?"

"No. I've been out back since I got up."

"What about over the weekend?" Zac asked.

The man paused as if in thought and then shook his head. "Nope."

Trace narrowed his eyes at the man. "Are you sure?"

Turner lowered his gaze. "Of course I'm sure. I haven't been out front all weekend."

"Where were you last night?" Zac asked.

"Here."

"All night?" Trace asked.

"Yeah."

"Can anyone verify that?" Zac asked.

"Yeah. My girlfriend. She was here, too."

"What's her name?" Trace asked.

"Mandy. Mandy Goodwin."

"Is Mandy home?"

"Yeah."

"Go and get her. We'd like to talk to her."

Turner disappeared. A few moments later, a thin woman of indeterminate age with brassy blond hair and a cigarette in her mouth met them at the door.

"Are you Mandy Goodwin?" Trace asked.

"Yeah. Who wants to know?" the woman replied in a belligerent tone.

"I'm Detective Barrington from Broken Police Station. This is...Detective Barrington."

The woman looked from one to the other. "Are you shittin' me?"

"No, I'm not," Trace replied. "We're brothers."

They looked enough alike that Trace was sure she'd accept his explanation. She looked from one to the other and then nodded, seemingly satisfied.

"What can I do for you, Detectives?"

"What's your relationship to Kevin Turner?"

"He's my boyfriend."

"How long have you been together?" Trace asked.

"Five months."

"Do you live here with him?" Zac asked.

"Yeah. That's not a crime, is it?"

"No, of course not," Zac replied.

A sudden thought occurred to Trace. "Do you have any children, Ms Goodwin?"

She looked at Trace. "Not that it's any of your business, but yes. I have two kids."

Trace's gut clenched. "Do they live here with you?"

Mandy stared at the ground. "No."

Trace hid his relief and posed another question. "Where were you last night?"

"I was here. With Kevin."

"All night?" Trace persisted.

"Yes. We had dinner, watched a movie and went to bed."

"What time was this?" Zac asked.

The woman took a drag of her cigarette and blew out a plume of smoke. "Let's see. We had dinner about seven. The movie went for a couple of hours. We were in bed by half-past ten."

She eyed Trace with curiosity. "What's this about, Detective?"

"We're looking for Oscar Webster. A young teenager. He's gone missing. His family's worried about him."

"Do you know Oscar Webster?" Zac asked.

The woman shook her head. "No. Should I?"

"He lives not far from here. Kevin said he's seen Oscar passing by here sometimes on his way home from school."

"What does he look like?"

Once again, Trace pulled out his phone. He showed her the picture.

The woman gazed down at the image for a few seconds and then shook her head. "Sorry. Can't say I've ever seen him before."

Trace eyed her steadily. "Are you from Broken, Ms Goodwin?"

"No. I moved here from Blacktown about six months ago. Needed to get out of the city. Too many people. Too much crime.
I much prefer it out here, in the country. I feel safer here."

Trace nodded in acknowledgement. "We do our best to keep it that way. But right now we have a teenage boy missing and we'd appreciate any help you could give us."

"Of course. I wish I knew more. I'll keep my eyes open and let you know if I see him."

"Thanks." Trace dug into his wallet for a business card and handed it over to her. "If you or Kevin think of anything else or you see Oscar, please give me a call."

She tucked the card into her cheap cotton bra. "Sure thing, Detective. You have my word."

Once again, Trace murmured his thanks. Together, he and Zac headed for their car.

CHAPTER THREE

Kevin Turner's gut churned with nerves. He threw himself in his favorite armchair and tried to get his heart rate back under control. It was like that day all over again. The day his life had changed forever. Two detectives at his door, asking questions about a kid. Only this time it was a boy and they weren't accusing him of raping him. At least, not yet.

The nightmare was happening all over again and there was nothing he could do about it. A strangled sound of fear escaped his dry throat. From her position on the couch in front of the TV, Mandy turned to him and frowned.

"Do you know the kid they're talkin' about?"

He fought for nonchalance. "Yeah." His voice came out a squeak. He cleared his throat and tried again. "What I mean is, I recognized him. Like I told the police, he passes by here now and then. Seems like a nice boy. Friendly. We've talked a few times. He likes the flowers in the front garden."

Mandy's frown deepened. "How come I've never seen him?"

"I don't know. Probably because you're never out in the garden."

She gave him a dubious look. Kevin's gut clenched. He tried to ignore the guilt that coursed through him. "Don't look at me like that. I've never hurt a child in my life."

She curled her lip up in disgust. "Don't be stupid. Why would I think that?"

Kevin drew in a deep breath and tried harder to slow his pulse. He was overreacting, seeing accusation where there was none. Of course she didn't suspect him of hurting the kid. Though she knew he'd done time, she had no idea why he'd been inside and that's how it was going to stay.

What he really wanted to do was tell the police about the boy's stepfather. That asshole was bad news. Oscar had shared enough about his troubles with the guy that Kevin knew the cops should be looking at Malcolm-bloody-Russell if they wanted to know why Oscar was missing.

But of course, he couldn't tell the cops anything because then he'd have to admit he'd done more with Oscar than see him pass by every now and then. He'd have to admit that the two of them had struck up a friendship over a mutual appreciation of flowers and that the kindhearted teenager was one of the few people in Broken who didn't judge him.

Though none of the townspeople knew he was on the register for sex offenders, a lot of them knew he'd done time. People looked at you differently when they knew you were an ex-con. They didn't trust you. They gave you a wide berth. But not Oscar. He'd treated him with kindness and respect. He'd always been pleased to see him. To stop in for a chat.

To discover his little mate was missing filled Kevin with concern. He wanted to join in the search party. He wanted to do what he could to help. But he couldn't do any of that. Just like he couldn't tell the police they were friends.

No, for his own sake, he had to stay the hell away from anything to do with Oscar Webster. As long as he convinced the police he had nothing to do with the missing boy, he'd be fine.

Cassie did her best to concentrate on her Year nine history class, but it was difficult. She was trying to teach her students about the Freedom Rides, but her thoughts kept circling back to Oscar. She'd left strict instructions with her mother to call her if he returned, but so far her phone had remained silent. She bit back a sigh. She wished she'd gone to the police last night and not waited until the morning, but she'd kept hoping Oscar would get scared being out in the dark on his own and would come home.

She hated to admit she was also embarrassed to air their dirty laundry in public and draw unwanted attention to their family. Their mother especially took pains to stay out of the public eye. Cassie had honored that unspoken rule for as long as she could remember, but Oscar had never stayed away so long and she was worried. Her mother would just have to cope with whatever attention the situation garnered. Cassie needed her brother found.

As soon as the bell went for recess, she hurried out of the classroom. Kids streamed out of rooms and filled the hallways, talking and laughing and clowning around. On any other day, Oscar would be among them, grateful to be released from the confines of the classroom and into the play areas.

She sent a silent prayer heavenwards that her brother turn up safe and sound and headed toward the Year eight area. Among the crowd of students, she sought out Joe Lahood. Like her brother, Joe was also small for his age, but instead of red hair and freckles, Joe had black hair and dark eyes and swarthy skin inherited from his Lebanese parents.

Last night, when she'd spoken to him, he'd been just as upset as she was that Oscar hadn't come home. She hoped now to discover Joe might have heard from him that morning, or at the least might have thought of somewhere they could look for him.

Spying Joe's dark head among a group of boys, she shouldered her way through the crowd and drew him aside, away from the other students so they could talk in private.

"Hi, Joe."

"Hi, Miss."

"Have you heard from Oscar?" she asked as casually as she could manage.

"No. Have you?"

Her heart sank. "No. Have you thought about where else he might be hiding?"

The boy shook his head. "No. The only place I can think of is the forest. We've been camping there before. Not all night, of course. Oscar would never stay out all night..."

His voice drifted off. Cassie could tell what he was thinking. She was thinking the same. Oscar was scared of the dark, even when he was with his best friend. And yet he hadn't come home. He'd spent the entire night on his own. She didn't want to think he might be hurt, that that might be the reason he hadn't returned, but reality was fast setting in. She couldn't ignore the possibility any longer. It was the only thing that made sense.

"Are you sure you didn't speak to Oscar last night? Or even yesterday afternoon?"

"No. Like I said, the last time I saw him was at school on Friday afternoon."

"Did he talk about his plans for the weekend? Mention anywhere he was going?"

Once again Joe shook his head. "No, Miss. Nothing like that. I'm sorry."

The boy looked so distressed, Cassie gave his shoulder a reassuring squeeze and put an end to her questions. Joe couldn't help her and it wasn't fair for her to keep pressuring him to provide answers he didn't have.

She gave him a reassuring smile. "Don't worry, Joe. I'm sure he'll turn up."

Joe's answering smile was just as strained. "Sure, Miss. Of course he will. I promise to let you know if Oscar calls me. Or texts. Anything. I-I'll let you know."

It was all she could hope for.

It was mid-afternoon when Trace and Zac arrived at the Russell house to interview Cassie's mother. The house was circa 1970s and was a traditional red brick and tile single story house that blended in with the other houses of a similar age and style in that street. As they climbed out of the police cruiser, Cassie pulled up behind them in a late model Honda. In her hand she carried a leather briefcase bulging with papers. She joined them on the nature strip, looking wan and pale.

"Any news?" Trace asked.

"No, not as far as I know. I've been at school all day, but no one's called."

Trace introduced his brother and then both men waited for Cassie to precede them through the front gate that led up to the house. The yard was neat and tidy. Native shrubs and bushes that were hardy and required little maintenance had been planted along the border in lieu of flowers. Not that Trace judged them for that. He didn't have time for flowers, either.

Cassie walked up the three stone steps and crossed the concrete verandah and then opened the front door. It squeaked in protest. Trace saw her draw in a deep breath before she ushered them inside. Trace found himself in a long narrow hallway that ended in a modest kitchen at the back. On either side of the hallway there were open doors. The front rooms were bedrooms. They followed Cassie into a living room. Trace pulled up short.

On the couch sat the most enormous woman he'd ever seen. The couch was a three-seater, but there wasn't an inch of space to spare. It sagged alarmingly. He guessed she must weigh around two hundred kilos. No wonder she hadn't made it down to the station. She probably struggled to move from the couch to her bedroom, let alone venture outside.

Trace fought to conceal his shock. He glanced at Cassie. Her expression was carefully blank. She kept her gaze fixed in the vicinity of her mother.

"Mom, the police are here. They want to talk to you about Oscar."

The woman on the couch let out a wail of despair. "My baby! Where's my baby! Have they found him?"

She turned a desperate gaze toward her daughter. The enormous rolls of fat that covered her stomach and arms jiggled alarmingly. Now Trace understood the weird vibe he'd gotten from Cassie when he'd asked her why she was there reporting her brother missing and not her mother.

Cassie moved closer to her mother. She stroked her mother's bare arm and made soothing noises.

"Don't upset yourself, Mom. It's going to be okay."

The woman continued to gaze at Cassie, her expression beseeching. "Where's Oscar? Have they found him?"

"Not yet, Mom. But they will. I'm sure Oscar will be home any minute."

Trace stepped forward and introduced himself and Zac. The woman turned to look at him through eyes that were filled with confusion and pain.

"I'm Marie Russell. Oscar's mom. Please find him, Detective. I need you to find him. I need my boy home."

"We're going to do all that we can to find him Mrs Russell," Trace assured her, "but first we need to ask you some questions."

The woman waved a plump hand in the vague direction of an armchair that stood adjacent to the couch.

"Take a seat. It hurts my neck to look up at you like that."

Trace glanced at Zac who parked himself in a corner. Trace perched on the edge of the armchair and leaned toward Oscar's mother. The woman's gaze kept darting about, as if expecting to see her son jump out from behind the curtain or fill the open doorway. Trace cleared his throat.

"Tell me about Oscar."

A smile filled Marie's face, making her look almost beautiful. "Oscar," she breathed. "My baby. He was the most perfect child. Slept through the night almost from the time I brought him home from the hospital. So placid, so happy, so serene. Always smiling. He's still like that. Always has a smile on his face."

"What does he like to do? Are there any places he likes to hang out?"

"He loves going to the park and walking through the gardens. He loves flowers." She smiled. "He loves the way they smell, he loves their pretty colors. I told him when he grows up he could work in a nursery. He loves that idea."

Trace glanced at Cassie.

"We checked the park last night and again first thing this morning. He wasn't there. We talked to some children who were playing on the swings. No one had seen him."

Trace turned back to Cassie's mother. "What about when he hangs out with his friends? Where do they go?"

"His best friend is Joseph Lahood. They usually just hang out in Oscar's room or at Joseph's house. Sometimes they ride their bikes down the street or hike the trails behind our house." Her expression became more frantic. "You have to understand, Detective. Oscar's a homebody. He doesn't like being out for too long and even when he is outside, he never ventures far. That's why I'm so scared. He's been out all night. On his own. My poor baby must be terrified."

Huge tears filled the woman's face. Cassie moved over to her and patted her shoulder. "It's all right, Mom. Don't get upset. We don't know that he spent the night outside. He might be with a friend. Or anyone."

"He doesn't have any other friends!" her mother wailed. "He wouldn't just go with a stranger. He knows better than that."

From the look Cassie gave Trace, he could tell she also agreed. Trace cleared his throat.

"Tell me about your husband, Malcolm. I understand he and Oscar got into an argument last night."

Marie nodded, her eyes downcast. Her double chins wobbled.

"Do you know what they were arguing about?" Trace asked.

"I think... I think it was something to do with Oscar not doing his chores. Malcolm got home late and was upset that

Oscar hadn't done them." She lifted her gaze. "It's Oscar's job to feed the dogs and chop wood. We're stockpiling for the winter."

"Did you witness the argument?"

"Just the start of it. Malcolm came home and realized Oscar hadn't done his chores and started yelling at him. Then they went outside. I didn't see or hear anything after that."

"Do you know why they went outside?" Trace asked.

The woman shrugged. The movement sent an alarmingly amount of fat wobbling. She kept her gaze directed at a point on the carpet.

"I don't know. Maybe they were going up to the wood heap."

Cassie glanced at Trace and shook her head. She'd already told him she'd guessed Malcolm was headed to the shed with Oscar so he could discipline him.

"How do Oscar and Malcolm usually get on?" Trace asked.

Another shrug.

"Please, Mrs Russell. We're not here to judge you or your family. We're here to find your son. We can't do that if you don't answer our questions."

At that, a fresh wave of tears filled the woman's eyes. She sniffed and swiped at them with the back of her hand.

"Malcolm's a good man. He's a good husband and father to my children."

"I'm sure he is," Trace agreed.

"He works hard to provide for us. He works such long hours. He comes home tired. I don't blame him for being irritable. That happens when you're tired."

"Of course," Trace said in a soothing voice. "Like I said, we're not here to judge you. We just want to find Oscar."

A few beats passed. Then Marie spoke again. "Malcolm and Oscar don't always get on. But it's not a malicious thing on Malcolm's part. Oscar... He can be difficult. You know he's...?"

"Autistic?" Trace supplied.

"Yes. But that doesn't hold him back. And he's as smart as a whip," Marie responded, her expression fierce.

"Of course. Your daughter told us he's a good communicator." Trace paused and then added, "Has Malcolm been violent toward Oscar in the past?"

Once again, silence fell in the small room. Trace saw Cassie regarding her mother with a pleading look on her face. Finally, Marie responded.

"Violent sounds so ugly. It's not like that. Malcolm loses his temper sometimes with Oscar and... Sometimes it gets physical."

"Have you ever seen Malcolm hit Oscar?" Trace asked softly.

Marie shook her head. "No."

"Then how do you know Malcolm gets physical with your son?"

The woman heaved out a weary sigh, once again setting her enormous belly wobbling. "They go up to the shed. That's where they go when Malcolm wants to discipline Oscar. I know it sometimes turns physical because Oscar has told me."

"How physical? Had Malcolm punched Oscar before?" Trace asked.

"No, not that I know of. But sometimes he's hit him with a strap or something like that around the back of the legs."

"And Oscar told you this?"

The woman stared down at her lap. Once again, her eyes welled with tears. She gave a jerky nod.

"What about last night? Did you talk to Oscar after he went to the shed with Malcolm?" Trace asked.

"No. I saw them walk out of the house and that was it."

"What about Malcolm? Did he return to the house afterwards?" Trace asked.

"No. I only knew he'd left because I heard his truck roaring out of the driveway."

"How did that make you feel?" Trace asked.

Marie shrugged. Fresh tears glinted in her eyes and slid down her cheeks. "I don't blame Malcolm. He tries hard with Oscar. He really does. But like I said, sometimes he loses his temper. I hate it when he lashes out at Oscar, but I understand it. Oscar's not his son."

She lifted her gaze and stared at Trace almost defiantly. "It's not easy living with an autistic child. Malcolm's a good man. He takes care of his family. Sometimes he just…let's himself down."

"What about with you? Is he ever violent toward you?" Trace asked.

Broken Bonds is available for pre-order from all digital retailers and will be released in January, 2022

Get a free book when you sign up for Chris Taylor's newsletter at: http://www.christaylorauthor.com.au

Other books by Chris Taylor

The Munro Family Series

(in order)

The Profiler

The Investigator

The Predator

The Betrayal

The Deception

The Negotiator

The Christmas Vigil (A novella)

The Ransom

The Defendant

The Shooting

The Maker

The Sydney Harbour Hospital Series (in order)

The Perfect Husband

The Body Thief

The Baby Snatchers

The Final Bullet

The Debt Collector

The Lab Test

The Stolen Identity

The Cliff-top Killer

The Likeable Fraudster

The Sydney Legal Series
(in order)

An Accidental Murderer

At the Hand of her Father

A Woman Scorned

Lies and Deception

Ordinary Evil

The Ties that Bind

The Perfect Crime

A Toxic Inheritance

Malicious Love

The Craigdon Family Series

(in order)

Callum

Joel

Isabella

Nicholas

Sophia

Flynn

Noah

Logan

Elizabeth

The Barrington Family Series

(in order)

Broken Lives

Broken Promises

Broken Bonds

Broken Spirits

Broken Minds

Broken Vows

Broken Hearts

Broken Dreams

Broken Homes

The Fairfax Family Series (in order)

A Cattleman in Disguise

A Cattleman's Quest

A Cattleman's Daughter

A Cattleman's Secret Baby

To Catch a Cattleman

The Doctor and the Cattleman

To Rescue a Cattleman

A Cattleman's Heart

For the Love of a Cattleman

Bachelors and Brides Series (in order)

Matilda

Austin

Farrah

Benjamin

Verity

Denver

Ebony

Tyrone

Willow

Books by Chris Taylor

Writing as

Bella
Christian

This Is Where It Ends Series
(in order)

Jessie's Story

Ryan's Story

Holly's Story

Sarah's Story

Veronica's Story

Love audiobooks? Check out Chris Taylor Books on audio

iTunes   Amazon Audible

Join Chris Taylor's Facebook reader group/fan page and be among the first to receive news of book releases, read and review books prior to release and other amazing offers.

Join Now!

Acknowledgments

As usual, no book comes into being without a lot of help and support by my friends and family. A world of thanks must go to my wonderful editor, Pat Thomas. Thank you for everything that you do to make my stories even more amazing than I could ever dare to dream. To former Detective Superintendent Michael Kilfoyle, thank you for lending my story credibility. Any mistakes are wholly my own.

To Justin Mendez and all of the team at 100 Covers, thank you for the fantastic book cover. To my sister, Nicole Guihot and to my friends, Ally Thomson and Sue Ricardo, thank you for your excellent editorial comments, proof reading skills and suggestions. I hope you like the final result.

To the fantastic writer organizations such as Romance Writers of Australia, Romance Writers of America and Romance Writers of New Zealand for all the help, support and encouragement they offer new and aspiring writers, including me.

To my readers, thank you for your support and love for my stories. Your encouragement and enjoyment make this journey all worthwhile.

And lastly, to my friends and family, especially my husband and children. Thank you for putting up with late dinners and even later conversations as I've emerged day after day from the sometimes scary but always enthralling world I've created on my computer.

About the Author

Chris Taylor grew up on a farm in north-west New South Wales, Australia. She always had a thirst for stories and recalls writing her first book at the ripe old age of eight. Always a lover of romance and happily-ever-afters, a career in criminal law sparked her interest in intrigue and suspense. For Chris to be able to combine romance with suspense in her books is a dream come true.

Chris is married to Linden and is the mother of five children. If not behind her computer, you can find her doing the school run, taxiing children to swimming lessons, football, ballet and cricket. In her spare time, Chris loves to read her favorite authors who include Richard North Patterson, Sandra Brown, Kathleen E Woodiwiss and Jude Devereaux.

You can find out more about Chris and get a free book when you sign up for her newsletter at her website:
http://www.christaylorauthor.com.au

Join Chris on Facebook at:
https://www.facebook.com/christaylorauthor/

www.ingramcontent.com/pod-product-compliance
Lightning Source LLC
Chambersburg PA
CBHW060753190726
48285CB00002B/414